Falling for
the Rancher Father

LINDA FORD

HARLEQUIN® LOVE INSPIRED® HISTORICAL

Recycling programs
for this product may
not exist in your area.

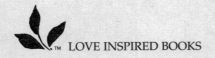

LOVE INSPIRED BOOKS

ISBN-13: 978-0-373-28262-3

FALLING FOR THE RANCHER FATHER

Copyright © 2014 by Linda Ford

www.Harlequin.com

Printed in U.S.A.

"I would like to ask you to consider coming a bit longer.

"I could get my work done so much faster if I didn't have to watch the twins, and they really enjoy having you here."

That she knew to be true. But what did Abel think of her presence? Mercy dared not ask. "I enjoy keeping them company."

"So you'll think about it?"

It was a beginning. More time would allow him to see how ordinary she could be. "I don't need to. My answer is yes."

He jumped to his feet and stood by her chair. "That's great."

She took her time inserting the threaded needle into the fabric she held. Carefully, she folded it, keeping the needle visible on top, and set it on the basket of other items to be mended. Only then did she lift her gaze to him.

He grinned widely. She wondered if his eyes revealed approval or only relief.

Books by Linda Ford

Love Inspired Historical

The Road to Love
The Journey Home
The Path to Her Heart
Dakota Child
The Cowboy's Baby
Dakota Cowboy
Christmas Under
Western Skies
"A Cowboy's Christmas"
Dakota Father
Prairie Cowboy
Klondike Medicine Woman
*The Cowboy Tutor
*The Cowboy Father
*The Cowboy Comes Home

The Gift of Family
"Merry Christmas, Cowboy"
†*The Cowboy's Surprise Bride*
†*The Cowboy's Unexpected*
Family
†*The Cowboy's Convenient*
Proposal
The Baby Compromise
†*Claiming the Cowboy's Heart*
†*Winning Over the Wrangler*
†*Falling for the Rancher Father*

*Three Brides for Three Cowboys
†Cowboys of Eden Valley

LINDA FORD

lives on a ranch in Alberta, Canada. Growing up on the prairie and learning to notice the small details it hides gave her an appreciation for watching God at work in His creation. Her upbringing also included being taught to trust God in everything and through everything—a theme that resonates in her stories. Threads of another part of her life are found in her stories—her concern for children and their future. She and her husband raised fourteen children—four homemade, ten adopted. She currently shares her home and life with her husband, a grown son, a live-in paraplegic client and a continual (and welcome) stream of kids, kids-in-law, grandkids and assorted friends and relatives.

Thou knowest my downsitting and mine uprising,
thou understandest my thought afar off.
—*Psalms* 139:2

To my grandson, Julien, as he graduates
from high school. Good for you.
I know you've worked hard. We're so proud of you.

Chapter One

Eden Valley Ranch, Alberta, Canada
Fall 1882

She was gone.

His heart slammed against his ribs. He scanned the entire clearing again just to make sure but she wasn't there.

"Allie." Abel Borgard yelled his daughter's name. One minute ago the nine-year-old sat on the chair by the cabin. He'd warned her to stay there while he unloaded the supplies, but now she'd disappeared. "It's not like her," he complained aloud. Ladd, her twin brother, was a different matter. He'd set off exploring the moment they'd alighted from the wagon. Abel had warned him to stay nearby, but it didn't worry him when Ladd got out of sight. The boy had learned at a young age to be self-reliant. Allie, on the other hand, needed rest and protection. The doctor's warning reverberated through Abel's brain. "She's extremely fortunate to have survived scarlet fever, especially under the circumstances."

"Allie." He didn't bother calling this time, just muttered the word under his breath. He again turned full circle, studying his surroundings. The tiny cabin would provide temporary shelter until he could erect a larger one, which he had to do before winter. The chill in the air reminded him time was short.

The trees, a nice mix of spruce and aspen, were far enough from the buildings to allow plenty of sunshine to reach the living quarters yet provide protection and privacy. The mountains rose to the west in all their fall majesty.

He completed his inspection of the surroundings but saw no little girl. Not so much as a hint of the blue dress she wore.

Abel understood the doctor's warning. Abel had come home from a three-month absence as he sought work to discover his wife had left days before, abandoning the then eight-year-olds to care for themselves. He'd found them huddled together, hungry and afraid. According to what he could get from the children, Allie had been sick even before Ruby left. Though in all fairness, Ruby likely hadn't known at that point it was anything more than a chill. Perhaps she hadn't even meant to leave them for more than a night but she'd fallen into the river and drowned. He liked to believe it had simply been misfortune, but he guessed she'd spent too much time in the back room of the saloon sharing drinks.

He strained to catch any sound of the children. Wasn't there a thud to his right…like distant horse hooves? Every nerve in his body tensed. An intruder? Were the children in danger?

The doctor had left Abel with no misconceptions as to the seriousness of Allie's situation. "I fear she will have damaged her heart. You'll need to limit her activities for the rest of her life or..." At this point, he'd shaken his head as if expecting the worst.

Abel had vowed on the spot that Allie would be treated as gently as a fragile china doll. He couldn't lose her. If anything happened to her he would never forgive himself. Any more than he forgave himself for the fact the children had been abandoned by his wife while he went in search of work. Ruby had never wanted to settle down and from the beginning had found the children a heavy burden, while Abel discovered they gave him reason to leave off being a wastrel. He regretted having started down that wayward path in the first place. The only good thing to come of it was his children and his determination to live a responsible, careful life from now on. He was twenty-nine years old and would devote the rest of his life to the well-being of his children. Never again would he allow his foolish emotions to lead him down the slippery path into the arms of a woman. Any woman. He would not risk his children's health and happiness by trusting a woman to settle down and be wife and mother.

Another thud. No mistaking the sound. There was a horse in the nearby clearing. His heart thumped him in his ribs hard enough to cause him to catch his breath.

He broke into a gallop and headed for the spot.

If anything happened to either of the twins...

He saw Allie ahead, rocking back and forth on the balls of her feet, her hands clasped together as if she tried to contain some emotion. Already her cheeks had turned rosy—a sure indication of her excited state. A danger sign.

He raced toward her and scooped her into his arms.

He brushed strands of her long blond hair off her face. "Baby, are you okay?"

"I'm fine, Papa. Isn't she glorious?" She twisted and pointed.

Abel jerked his gaze from his precious daughter and followed the direction she indicated. His eyes lit on a woman who reminded him of those he'd seen in saloons. Only instead of bright-colored, revealing dresses, she wore a dark red shirt, fringed gloves and riding pants. It wasn't the clothes that brought those other women to mind—it was the look of sheer abandon on her face. Her mahogany-colored hair rippled down her back, held in place by a small cowboy hat secured under her chin. She sat on a beautiful palomino gelding.

She waved a hand over her head and the horse reared on its back legs.

Abel clutched Allie tight. "She's going to be hurt."

"Oh, no." Allie's voice was round with awe. "She does it on purpose. She's a trick rider. She's going to join a Wild West show."

"She is, is she?" The gal made a beautiful picture of horse and rider but she posed a threat to his children if she hung about, filling Allie's head with admiration.

The horse returned to all fours and clapping caught Abel's attention. Ladd stood on the other side of the horse, his eyes round with awe. "Can you show me how to do that?"

"It's not hard." The woman's voice rang with humor and what he could only explain as love of life.

That was all well and good. He had no objection to her joining a Wild West show, loving life or doing dangerous things on back of a horse, so long as she stayed away from his kids.

"Can you show me?" Ladd asked.

"Sure thing. All you do—"

Abel crossed the clearing to clamp his hand on Ladd's shoulder. The boy jerked, surprised, no doubt, at the sudden appearance of his father. Hopefully he was also feeling a little guilty at having brought Allie out to the woods when she was supposed to rest. "Ladd, take your sister back to the cabin. Allie, you know you shouldn't be here."

Allie patted him on the cheek. "I'm okay, Papa. You worry too much."

"Maybe I do. Maybe I don't. I only want you both to be safe." He set his daughter on her feet, patted them both on the back and sent them on their way. He didn't turn until they were out of sight.

Sucking in air, he tried to calm the way his insides rolled and bucked at how this woman had intruded on his hope of peace and quiet. He didn't want to say anything he'd later regret, so he pushed aside his inner turmoil as he slowly faced the woman. "You're trespassing."

She lounged in her saddle as if she meant to spend her entire day there. "I think you are mistaken. This land belongs to Eddie Gardiner. He's given me permission to be here."

"That might have been so at one time, but I've rented the cabin and the surrounding land from Mr. Eddie Gardiner." He planned to raise cows. His ranch would be insignificant compared to the Eden Valley Ranch, but it was all he wanted. Besides— "I want peace and quiet for my children." At the cold way she studied him, his resolve mounted a protest. "I don't want them learning reckless ways. Nor do I want my daughter overexcited by witnessing your activities. What you do in your own time and space is your business. But what you do around my children is my business."

The grin she wore plainly said she didn't take him seriously.

His spine tingled as he held back a desire to tell her exactly what he thought. He mentally counted to ten then widened his stance, narrowed his eyes and gave her his best don't-mess-with-me look, the one that made the twins jump to obey. "I suggest you leave and don't come back."

She laughed. A cheerful-enough sound, but one that dug talons into his backbone. It reminded him of Ruby and the way she laughed when he suggested she should settle down and be a mother to the children. And it filled him with something hard and cold. But before he could put words to his feelings, she spoke.

"Pleased to meet you. Nice to know there'll be a kind neighbor nearby." She reined her horse into a two-legged stand and let out a wild whoop. "I'll no doubt be seeing you around since we're neighbors." She drawled out the last word in a mocking way, then rode away at a gallop, bent over her mount's neck as they raced through the trees.

"You won't be seeing more of me and my family if I have anything to say about it," he murmured then headed for the cabin and his kids. He had to make sure they were unharmed after encountering the crazy wild woman on horseback.

Twenty-year-old Mercy Newell galloped through the trees, not slowing until she reached the barn on the Eden Valley Ranch—her home in Canada. She'd come from London to this raw new country a little more than two months ago with Eddie's sister, Jayne, and their mutual friend, Sybil. Both were now married and living in small log cabins on the ranch though both said they and their new husbands would be starting their own ranches come spring. She wished them all the best, but she didn't intend to marry and settle down. Not when there were things she wanted to do. Number one on that list was to join a Wild West show. Since the day she'd seen one in Benton, Montana, on their trip here she'd known she wanted to be part of such a show. The excitement, the thrill, the roar of the crowd's approval...

While there, she'd even managed to get a few lessons in doing the stunts and instructions on more things she could learn. Since her arrival at Eden Valley Ranch, she'd also been taking lessons from anyone who would help her.

She reined in, pulling Nugget to a halt, getting him to rear up. She jumped from the saddle before he returned to all fours and led him to the barn where she brushed and fed him.

All the while she muttered about the man in her clearing. "Who does he think he is? Telling me to leave like I was common trash. As if he has the right. He says he rented the cabin. I'm not about to take his word on it, though. But even if he did, that doesn't give him the right to chase me away."

Nugget nudged her aside as if to say he was tired of her grousing.

"Fine. You're not the only one I can talk to." Finished caring for the horse, she stalked across to Jayne and Seth's cabin. All the men were at the fall roundup except for Cookie's husband, Bertie. She didn't even spare a glance toward the cookhouse. Cookie and Bertie would both tell her to calm down and be sensible.

Mercy had no intention of doing either.

She knocked and strode in without waiting for an answer. Besides Jayne, both Sybil and Linette, Eddie's wife, sat around the table. "Good. The three of you are here. You can all hear my story at the same time." She plunked down on the only available chair. "I met the most rude man."

Sybil sat up straighter. "Where? Mercy, what have you been up to this time? I do wish you wouldn't roam about the woods as if—"

Jayne spoke as soon as Sybil paused for breath. "Please don't tell us you've met a man while out there. What kind of man? What did he do?"

Mercy waved aside their concerns. "He says he's rented that little cabin southwest of here. He informed me I was trespassing. Pfft. If he thinks he can order me around, well, he'll soon learn otherwise."

Linette waited for Mercy to run out of steam. "That must be Abel Borgard. Eddie told me he'd let him have the little cabin for himself and his children. Twins, Eddie said. A boy and a girl. Did you see them?"

She smiled. "I didn't realize they were twins. The little boy is sturdy and filled with curiosity. He wanted me to show him how to teach a horse some tricks." She ignored the way the others looked at each other and shook their heads. They simply did not understand why she had to do this. They'd asked and she'd only said it was an adventure. But it was more than that. A need deep inside. A restless itch that had to be tended to. She'd been that way most of her life. Probably since her brother died when he was eight and she, six. It was not a time in her life she liked to think about so she gladly pulled her thoughts back to her waiting friends. "The little girl is tiny but a real beauty. Her father swept her into his arms as if she was a—" She couldn't finish. She'd been about to say a precious princess. "A much younger child." She'd seen the way the little girl patted his cheeks and how his expression softened with what Mercy could only interpret as devotion. "He said I was too reckless to be around his children. Really? I am never reckless."

The others laughed.

Mercy tried to scowl but ended up laughing, as well.

Sybil sighed. "It sounds romantic. A man raising two children on his own. So protective of them."

Linette patted her rounded tummy. She was two months from having her firstborn. "Eddie will be a good father. I've already seen it in the way he treats Grady." Grady was the little boy they were raising as their own.

"Where is Grady?" Mercy asked.

"He's over at Cassie's playing with the children." Cassie and Roper and the four children they'd adopted lived beyond the barn in a house big enough for the six of them.

Linette returned immediately to Mercy's situation. "It seems to me you'll have to respect Abel's wishes and stay away from the cabin. Maybe now you'll remain at the ranch. Tell me you will. I worry about you out there on your own."

Mercy didn't bother to again say she could take care of herself. "Guess I will be practicing my riding and roping around here until I find another place. But—" She leaned forward and gave them each a demanding look. "I don't want anyone hanging about warning me about the dangers. Agreed?"

Jayne and Linette exchanged a look then together shook their heads. "We aren't agreeing to any such thing."

"Nor am I," Sybil said. "From the beginning I've opposed your dream to join a Wild West show and will continue to do so."

Mercy groaned. "I can see I'll have to find another place to practice." In the meantime, the corrals were virtually empty, with the cowboys and horses gone on the roundup. She'd be able to work on her tricks without a lot of interference. She'd simply deflect her friends' needless worry should they voice it.

The next morning she slipped from the house before Linette or Grady stirred and hurried down to the corral behind the barn. The guns she used for her fancy shooting worried the others the most so she did her gun work in the cold dawn. The pearl-handled guns, one of her greatest treasures, had been acquired through Cal, a cowboy who had worked at the Eden Valley Ranch before he'd been fired. She'd encouraged Cal to do a number of things Eddie didn't approve of. He'd even coached her roping stunts. Thankfully, it was his own actions that got him fired, and nothing she could feel responsible for.

After an hour, her wrists grew tired and she saddled Nugget and brought him out to the same area. She practiced a number of tricks—bowing, rearing up, sidestepping. Then she turned her attention to a new trick—teaching Nugget to lie on his back and let her sit on his chest.

She finally got him to lie down and roll to his back and rewarded him with a carrot.

The sun had grown warm. Her stomach growled, reminding her she'd eaten nothing but a slab of bread she'd grabbed on her way through the kitchen. Linette and Grady would be up and about by now. Time to climb the hill and find breakfast. She'd heard Cookie call good morning to Jayne a short time ago. Overhead, a flock of geese honked, and a crow called from the trees. The chickens cackled and crowed. The world had come alive.

She stepped into the house and traipsed down the hall to the kitchen.

Grady ran to her, almost tackled her. She caught him. "Whoa, cowboy. What's your hurry?"

"We got company."

Warning trickled down Mercy's spine. Surely Abel hadn't stepped into her corner of the ranch. She slowly raised her eyes. The twins sat at the table watching her. She shifted her gaze around the room until she met Linette's eyes. No one else was there.

Her breath whooshed out.

"Papa says we can stay here while he works," Allie said.

"That's nice."

The children eyed her. She eyed them back. Then they all grinned.

Linette brushed a strand of hair off her face. "I thought you might like to take the three of them out after breakfast and amuse them while I do some things around the house."

Mercy laughed, as much out of relief as amusement. She didn't mind spending time with the children. Over breakfast, she considered the day. "Who wants to watch me do some roping?"

The boys yelled yes and Allie nodded, her blue eyes sparkling.

"Good. Then finish your breakfast, help me clean up and we'll go do it."

The boys ate hurriedly but Allie picked at her food.

"Come on, Allie," Ladd said. "We can't go until you finish."

Slowly she cleaned her plate, then the three of them helped Mercy do the dishes. Ladd dried the dishes so fast they barely got introduced to the towel. He was darker than his sister, his blue eyes so dark they almost seemed black until the light hit them and the blue became evident.

Grady, five years old, carefully placed each dish on the table and dried it with both hands.

Allie dried each dish as slowly as she ate.

Ladd nudged his sister. "Go faster."

"I can't."

They studied each other. Mercy thought Ladd would press the point and then he patted her shoulder. "Do your best."

Mercy turned away and stared at the soapy dishwater. The boy's gentleness with his sister tugged at her thoughts. Had her brother, Butler, treated her with such kindness? She tried to remember. But it seemed she could only recall the loneliness of his illness and the emptiness of the house after he died. And how her parents had mourned so deeply they plumb forgot they had a daughter.

That was in the past. The future and adventure beckoned.

She handed the last dish to Ladd and dumped out the dishwater. "Are we ready?"

The boys cheered in affirmation and Allie merely nodded, but her eyes said she anticipated the outing as much as the boys.

They called goodbye to Linette and headed down the hill.

Thor, the tame fawn, saw the children and bounced over to join them, eliciting squeals of laughter from Allie.

Mercy stopped to let them enjoy the antics of the rapidly growing deer before they moved on. Soon Thor would disappear in the woods to join other deer, but she wouldn't inform the children of that fact. Let them enjoy the pet while they could.

Thor bounced away in search of amusement elsewhere and Mercy shepherded the children onward.

She had them sit against the barn and showed them how to swing the rope overhead. How to drop it over a fence post. How to spin a circle of rope just above the ground and jump in and out of it. "I have lots more to learn," she said.

"But you're pretty good," Allie said.

Ladd bounced to his feet. "You said you'd show me how to make the horse bow."

It wasn't exactly what she'd said but close enough. She'd spent a few days getting Nugget to follow the offer of a carrot until his head almost reached the ground. Then she'd taught him to pull one leg back and put the other forward. He was getting good at bowing. She figured he'd perform for Ladd and handed a carrot to the boy. "Stand here. Show him the carrot then lower it toward the ground. He'll do the rest because he knows what to expect." Nugget performed perfectly. "Now give him the carrot."

Ladd held the carrot out but drew back as the horse tried to take it.

Mercy guided his hand so Nugget got his treat.

"What else can I make him do?" Ladd asked.

"Before I show you, maybe Grady and Allie would like to do a trick." She held a hand toward the pair.

Grady jumped forward. "Can I get him to bow, too?"

"You sure can." She repeated the trick with Grady and helped the boy feed Nugget his treat.

Allie stood nearby, rocking back and forth in anticipation. "Can I do something different?"

"What would you like to do?"

"Me and Ladd saw you standing on his back. Can I do that?"

Mercy considered the request. Nugget was still saddled and he wouldn't protest, and if she held Allie, she could see no problem. The child would be perfectly safe. "I don't see why not. Come on, I'll show you how."

She lifted the featherlight child to the saddle, placing her feet so she balanced then held her hand as she straightened. "There you go. What do you think?"

Allie giggled. "I'm a bird." She held out her free arm.

A man came out of nowhere direct to Mercy's side. Although alarmed at the sudden appearance, she held Allie firmly.

He lifted Allie from the horse and stepped back. "How dare you put my child at risk?"

"You! Mr. Abel Borgard, I presume. Haven't we met before?" She didn't much care for the dark expression on his face.

"And you would be…? Just so I know to avoid you in the future."

"Mercy Newell. So pleased to make your acquaintance." But her sarcasm was wasted on him.

"Papa," Allie patted his cheek to get his attention.

"Yes, baby."

Baby! This child was no baby. Why did he call her that? Worse, why did he treat her like an infant?

"It was fun," Allie said. "And she held my hand really tight."

"It was exceedingly foolish. Ladd, didn't you think to say something?"

Ladd faced his father without a hint of fear. Or remorse. "Miss Mercy held her real good. She is smart about horses and—"

"Children are different than horses, Miss Mercy. Mrs. Gardiner knows I've come for the children. I'm taking them home." He still carried Allie in one arm and took Ladd by his free hand. "Where they'll be safe." He hurried away.

Ladd and Allie sent Mercy pleading looks. She couldn't say if they were silently apologetic or simply regretting that their enjoyment had been cut short. Regardless, something about their silent appeals released her own caution and she trotted after them, reaching Abel's side before he made it to his horse. She grabbed his shoulder and forced him to stop.

"Sir, you are mistaken if you think I was about to let something happen to your children. I was only allowing them a bit of harmless fun. Everyone should be allowed to enjoy life and not shoved into a corner."

He put Allie down and released Ladd. "You two go wait by the horse."

They scampered away and stood watching the two adults.

Abel turned his back to the children. "Miss Newell, whether or not you agree with my choices on my children's behalf is immaterial to me. But Allie has been very ill. Her heart has been damaged and the doctor says she must not get overly excited, nor can she be allowed to overexert herself. It could have very bad consequences."

There was no mistaking the agony in his voice as he spoke those words and then he strode away, swung to the back of his horse and lifted the children, Ladd behind him, Allie sheltered in his arms.

How was she to have known about Allie? The last thing she would ever do was put a child at risk.

Abel reined his horse about. He was about to leave. She couldn't let him go without trying to explain.

"Wait." She raced to the head of the horse, forcing Abel to pull up. "I'm sorry. I didn't know. But believe me, I would never put a child in danger."

Abel studied her a moment. Then he shifted his gaze to Allie. He cupped her head then reached back and pulled Ladd closer. He lifted his gaze to Mercy.

"So you say. But it is immaterial to me. My one and only concern is my children."

She fell back, struck by the depth of emotion in his eyes.

"Whatever foolish thing you choose to do with your time is your business." He rode away. Ladd lifted a hand in a wave.

Mercy stared after them, her insides churning. She knew the look in Abel's eyes. Not because she remembered ever seeing it but because she had longed for it all her life. Instead, all she'd ever seen was indifference. Seems Butler was the only child who had mattered to her parents and when he died, Mercy became a necessary nuisance. She could never do enough to get them to acknowledge her. No matter how absurd her behavior.

She shook off the feeling.

She'd hoped she'd found the acceptance she longed for when, at seventeen, she fell in love with Ambrose, the preacher's son. They'd enjoyed many adventures together. But after their romantic summer—oh, how mistaken she'd been about that—he'd introduced her to a sweet, young thing he identified as his fiancée. When Mercy confronted him, he said he couldn't live with a person like her who longed for adventure. A man wanted to come home to peace and quiet, not restlessness. Mercy realized then that men, in general, preferred a woman to be invisible in her husband's shadow. Mercy could never be that.

The circle of her thoughts widened. Wasn't the Wild West show exactly the kind of thing she'd wanted since she was sixteen years old and watching Cleopatra's Needle unveiling in London? They'd buried a time capsule beneath it that included pictures of the twelve most beautiful women. That struck her as unfair. What if a woman was born ugly? Was she to be ignored? What if she was beautiful but no one noticed? No, a person had to be able to *do* something to earn notice and value.

She would do something. She would join a Wild West show and perform for others. The audience would appreciate her skills. It didn't matter what Mr. Abel Borgard thought.

Chapter Two

Abel held Allie tight as he rode toward the cabin. He found comfort in Ladd's arms about his waist. Miss Mercy was a menace to his kids and likely to herself, though that didn't concern him. It surprised him, however, that Eddie allowed such conduct. Like his parents said, "You reap what you sow. If you sow to the wind, you reap sorrow." He'd learned the truth of their words the hard way. He'd left home at sixteen to follow a sin-filled path, thinking it meant excitement. It had led him to marriage with Ruby. She wanted to continue their wayward path but once the twins were born, Abel wanted only to provide them with safety and security. Poor Ruby hadn't signed up for that sort of life. So she paid in frustration. With an unpredictable, unreliable mother, the twins paid, too, and unable to stop the train wreck of his marriage, Abel would likely spend the rest of his life making up for his foolish decisions.

And he would not allow Miss Mercy to undo the good he aimed to achieve by settling down and giving the twins a home like they'd never known.

The children were quiet on the trip home. He let them

off in front of the cabin. "Go inside. I'll be there as soon as I take care of Sam." The faithful horse would get a few oats and some hay, which reminded him of another job awaiting him. He must find feed for the horse and the milk cow he hoped to obtain. This late in the year, locating feed would prove a challenge.

He returned to the cabin, ducking his head to enter. The inside was as inadequate as the door—barely big enough for a table, four chairs and a narrow bed. Beyond that, a corner of the roof had been damaged. He'd repaired it, but a good wind or a heavy snowfall would threaten the entire roof. He had to get a bigger, sturdier cabin built before winter set it.

Allie and Ladd stood shoulder to shoulder and watched as he hung his hat on a hook. He faced them. "What's on your mind?"

"You were rude to Miss Mercy," Allie said, her face wreathed in distress.

"Oh, honey. I was only concerned about you. Can you imagine how I felt to see you standing on the back of her horse?" His heart had punched his ribs with such force they still hurt.

"She wouldn't let me fall."

His daughter's loyalty was commendable but misplaced.

Ladd nodded. "She let me and Grady make her horse bow. She knows what she's doing. Someday she's going to be in a Wild West show and I bet she'll be the best person in the whole show."

"Don't say bet." He spoke automatically as his thoughts raced. When had the twins ever been so passionate about defending anyone? Never, in his mind, though they often refused to reveal the truth about what Ruby had been doing in his absences. In that case he decided he preferred not to know too much so long as everyone was safe.

There seemed no point in continuing the discussion about Mercy's reliability. "Who'd like bannock and beans?"

Soberly, they both nodded. "We do."

Seeing as it was one of their favorite meals he expected slightly more enthusiasm, but he'd settle for changing the subject.

As he mixed up the ingredients for the bannock and put it in a cast-iron fry pan to bake in the oven, he told the children about his trip to the woods. "I need to get the logs in to build a nice cabin for us. Something bigger than this. And I need to chop firewood." The enormity of what he had to accomplish in the few weeks before the snow came settled heavily on his shoulders. He didn't need to deal with Mercy on top of it, yet she had become a fly buzzing about his head. He couldn't go to the woods and leave the twins alone, but obviously taking them to the ranch had been a disaster. He didn't have a lot of options open to him.

He warmed the beans and checked the bannock. "Almost ready. Anyone hungry?"

"I am." Ladd's answer was expected.

"Me, too."

Abel jerked around to stare at Allie. "You're hungry?"

"Starving."

"Well." That was good. Did it signal she would not have lasting damage from her illness? He swallowed back his reaction. He wished he could hope for her to someday be healthy, but the doctor had offered no such hope and Abel would not be taking any risks with her health.

He placed the food on the table and asked the blessing, then they dug in. Ladd ate heartily as usual but when Allie cleaned her plate and asked for seconds, Abel shook his head. "I can't believe how much you're eating. Are you okay?" His spine tightened. Did it mean she was getting better or did it signal something awful?

"I guess helping Mercy gave me an appetite."

"See, she's a good person. She made Allie feel better." Ladd grinned as much as his sister.

Abel shook his head. "She does foolish things and there is always a price for foolish choices. Doing wild things leaves a person with regrets."

The twins simultaneously put down their forks, placed their hands beside their plates and studied him with serious expressions. They turned to look at each other, then returned their gazes to him.

He felt their unasked questions and waited.

Ladd finally spoke. "Like Mama."

He wasn't sure what Ladd meant and didn't want to guess. "What do you mean?"

Allie answered. "Mama said we were nothing but a nuisance."

Ladd nodded. "A stone about her neck."

"We were the payment for your wild life, she said."

Oh, the pain he'd inflicted on these precious children. And, he admitted yet again, to Ruby. It was true. He'd changed his mind about what sort of life he wanted to live. She hadn't. But it was the twins that mattered. And always had. How could he make up to them for the choices he'd made, or would they always pay?

He pushed his chair back. "Ladd, Allie, come here." He patted his knees and the pair scrambled into his lap.

Their arms cradled his neck and he wrapped his arms about them both and held them tight.

"I love you two deeper than the ocean, higher than the sky and wider than forever. You are the very best thing that has ever happened to me. I wouldn't trade either of you for gold nuggets the size of this cabin." His voice trembled with the enormity of his love for them. "And don't you ever forget it."

"We won't," they chorused as they burrowed into his shirtfront.

He held them close as long as they would allow, but all too soon they wriggled away. "Get ready for bed while I clean the kitchen. Then I'll read to you."

A few minutes later, Ladd lay on the narrow bed he would share with Abel, and Allie crawled under the covers of the trundle bed right beside them.

"First, let's say our prayers."

The children closed their eyes and murmured their usual prayers, asking for blessings on the people in their lives. But then Ladd added, "And thank You for Mercy. I like her."

Before Abel could protest, Allie added, "Bless Miss Mercy and help her be the best Wild West person ever. Amen."

"Children, I don't think you should be including Mercy in your prayers." He hated to say it. Knew it didn't make for sound theology.

Allie gave a gentle smile. "I think God would approve. He loves her, too, you know."

What could he say? The child was right. And yet her defense of Mercy worried Abel. The woman signified danger for his children. But he simply said, "I suppose

He does at that," then opened the storybook he'd been reading to them.

This was his favorite time of the entire day. And he didn't intend to let a certain wild woman ruin it for him.

He read for a few minutes as the children grew drowsy, then closed the book and prepared to tiptoe away, though he could only move a few feet before he ran out of space.

"Papa?"

"Yes, son?"

"Mercy is the smartest woman ever and would never do anything foolish."

Abel's sense of contentment and well-being crashed. Mercy again! How had she so quickly and thoroughly beguiled his children? He had to keep her away from them. How hard could it be? Yes, he needed help with the children. But he'd take them to Linette and leave instructions that they were to stay away from Mercy and she from them.

It was simple enough. Linette would surely understand and agree. Beside, how could she refuse if he gave instructions?

The next morning, Linette and Grady were sick with colds and Linette didn't think it was wise for the twins to come for the day.

Mercy would deliver the message to Abel on her behalf, and then maybe she'd never see the man again. She could certainly live without his scorn. Yes, he had his reasons for concern over his daughter. Momentarily she felt a silly sense of longing at his affection for his kids. But more and more his final words churned inside her head. Foolish ways, indeed! Humph. He'd soon see firsthand how foolish she was when she became a star in a Wild West show. Not that she cared what he thought or whether he ever saw her perform.

She passed through the clearing that surrounded the ranch site and climbed the hill toward his cabin. Soon she entered the woods, where the cooler air made her pull her jacket tighter.

A dark shadow to her right caught her attention and as it slipped out of sight, her nerves tingled. An animal of some sort. Her pearl-handled pistols were stowed in her saddlebags, but she mostly used blanks in them. However, she had a business pistol and a rifle and both were loaded. She palmed the pistol and kept alert. Again she noticed the shadow. It passed so far to her right she wouldn't have noticed it if she hadn't been watching so carefully. Whatever it was followed her. Her skin prickled. This required further investigation. She guided Nugget off the trail, dismounted and slid through the trees toward the shadow, her gun at the ready. She paused and listened. There came a rustle of leaves as they fell to the ground to join the other yellowed and browned ones. Wind whispered through the trees. Birds cooed and called.

Then a metallic click froze her blood.

"Drop your gun and turn around real slow."

She considered the order for about two seconds. But, knowing she had few options, she obeyed and with her arms raised to indicate she didn't pose any danger, she turned to confront a man, short of stature, wide of beam with enough black whiskers to cover most of him for the winter.

"Why you sneaking up on me?" he demanded in a voice that sounded like he used his throat to store nails.

"Seems I didn't do any sneaking up on anyone."

"Only 'cause I'm better 'n you in the woods."

Her grin felt crooked. "You are that all right."

"Sure am. Now why you following me?"

"I didn't know it was you, now did I? I thought it might be a wolf."

He made a derisive sound. "And if it was, were you figuring to shoot him with that?" He nodded at her pistol on the ground.

"I figured to scare him off."

"Missy, you sure are a greenhorn. What if I'd been a bear?" He lowered the gun and hooted like he enjoyed finding someone so foolish. There was that word again. It burned clear up her throat that she'd inadvertently proved Abel's opinion of her. Not that he'd ever know.

"I guess in hindsight, I was a little careless." She let her hands fall to her side and her breath eased out when he didn't object. "Who are you?"

The man's dark eyes narrowed. "Ain't none of yer business. Just leave me alone if you know what's good for ya."

"Gladly. Now can I go?"

"Where ya going?"

"Don't see that's any of your business."

He waved the gun as if to remind her he had the upper hand.

She shrugged. "Just delivering a message to a man, then I'm going about my own business." She emphasized the final two words.

"Then git. And forget you ever saw me."

She started away.

"Not that you'll ever see me again."

"Suits me fine," she muttered when she was well

out of hearing. The woods were getting overrun with crazy men.

As she continued on her journey, something about the whiskered man bothered her. She'd seen him somewhere. But where? She couldn't place him. Had it been under good circumstances or bad? Was he a danger, or harmless except for his craziness? She shrugged. What difference did it make? He was likely only passing through.

She reached Abel's cabin. His horse stood saddled and waiting. He opened the door as she approached, the twins at his side. As soon as he saw who it was he eased the children back to the cabin and pulled the door closed.

She gritted his teeth. A person could almost think he didn't welcome her presence. Almost? It couldn't have been plainer unless he hung a big sign over the door.

"Can I help you?" he asked.

Although his words were polite enough and his tone moderate, she felt the sharp edge of each syllable, and if not for her concern for Linette and Grady she would have reined Nugget around and left him to find out on his own her reason for coming. Instead, she swallowed a huge amount of resistance. "I brought a message from Linette. She and Grady are sick with colds and she asked you not to bring the children today."

The harshness in his face fled, replaced with concern. "I trust they are not seriously ill."

"Me, too." Mercy's heart had clenched at the thought of a sick child, but Linette assured her it was only a cold and normal for this time of year.

"Thank her for letting me know. I wouldn't want Allie to get sick."

"That's what Linette said."

The door creaked open and two little heads peeked out. "Hello, Miss Mercy," the twins called.

"Hello, you two. How are you?"

"Good, thank you," Allie said.

"Papa, are you going to take us with you to the woods now?" Ladd asked.

Abel looked toward the sky. The clouds had been thickening all morning. "I can't. It looks like rain."

Or snow, Mercy added silently.

"Then what are you going to do?" Ladd's voice carried a huge dose of worry. "You said you had to get logs. Papa, we'll be okay by ourselves. Won't we, Allie?"

Allie nodded her head and looked determined.

"I'll take care of Allie." Ladd's voice carried a hefty dose of concern.

Mercy's eyes stung at Ladd's sense of loyalty and responsibility. From the far recesses of her memory came a picture. She was about four, which would make Butler six. He'd held her hand tight as he helped her cross a bridge. As she looked at the memory, she realized there had never been any danger. The bridge was plenty wide enough that she wouldn't fall off but only Butler's hand had given her the courage to venture across.

Ladd's promise to protect his sister reminded her of that moment.

Abel sighed deeply. "I really need to get those logs home."

Was he going to leave the kids alone? "How old are you?" she asked them.

"Nine," they answered together.

"But we're very responsible," Ladd assured her.

Mercy thought of the whiskered man in the woods. "Why don't I stay with the children?" What had prompted her to make such an offer? He'd refuse without even considering it. After all, he'd made his opinion of her very plain. Foolish. The word stuck in her throat.

"Oh, please, Papa. Please." Allie clasped her hands in a beseeching gesture and rounded her blue eyes.

Mercy hid a grin. Anyone who could deny such a plea would have to have a heart of stone.

"It's an excellent idea, don't you think, Papa?" Ladd added reasonableness to the request.

Mercy chewed her lip to keep from revealing her amusement.

Abel had his back to her, considering his children. Slowly he turned and faced her. His mouth drew back in a frown. Lines gouged his cheeks.

Even before he spoke, she knew he'd refuse.

Then Ladd tugged at his arm and Abel turned back to the children.

"Papa, you know you don't have many days before winter."

"You're right, but still—" His shoulders rose and fell. He caught Allie's chin. "Baby, you have to promise to take it easy."

"I will, Papa."

He placed his hand on Ladd's head. "Sunshine, you have to promise to watch your sister." He leaned closer and lowered his voice. "And no Wild West stuff."

Mercy coughed. "Shouldn't you be giving me the instructions?"

He faced her, rather reluctantly, she figured. "I will

accept your offer but only because I'm desperate. It's late in the season to be starting out and I must make up for lost time."

"My," she said, sighing as she pressed a palm to her chest, "your enthusiasm is overwhelming."

Allie giggled, then seemed to think better of it and smothered it with her hand.

Abel's eyes narrowed. They were the same dark blue as his son's, Mercy noted. And he had the same unruly dark blond hair half controlled by his hat. "You can put your horse in the pen." He nodded in the general direction. "And thank you for offering to watch the children."

His thanks was so begrudging that she laughed as she reined about and took care of Nugget.

He was in his saddle when she sauntered back to the cabin. "The children know where everything is. If you need anything, ask them." But he made no motion toward leaving.

She favored him with the most innocent, sweet look she could manage when inside she bounced back and forth between amusement and annoyance. "We'll do just fine. Don't worry." She knew full well that every minute he was gone he would worry she might do something foolish. Some rebellious portion of herself that she'd never tamed urged her to add, "I'll try not to do anything foolish."

At the look on his face, she laughed.

Ladd and Allie stood in the doorway. "We'll be good, Papa. Truly we will."

"I'll hold you to it." He rode away.

Mercy didn't wait for him to disappear from sight before she shepherded the twins inside and closed the door. "It's getting colder by the minute," she said by way of explanation for her hurry. She'd never been in the cabin before. Hadn't been the least bit interested in it. Now she glanced around taking in every detail. Which didn't take more than a minute. The cabin was smaller than Jayne and Seth's. Only one tiny room. The small cookstove would more than heat the place on most days. She expected by the time the fire was hot enough to boil water the room would be hot enough to make a grown man drip with sweat. Only one tiny window allowed in light. The few shelves lining the wall overflowed with books, clothing, hardware. One corner of the ceiling had a definite sway to it. She recalled noticing damage to the roof outside. Abel had real cause for hurry if he meant to give these children a warm, safe place for the winter and she knew he did.

"What would you like to do?" she asked the pair.

"I'm not supposed to do anything," Allie said, a little tremor in her voice.

"Your father said you were to take it easy. There are still lots of things you can do."

"Like what?" Both children leaned forward, eagerness in every muscle.

She looked about. "Lots of things." And she'd dream them up in the next few minutes.

She'd prove to Mr. Abel Borgard that she could be trusted not to act foolishly. Not that she ever did. No matter what his opinion of her activities.

Chapter Three

Abel considered the work he'd accomplished. Trees selected for the cabin and cut down. Some firewood gathered. Despite the crisp air, he worked with his shirtsleeves rolled up, sweat trickling down his back. Today held more urgency than just the approaching winter. Mercy was back at the cabin with his children and his nerves tingled at the idea. He'd only seen the woman twice and both times her behavior had given his heart a fit. Would he get home to find the children swinging from the rafters or jumping off the bed?

He swung his ax with renewed vigor. The best thing he could do was get as much work done in as little time as possible.

A few minutes later he paused to wipe the sweat from his brow. That's when his neck muscles twitched. Something or someone watched him. He could feel it. He jerked about. A dark shadow ducked into the bushes. But not before he'd seen enough to know it was not an animal but a squat man with a dark beard down to his chest.

His heart did a persistent two-step inside his chest, making it hard to get a decent breath.

He pretended to study a tree as if considering how best to chop it down, hoping he'd see the man again. He didn't much care for someone to be spying on him, but at least if Abel could see him he'd know the children were safe. Maybe he should forget getting logs and head back.

He warred between the urgency of his task and the need to assure himself of the children's safety.

One simple fact persuaded him to return to swinging his ax.

Mercy had a gun—he'd seen the bulge in her jacket as she returned to the cabin after penning her horse. He had no doubt she knew how to use it. Nor did he think she would hesitate to do so if the need arose. She'd probably jump at the chance.

He chuckled softly as he realized her foolish behavior provided him with a bit of comfort at the moment.

Twice more he glimpsed the dark shadow of the man. What kind of person spied on another? But after a bit he stopped worrying about the mysterious man, who did nothing to make Abel feel threatened. And as long as he was content to watch Abel, those back at the cabin were safe.

He worked steadily into the afternoon, pausing briefly only to drink from his canteen, chow down a sandwich or wipe his brow. As the shadows lengthened, he headed back to the cabin. He'd seen no sign of the intruder for the past hour and hoped the man had left the vicinity. But he wouldn't be completely at ease until he reached the cabin and saw the twins for himself.

He tended Sam first, knowing he would not want to return to the job once he entered the cabin. He put the saddle and blanket in the little shed that offered a modicum of protection, then crossed the yard, threw open the door and ducked inside.

The aroma that greeted him filled his mouth with saliva. How pleasant to come home to a hot meal after a hard day of work. He'd always hoped Ruby would change, would someday decide she liked being married, liked being a mother, liked tending the home. It had never happened and now it was too late for dreams. He would never again risk his children's happiness for the hope of a happy home, and certainly not for the sake of a hot meal. Though it would be pleasant to have something besides beans and bannock for a change.

"The place is getting cold," Mercy said, reminding him he stood in the open doorway.

He closed the door and swung the children off their feet in a big hug. He studied each face. No guilt on either. No heightened color in Allie's cheeks. That was good. And no one mentioned a whiskered man visiting. The last of his tension slipped away.

"Your supper is ready." Mercy shrugged. "I thought you might be hungry." She slipped past him and snagged her jacket from the hook by the door. "I'll be on my way."

"Do you think Mrs. Gardiner and her son will be recovered by tomorrow?"

Mercy gave him a look so full of disbelief he felt a little foolish. "I wouldn't think so. It usually takes a few days to get over a cold, doesn't it?"

"I guess so." Abel's thoughts raced. He still had a lot of work to do and he couldn't leave the children unsupervised while he was away. He looked about again. The children were in one piece. A meal awaited him. That left him one option. He made up his mind and had to act quickly before he thought better of it.

"Can I persuade you to work for me until such time as the children can go to the ranch again? I'll pay you a fair wage."

The children grabbed his hands and grinned up at him then turned to Mercy.

"Please, Mercy," they chorused.

He wondered if he should correct the way they addressed her but, instead, he waited for her to answer, finding himself as tense and eager as they seemed to be. Eager? No. Simply desperate.

Mercy looked at each of the children, then brought her gaze to him, regarding him steadily as if daring him to voice any objection to the way she had managed.

He couldn't and returned her look for look, noting, for the first time, the deep brown of her eyes and how her mahogany hair framed a very pretty face.

"I enjoyed spending the day with the children," she said, smiling at them. Her smile disappeared as she again looked at him. "I'd love to come as long as they need me."

"Thank you." It was only for the children, he silently repeated. She made it clear she felt the same way. Not that it mattered to him one little bit.

"I'll return in the morning then." She brushed her fingers across Allie's cheek and then Ladd's. "See you two tomorrow." And she left without a word of farewell to him.

Not that he cared, he insisted. But the tiny cabin seemed empty...a feeling that intensified after the twins went to bed.

Determined to dismiss such irrational thoughts, he

pulled the Bible off the shelf and read it. His parents had raised him to look for answers to life's problem in the words of scripture and to obey unquestioningly the precepts set out there. Since the twins' births he had found strength and guidance in the pages of the Bible, just as his parents had taught.

But tonight he found no solution for the restlessness that plagued him.

Finally he gave up and prepared for bed. Thankfully the cold air and hard work of the day enabled him to fall into a sound sleep.

The next morning, the children could barely be persuaded to stay in bed long enough for him to start the fire and take the chill off the room.

"When will Mercy be here?" Allie asked for the twentieth time.

"Let's have breakfast first." He tried to corral them both to sit at the table, but they kept bouncing up to throw open the door and see if Mercy approached.

After a few such interruptions, Abel grew annoyed. "Miss Mercy is only helping for a few days. You're simply asking for trouble if you think it's anything more."

Wide-eyed and disbelieving, the twins stared at him.

"Didn't she say she meant to join a Wild West show?" he added to press home his point.

Their gazes grew wary.

"That means she'll be traveling all over the country, living with the others in the show." It sounded like a restless sort of life he wouldn't welcome. He'd tried it already and knew it offered adventure but gave only emptiness. But to each her own. "You won't see her much after that."

Allie brightened. "We could go with her."

He blinked before the eagerness in his daughter's expression. "You could not." What a dreadful, sordid life for a child.

Ladd sighed long. "She's not going for a while. She might change her mind after she gets to know us better." His shoulders sagged. "But she's very good. I guess she won't change her mind."

"There you go." Abel should be relieved that they'd accepted the facts of Mercy's friendship but, instead, he felt as if he had jerked a rug out from under their feet.

A noise against the side of the cabin snapped Abel's head in that direction. Both children bolted to their feet. "Mercy," they yelled.

He grabbed two arms and planted the pair firmly back in their chairs. "Mercy would not be rubbing against the house. Sit here and be quiet." He grabbed his rifle from over the door. If that whiskered man from the woods thought to bother Abel and his children…

"Don't shoot her," Allie whispered.

"Sit and be still." He tiptoed to the door, quietly opened it and inched out far enough to see the side of the cabin. A deer. They sure could use fresh meat, but he wouldn't shoot an animal with his children watching. Besides, this was a doe. He'd find a buck out in the woods. He signaled to the children to come and held his finger to his lips so they'd know enough to be quiet.

They joined him.

"Awww," Allie whispered, the faint noise startling the doe, who bounced into the trees and disappeared.

Allie stared after her. "What did she want?"

He shepherded them back inside though the wind was still and the air promised a warm day. "I don't know. Maybe she is curious. Maybe she's been here before when no one lived here."

"Maybe she thinks this is her house." Allie looked about ready to burst into tears.

"No, baby. I don't think so. Deer like to be among the trees. They don't live in buildings."

Allie sniffled. "You're sure?"

"Very."

Ladd had remained at the door. "Here she comes."

Abel didn't have to look up to understand he meant Mercy. Allie raced to join her brother. Abel took his time going to their side, though truthfully he was as relieved as the twins to see her ride to the cabin. But only because he needed to take advantage of the autumn weather while it lasted.

She called, "Hello," then led her horse to the corral.

Which gave him almost enough time to convince himself he only cared because he had work to do and her presence would enable him to get at it. Besides, he still wasn't persuaded the twins were completely safe with her. What if she decided to shoot her guns off? Or race her horse around with the twins on its back?

He hurried inside to get his coat and hat and leave before she entered the tiny space. They met at the doorway.

She carried a bulging gunnysack.

Both curiosity and caution stopped him in his tracks. "What's in there?" He couldn't keep the ring of suspicion from his voice.

She chuckled. "You needn't sound like you wonder if I've brought knives to let the children throw. Or guns to shoot."

He worked to hide his discomfort; she'd correctly gauged his concern. "I am their only parent."

"Yup. I figured that out. Relax. I merely brought some things to keep the children occupied. See for yourself." She opened the sack and held it out for him to peer in.

Papers, books, cookies? His mouth watered. How long since he'd had cookies? He swallowed back the saliva and nodded. "Looks harmless enough."

"I keep telling you I am not so foolish as to do something to hurt a child."

He looked at her and saw the way she tried to hide her emotion. But she didn't quite succeed. Her lips tightened slightly and her eyes were too wide.

With a stab in his gut, he realized he'd hurt her feelings. "I'm sorry. I didn't mean to suggest you would." Yet hadn't he, despite how well she'd done yesterday? The children had told him about their day in great detail. How they'd shown her all the things he'd bought before their arrival—new clothes, food and winter supplies. They'd shown her their books and their few toys. Told him how they'd played a fun game of pretend family, then she'd let them help her prepare the meals.

His suspicion was unfounded. Yet his caution must remain. He had to keep the children safe. And somehow he knew Mercy was a risk to them. And to him, too, though he couldn't say why he included himself. He had no intention of letting any woman upset the stability he'd worked so hard to establish for the children. Especially a woman whose stated goal was to join a Wild West show. He'd had enough of women who wanted only to run off for whatever reason.

His jaw creaked as he warned himself of all the dangers he invited into his life by asking Mercy to watch the children, but he didn't see what else he could do at the moment.

It would only be for a day or two, he told himself, then he'd insist Mercy stay away from all of them.

Mercy watched Abel ride from the yard, then got the children to help her clean the little cabin. When they were done she lifted the gunnysack. "I brought something for you to do."

"What? What?" Ladd jumped up and down.

"Can we see?" Allie bounced on her feet, then sighed and stood still.

Mercy wished she could tell the child to enjoy herself, but Abel said her heart might be damaged. Must the poor little girl live like an invalid all her life? Mercy had planned things to amuse both children— quiet, imaginative play for Allie, more vigorous activity for Ladd.

She pulled pieces of paper from the sack. "It doesn't look like much yet, but this is everything we need to take a long, adventuresome trip."

Both children studied the paper as if expecting a covered wagon to emerge.

The sun had already driven away the cooler night air. "It's going to be a lovely day. Let's sit outside and enjoy it while we have our adventure." She grabbed a quilt off the bed and spread it under a tree that allowed her a good view of the clearing. She hadn't seen the whiskered man again, nor had she placed him in her memories, but she meant to be cautious until she was certain he was either gone or posed no threat to them.

The three of them sat on the quilt, the children's expressions eager.

"Would you like to go on a ship?"

"Where to?" Allie asked, her eyes gleaming.

"Where would you like to go?"

They looked puzzled.

"I crossed the ocean from my home in England in order to get here." She described the ship. "Do you want to come with me?"

They both nodded, Ladd curious, Allie excited. Her porcelain cheeks had a healthy rosy tint to them. Or did the color signal heart problems? She'd asked Sybil and Linette about the child and both had warned her to watch for breathlessness, fatigue, chest pain or nausea. Sybil said she once knew a boy who had heart problems and his lips would get blue. Mercy saw none of those signs, so unless she witnessed evidence to the contrary she'd take it for natural coloring.

"I'll show you how to make boats." As she talked, she folded the paper into a boat shape and then made sailor hats for them.

"Let's get ready for an adventure." She told them of the tall smokestacks on the ship, the storms that blew and the way the waves rose so high.

She guided their play, letting Ladd climb the tree beside them and be the lookout while Allie stood on the ground acting as the captain, giving orders to Ladd.

Mercy watched Allie closely for any sign of fatigue or blueness around her lips. But the children played for a couple of hours before she felt she should direct them to quieter play.

She pulled out an atlas she had borrowed from

Linette and Eddie's library. "Let's see some of the places we could go."

For the rest of the morning they pored over the book and she told them things she knew about each country they decided to visit. It was a good thing she had paid attention to her geography and history lessons.

"Now it's time for the travelers to have something to eat."

She made sandwiches and they ate outside. "I'll make tea for us." She left them on the quilt and made tea thinned with tinned milk and rejoined them on the quilt.

The thud of approaching horse hooves and rattle of a chain jerked her to her feet and instantly at attention, but it was only Abel dragging logs into the clearing to the spot where he meant to build a new cabin.

The children rose, too.

"Papa," Allie called.

"Stay there until I finish."

He unhooked the chains, then straightened and wiped his arm across his brow. All the while, he studied the children until Mercy fought an urge to jump up and down and say she hadn't been doing anything wrong.

But she would not let his suspicious nature affect her.

His gaze settled on her. She met his look without flinching because—she told herself firmly—she had no reason to be nervous. Sunlight flashed in his eyes making them a warm blue. Their gazes held. The look went on and on until her lungs grew airless. She was overly aware of his study, of her own rapid heartbeat and of the shimmering air in the clearing.

He headed toward them and her ribs tightened so much her lungs could not work.

Ladd raced to him. "Papa, we have been having such fun."

Abel shifted his attention to the boy, and Mercy gasped in an endless breath. What had happened? Why had she felt so strange, as if the air between them pulsed with something she couldn't name?

Allie took two steps then waited for Abel to reach her and lift her to his arms. "We've traveled all over the world."

Abel lifted his eyebrows in surprise. "I sure am glad you got back before I did. I might have worried."

The twins laughed. "Oh, Papa," Allie scolded. "We were here all the time." She squirmed from his arms and ran to Mercy's side and smiled up at her. "Mercy took us on a pretend voyage. I was the captain."

"And I got to climb high and be the watchman."

"I am most glad to see you've all survived your adventure." His gaze bored into Mercy. She tried to tell herself he was warning her that the children better remain unharmed. But it wasn't suspicion she saw or felt. His look measured her, examined her and left her again struggling to fill her lungs.

"Of course everyone is safe," she murmured, then jerked away, saw the tin of cookies on the quilt and grabbed it. "Abel, we were about to have tea. Would you care to join us?" Oh no. Had she just called him by his given name? Surely another evidence of her unacceptable behavior. But it had somehow slipped out of its own accord.

"Oh, please do, Papa," Allie begged. "It's such fun."

"I think I shall." He sat cross-legged on the corner of the quilt. The children sat beside him.

His ready acceptance surprised her, made it impossible for her to think clearly. Shouldn't he be in a hurry to get his work done instead of lingering here? But for some crazy reason, she'd asked. And now she must do as she'd offered and she passed the cookies and poured milk tea from the jug she had prepared.

As he sipped from his cup, he continued to watch her.

What did he want? Why did he keep looking at her so intently? Did he like what he saw? She squirmed under his scrutiny, rearranged the five remaining cookies in the tin, set the tin on the quilt and adjusted it several times. Then, to see if he still stared at her, she lifted her gaze back to him. She blinked as her eyes collided with his blue ones.

Had he watched her all this time?

He jerked his gaze away and put his cup down. "I have to get back to work." He gained his feet in a flash. "I can get more logs hauled in this afternoon." He clamped his hat on his head and strode away.

"Bye, Papa," the twins called, then turned their attention back to their cookies and tea.

Mercy saw Abel pause at the edge of the clearing to glance their way again. His look slid past her and then returned. He shook his head as he guided the horse out of sight.

Mercy tried to analyze what had just happened. Why had he stared so long? Why had she found it so difficult to breathe? It didn't make sense. She had befriended all the cowboys at the ranch. She had been at ease with the sailors on the ship and with everyone—male or female—she met in between. But never had she felt such a strange tightness in her throat or a twitch behind her eyeballs.

Goodness. The man didn't even approve of her. He

only tolerated her presence because he had no other way of providing supervision for his children. Still, she couldn't help admiring his devotion to the twins. Many children didn't ever know such approval from either parent. As for her, he made his opinion crystal clear.

She shook her head, as Abel had done, and wondered if he was as confused as she was.

What was wrong with the pair of them?

They didn't much care for each other and yet... She shook her head again.

It must be the autumn sunshine so warm and deceptive when everyone knew it could change overnight. The temporary delay had lulled them all into a make-believe state.

She turned her attention back to the children. It was time to enjoy the present and forget the unexplainable.

Chapter Four

Abel shook his head several times as he returned to work. What had made him stop in the middle of a sunny afternoon to share tea and cookies with Mercy and the children? He couldn't afford to waste daylight when winter was hard on his heels.

He'd observed Mercy and the children a few minutes without them seeing him. The three of them sharing a picnic. Such a domestic scene. Mercy bending her head toward Ladd and then Allie as they talked. Touching their heads and laughing. The twins drinking her in with their eyes.

His throat had tightened. This happy scene was all he'd dreamed of since the twins were born. Only he'd hoped Ruby would be the one sharing the moment with the children. And he would be right at her side.

Mercy did not fit into the picture he imagined. She wore loose trousers. All the easier to ride in. Mercy obviously did not care about following any rules in her life. Remember, he warned himself, this woman wants to join a Wild West show.

Yet as their gazes connected across the clearing, he

seemed unable to remember his arguments. He tried to pull his thoughts into order as he unhooked the logs. This woman was different from Ruby only in her upbringing. Certainly not in what she wanted from life. He and the children didn't count in her plans. He must bear that in mind.

Then her gaze had snagged his again like some kind of rope trick—demanding, probing, searching...for what he could not say, but he felt as if she reached into his chest and sought to squeeze truth from his heart. How silly. He'd been nothing but truthful with her.

He spent the rest of the afternoon working in the woods. Despite his best efforts to the contrary, his thoughts kept harking back to the cabin and the trio on the quilt enjoying the sunshine. He straightened at the truth he'd discovered—they enjoyed each other while he worked alone. He shook his head at how foolish his thoughts had grown. Of course he worked alone. And the children were safe at home. That's what he wanted. Only he felt isolated.

He bent his back to the task and swung his ax with renewed vigor. He didn't let up until the late afternoon shadows lengthened. He knew he must return if he hoped for Mercy to reach the ranch before dark.

He should warn her of the whiskered man, he realized now. Even her guns and rope would be useless if this man in the woods got the drop on her.

Anxious to get back, he hurried Sam onward. Again, as he'd done earlier in the day, he paused before those at the cabin noticed his presence. Immediately, he saw Mercy. It was hard to miss her. She rode her fancy palomino. The horse reared back on his hind legs as she twirled a rope around the pair of them.

Like Allie said, she made a glorious sight. The words *fire* and *flash* sprang to his mind.

Then he saw the children against the cabin wall, clapping. Allie's eyes were bright, her color heightened. Abel's throat clenched tight. She was overexcited. Hadn't he warned Mercy about this?

He dropped the reins and raced to Allie to scoop her into his arms. He brushed his hand across her face, swept her hair from her forehead. Was she warmer than she should be? "Come along," he said to Ladd, and strode toward the cabin. He put Allie on a chair. "Stay here." He turned to Ladd. "You stay with her." He returned outdoors.

Mercy had dismounted and led her horse toward him.

He strode toward her. His insides churned and his fists clenched at his sides. "Do you have no concern for my children? Are you interested only in an audience for your riding?" He sucked in air to refill his lungs.

She opened her mouth.

Before she could get a word out, he held his hand toward her, silencing her.

"Did you not see how excited Allie was? Did you not notice her bright cheeks?" He shook his head. "I can't believe you could be so careless. I simply can't allow you near my children."

She tilted her head and gave him a hard look.

"Have it your way," she said, her voice hard as rock. "I'm tired of explaining myself. Do you mind if I get my things?" She stalked past him without waiting for his answer.

He followed her and saw the children, wide-eyed and stiff.

Mercy knelt before them, caught their chins and pulled them to face her.

Allie, lips trembling, said, "You can't go."

Ladd gave his father a burning look, then shifted his attention to Mercy. "I like you here."

"I must go. Be good." She kissed them both on the forehead, grabbed her sack and jacket then strode from the house. She swung into her saddle and reined about. At the edge of the clearing she had the horse rear on his back legs. "Goodbye, Mr. Borgard."

This afternoon he'd been Abel, and now Mr. Borgard. Alone again. Though why he thought it had ever changed defied explanation.

He watched until she rode out of sight before he returned to the cabin and the two children watching him with wide eyes and stubborn mouths.

"What do you want for supper?"

Tears welled up in Allie's eyes. "Mercy said she'd make us vegetable soup. But now—" Her voice quivered. "You chased her away."

Ladd clattered to his feet. "She wasn't doing nothin' wrong. You're mad just 'cause she likes to do fun stuff." He glowered at Abel.

Abel sighed. "You both know how careful Allie has to be. Do you want her sick again?" He directed his question to Ladd.

The boy's anger faltered as he considered his sister. He shook his head, then faced Abel squarely. "We were only watching."

Abel didn't intend to argue with his son. "I have to do what I think is best."

"Mama said you forgot how to have fun. She was right."

Abel ignored the boy's comment. Better to let them

blame him than to realize the truth that Ruby cared more about her fun than her children. "Who wants bannock and beans?"

"I want vegetable soup." Allie crossed her arms and pursed her lips.

Abel sighed. "So bannock and beans it is."

The evening did not get better and he was happy when the time came to tuck them in. They still refused to forgive him despite the fact he'd done nothing that required forgiveness.

And then he faced the lonely evening. Only then did he remember he had meant to warn Mercy of the man in the woods. He slipped outside and closed the door behind him. Had she gotten back safely? He strained to listen for any unusual noise in the woods. When he heard only coyotes howling and night birds calling he told himself he was being silly. Of course she'd gotten back safely. Surely someone would let him know otherwise.

He returned inside and prepared for bed but, despite his weariness, sleep did not come easily. How was he going to get a bigger cabin built and firewood brought in?

Still, hadn't he planned to manage on his own when he moved here? Really nothing had changed.

Only his wish that things could be different. But even that wasn't new. He'd wanted something more all his life. When he was sixteen he'd thought he'd find it in abandoning the principles his parents had taught him. When he married Ruby, he thought he'd find it with her. After the twins were born, he thought he'd find it in being a father and returning to his faith in God.

And yet... He dismissed the errant thought.

It *was* in obeying God and living a careful life and looking after the twins that he would find what he wanted.

His last thought before sleep claimed him was that Mercy had been glorious, all fire and flash. He meant to argue to the contrary but instead fell asleep with a smile on his lips.

His smile turned upside down the next day as he contemplated his work. The sky hung heavy with clouds threatening rain and making it impossible to consider taking the twins with him to the woods. That meant he must stay close to the cabin. Right after breakfast he went to the logs he had dragged in—the ones meant for firewood—and cut and stacked a supply.

The children stayed inside where they would be warm and dry. He returned to the cabin after a couple of hours to check on them and get a drink.

As he stepped through the door they both gave him accusing looks.

"There's nothing to do," Ladd said in his most disgruntled voice.

Allie nodded. "If Mercy was here she'd play games."

"Or tell good stories," Ladd added, with heavy emphasis on the word *good,* as if to say her stories were much better than any Abel had read or told.

He gave them both considered study before he said, "Or do something wild and woolly like this was part of Mr. Robert's Circus Side Show." He named a traveling circus.

Allie's eyes gleamed and pink filled her cheeks. "That was the best of all."

The mere mention of it overexcited his daughter. "It's not good for you." He downed a dipper of water and returned to the pile of wood. He wasn't arguing with a pair of disappointed nine-year-olds. They didn't know what was good for them. Even sixteen-year-olds couldn't know. Wasn't he proof of that?

At the end of the day, the twins ate their meals in accusing silence and went to bed without being told. Ladd reached over the edge of the cot and held Allie's hand.

Their displeasure with Abel festered. But what choice did he have? He sat alone after they'd fallen asleep and faced his quandary. Without help, he would have to abandon plans to build a bigger cabin. They could spend the winter in this one just fine, if he had enough firewood to ward off the cold. On nicer days he could take the children to the woods with him, but how many nice days could he count on? As if to answer his question, the wind moaned through the treetops. *God in heaven, I'm counting on You to help me. Maybe even send*—he didn't finish the request. *Send someone to help.* Mercy certainly wasn't an answer to prayer.

He woke slowly the next morning. His eyelids didn't want to face the day. His limbs felt heavy and unresponsive. But lying abed would not solve his problems.

He sighed and rolled over. The bed beside him was empty. He patted both sides to make sure. His eyelids jerked open. Where was Ladd? In the weak light Allie looked at him from her trundle bed, eyes wide and watchful.

He scanned the cabin. Ladd wasn't there. The small quarters offered no hiding place, but he sat up and looked about again to make sure he hadn't missed the boy.

"Where's Ladd?" he asked Allie.

"Gone."

"Gone?" Any remnant of sleep vanished as his blood raced through his veins. He grabbed his trousers and pulled them on under privacy of the covers. "Where?"

"To get Mercy. We want her to look after us. 'Sides, you need her here so you can get logs." She sat in the middle of her bed and watched him as calm as could be while his arms turned leaden and he couldn't seem to get them into the sleeves of his shirt.

"Mercy? She's six miles away. When did he leave?" He peered out the window. The sun had not yet risen but cold gray light filled the clearing. Had his son ventured out in the dark? Was he lost? What about that whiskered man?

He pulled on his jacket and grabbed his rifle. But at the door he stopped. He couldn't leave Allie here alone and wouldn't take her out in the damp cold.

His lungs so tight he could hardly force in air, he faced the door. All he could do for the moment was pray. *Oh, God, keep my boy safe.* As soon as the sun drove back the chill, he would bundle Allie to her teeth and take her with him to find Ladd.

Mercy tiptoed from her room. If Abel didn't want her help with the children, that was fine. It gave her more time to practice. She wanted to be able to twirl a big enough circle with her rope that she could swing it up and down over both herself and Nugget. She'd tried the day before yesterday. That's when Abel had shown up all glower and snort. He didn't bother to take into account that the children were content to sit quietly as they watched her. Nope. He simply ordered her off the place.

She missed the children. But she surely wouldn't miss dealing with a man like Abel any more than she'd miss stabbing herself in the eye with a hot needle.

Carrying her boots so as not to disturb Linette and Grady, who were still miserable with their colds, she glided down the hall and creaked open the door. She glanced back at the stairs to make sure she hadn't wakened them and slipped through the opening.

She turned and screamed as someone stood on the step before her. Heart in her mouth, she managed to croak out a greeting. "Ladd, you gave me a fright." She looked past him as she pulled on her boots, expecting to see Abel and Allie. "Where's your papa?"

Ladd ducked his head. "He was sleeping when I left."

Mercy heard the words but they made no sense. "Left where?"

"Home."

Surely he didn't mean— "You mean the cabin?"

"Uh-huh. I promised Allie I would come and get you." He grabbed her hand. "You have to come. Please. It was so boring without you. Allie even cried a little."

She stared at the boy. "Does your papa know where you are?"

"Allie said she'd tell him."

"But it's barely light. How did you get here?"

"I followed the trail, but it was hard to see." He glanced beyond her. "Someone helped me."

Someone? So far as she knew the men were all on the roundup and the women tucked safely in their beds. Except for that whiskered man she'd seen. "What did this someone look like?"

"I don't know. I couldn't see him. He carried me and left me there." Ladd pointed toward the barn. "I might have got lost if he didn't help me. Actually, I think it was God helping."

None of what the boy said made sense. Except one thing. His father didn't know where he was. Or if he was safe.

"You must be hungry. Come in." She opened the door and herded him to the kitchen, where she sliced a thick slab of bread and spread syrup on it.

Linette came into the room as he ate. Mercy drew her into the hall and explained Ladd's presence. "I have to get him back as soon as possible. Abel will be frantic with worry. His children mean more to him than anything in the world."

"You go. And don't let the man chase you away again. He needs your help even if he won't admit it."

"And he won't." But she couldn't let her annoyance at his rude dismissal matter at the moment. She returned to Ladd's side. "While you finish eating I'm going to saddle Nugget."

He nodded. "Be sure to bring some books and maybe cookies."

She chuckled. "I'll see what I can do."

Linette followed her down the hall. "I'll keep an eye on him until you return."

"Thanks." She trotted down the hill and saddled Nugget then rode him back to the house. Ladd came out and she swung him up behind her.

They rode down the trail toward the little cabin. Every one of Mercy's senses was alert for any strangers in the woods, although she saw nothing out of the ordinary. As they neared the cabin, Abel rushed to their side. He swung Ladd down and hugged him, remaining so close to Mercy's side she couldn't dismount.

He put Ladd on his feet, then reached up and lifted Mercy down. Even though she didn't need his assistance, she saw no point in arguing with the distraught man.

He didn't release her when her feet hit the ground but hugged her equally hard as he'd hugged Ladd. Then he held her at arm's length.

"Thank you." His voice was deep with emotion.

They studied each other. She couldn't say what he thought or felt except for the way his eyes darkened, which could indicate regret or any of a dozen things.

But his firm hands on her shoulders, the unexpected solid comfort of his chest and the warmth of his breath on her cheeks as he thanked her cut a wide swath through invisible barriers she'd been unaware existed. Something made her want to return to his embrace. Strangely, she felt safe in his arms. How ridiculous! She hadn't ever needed or wanted or received such foolish comfort. Her parents had never offered it. But a little voice from her depths pleaded for more of it.

Whoa…he wasn't offering it intentionally. He merely was grateful that she'd returned his son.

She stepped back out of his reach. "He's fine."

"Ladd," Abel said. "Go see your sister. She worried." He waited until the door closed behind the boy. "Where did you find him?"

"On my doorstep."

"He made it all the way to the ranch?"

She nodded, watching the emotions on his face change from worry to disbelief. "How is that possible? It was dark and a fair hike for a child."

"He said a man picked him up and carried him."

Worry wrinkled his brow. "I've seen someone in the woods. A short, stocky man. I meant to warn you about him."

"I've seen someone, too. A man with lots of whiskers."

"Sounds like it could be the same person." Abel scrubbed a hand over his hair, tangling it.

If she wasn't so concerned and confused at both his actions and her reactions she might have chuckled at how he messed his hair.

"I wonder who he is and what he wants," Abel said.

"I don't know, though I'm certain I've seen him somewhere before. I just can't place where or when."

"Did you get a good look at him?"

"I did. I know I should recognize him."

"Would you have seen his likeness on a wanted poster?"

She considered the question. "I don't know. I wish I could place him." She shrugged. "But if it was he who helped Ladd we can be grateful he didn't harm him instead."

Abel shuddered. "I don't like it." He messed his hair again and then, as if realizing what he'd done, he smoothed it. "The man could be crazy."

She'd momentarily shared the same thought but immediately dismissed it. A person should be judged on evidence, not on suspicion or caution. "Or maybe he likes living in the woods. Or for all we know, he has a cabin of his own."

"Wouldn't Eddie know if that is so?"

She gave silence assent.

"Has he ever mentioned this man?"

She shook her head.

"Then we'll have to be cautious and on guard."

We? When had they become we?

"Anyway. Thank you for bringing him home safely."

"You're welcome."

He smiled.

She knew her eyes widened but she couldn't help herself. His smile transformed his features and made him look…well, nice.

"Please come in."

"My horse…"

"I'll tend to him later."

She let herself be ushered to the door five steps away, let him reach around her and hold it open for her to precede him.

"Did you ask her?" Allie demanded.

Mercy knew what Allie wanted, but Abel hadn't asked.

He took her coat as she slipped her arms out. He hung it next to his and went to the stove. "Have you had breakfast?"

"No." Ladd had interrupted her plans for the day. Not that she minded.

"Then join us. We haven't eaten yet."

"Thank you."

"But first I have a son to deal with." He sat on the edge of the bed and pulled Ladd to his knee to face him. "I'm happy you're safe, but what you did was foolish and against the rules."

"Yes, Papa."

"Haven't I told you that there is a price to pay for foolish and sinful choices?"

"Yes, Papa."

"There is no escaping. The Bible says, 'Be sure your sin will find you out and whatsoever a man soweth he shall reap.' I simply want to save you the pain and sorrow of reaping a bad harvest. Do you understand?"

"Yes, Papa." Ladd spoke softly, his head bowed.

"You know I must punish you."

"I know."

Mercy wondered what form of punishment Abel had in mind. She'd witnessed how rigid he was about rules. Would he mete out unmerciful judgment?

"After breakfast, you will clean up the kitchen and do the dishes by yourself, and while you're doing it I want you to consider why I forbid you to go out on your own. You could have been hurt or lost."

"God sent a man to help me."

Mercy and Abel exchanged a look. His was full of concern and worry. For her part, she wondered how he'd deal with this.

"Son, like I said, I'm glad you're safe and sound. Let's leave it at that." He patted Ladd on the back and returned to the stove.

"Do you drink coffee?" he asked Mercy, then realized she still stood. "Please, have a seat."

She sat on one of the chairs. Allie hung over the back, her face so close to Mercy's she breathed in the sweet scent of her skin. "I like coffee fine," she answered.

He filled a new-looking coffeepot with water, ground some beans and tossed the ground coffee into the pot. In a few minutes he poured her a cupful.

She cradled her hands about the cup.

He sipped his coffee as he turned his attention back to the pot of porridge he cooked. He handed bowls to Ladd. "Set the table, please."

Mercy kept her attention on her cup as she tried to ignore his presence. It was impossible. He was so big in such a small space. And so vital. He touched Allie's head, brushed Ladd's shoulder, smiled at them.

Her mouth went dry. She gulped coffee but the dryness remained.

The children were fortunate to know such affection and approval from their father. What had happened to their mother, she wondered?

He filled bowls, set them on the table and sat down. "Let's thank God for the food." The children bowed their heads and Abel said a prayer of thanksgiving, not only for the food but for the safety of his son.

Allie and Ladd sent silent signals to each other across the table. They ducked their heads to eat their breakfast, then looked steadfastly at their father.

Abel cleaned his bowl and drained his coffee cup. "Mercy—you don't mind if I call you that, do you?"

"I answer best to it. After all, it's my name." She knew he meant to ask her permission to use her Christian name, but some perverse imp prompted her to answer indirectly.

His smile was fleeting. "Fine. Mercy, I find myself in a quandary."

She offered him no assistance. He had gotten himself into this quandary without her help. He'd have to get out the same way.

"I need to get wood and cut logs. I can't leave the children to do it. And they are quite insistent that they want you to stay with them. Will you?"

Although she understood what he wanted, he'd been much more direct about telling her to leave. He could be equally direct about asking her to come back. "Will I what?"

His eyes narrowed. He'd correctly read her resistance.

Just as she understood that he swallowed his pride to ask her straight out. "Will you please stay with the children so I can get at my work?"

She laughed, with relief at being welcomed back and also with a touch of victory that he'd had to lessen his rigid stand. "Why, I'd be pleased to."

The children grinned. Ladd immediately set to work cleaning the table and washing dishes.

Abel pushed back from the table. "Thank you." He wrapped slices of bread and syrup in brown paper, snagged a can of beans and then grabbed his coat and hat. "I'll be on my way." He hugged the children and hurried out.

She stared at the door for a heartbeat after he left. Two and then a third. His thanks had been perfunctory. His leaving hasty. And why not? He had to prepare for winter. Had to provide the children's needs.

No reason in the world to wish he could linger a bit and talk to her. No reason at all.

In fact, it was a relief to have him gone. He was too big. He crowded the tiny room and made her uncomfortable. Whew. She released the air from her tight lungs. Now she could breathe easy without concerning herself about his reaction to what she said and did.

She rubbed her arms, remembering his solid chest and warm hands.

Why had his hug felt so good? Like it filled up an empty spot in her heart. She shook her head. Where had such foolishness come from?

Chapter Five

Abel led Sam in the general direction he planned to go but, before he ventured farther, he left the horse waiting as he scouted around the cabin. If some crazy man hung about in the vicinity he wanted to know about it. Heavy gray clouds hung low in the sky. Dampness filled the air. At least the twins would be safe and dry in Mercy's care.

Mercy! The woman seemed destined to fill his mind with confusion.

Shoot! He was crazier than any wild man. He'd hugged Mercy. Only because he was so all-fired relieved to see Ladd safe and sound. Or at least that's the excuse he gave himself and initially it had driven his actions. But he'd felt a whole lot more than relief as soon as his arms closed around her. He'd noted a number of things—how she fit just below his chin, how small yet strong she felt, how her hair filled with the scent of summer flowers and fresh-mowed hay.

Momentarily, without forethought, his arms had tightened around her and then she'd stepped back, no doubt as shocked by his actions as he'd been.

A thorough search around the cabin yielded no evidence of anyone lingering in the area. So Abel returned to Sam and left to find firewood and good logs, though building a bigger cabin before winter seemed a distant possibility.

He worked steadily all day, grateful the rain held off. Shadows filled the hollows and hung around the trees as he returned to the cabin with logs. Rather than unload immediately, he headed for the cabin, driven by far more than concern for the children. All day his thoughts had tortured him with memories of Mercy in his arms. Yet only the day before he'd considered her a menace to his children's safety.

Likely she still was, and he needed to keep that in mind. A woman interested in pursuing a wild life in a show, a woman who ignored his warnings about involving the children in her activities, a woman who rode like a man and...

He reached the cabin door and paused to listen. Laughter came from inside and he forgot to list the other things against Mercy.

Ducking his head, he stepped inside and ground to a halt. Flour covered half the surfaces in the cabin and if he wasn't mistaken, dough spatters decorated the surfaces that had been spared the flour dusting. The children wore generous amounts of both and Mercy's hair had turned gray. When had he ever seen such a mess? Was this her idea of looking after the twins? "What exploded?"

The three looked up, saw his expression and glanced around. Their gaze returned to him, guardedness replacing the laughter.

"We made cookies," Ladd said, his words solid.

"Mercy helped us." Allie sounded a little more conciliatory.

Mercy didn't say anything and her gaze dared him to object.

He swallowed hard, the aroma of cookies from the oven overwhelming his annoyance. "Cookies, huh?"

"Want some?" Allie asked.

"They smell good." He'd overlook the mess in order to enjoy the cookies. And the company of those who had baked them. Tonight he'd clean the mess. At least he'd be too busy to be bored and lonely.

He sat at the table and tried not to look too surprised at the cookies set before him. One was small and slightly black around the edges, another was the size of a saucer, several were balls and one had been shaped into— He peered more closely at it.

"It's a horse," Ladd said. "Allie made it."

Allie stood at Abel's side waiting for his approval. Who'd have thought to make a horse out of cookie dough? Probably Mercy. "It's looks very nice."

Allie beamed her approval.

Mercy handed him a cup of coffee although she didn't join him and the children at the table.

He studied her out of the corner of his eyes. Was she uncomfortable around him? He had no one but himself to blame if she was. Nor could she find this any more awkward than did he.

He downed his coffee and ate two cookies—one each child had made—pronounced them delicious, then hurried back outside to deal with the load of firewood.

A couple of hours later, he returned to the cabin. When he stepped inside, he blinked at the transformation. The flour and dough had been cleaned up and the vegetable soup Allie craved simmered on the stove. The table had been set for three. No reason he should be disappointed, he told himself. Mercy had to get going if she planned to get back while she could see the trail.

She grabbed her jacket and he followed her out the door.

"Keep alert. I don't like to think what a man is doing out in the woods."

She chuckled. "I'll keep my gun and rope ready and, if need be, use them both."

He didn't ask how she'd use them both but, no doubt, she could.

She swung into the saddle and sat there. "I don't know if you were aware that there are church services at the ranch every Sunday. There's a service tomorrow, in the cookhouse. Everyone is welcome. If you're interested."

"I'd love to come. I want the children to realize that Sunday means church. What time?"

"We meet right after breakfast." She gave the time. "See you then."

"Yes. I look forward to it." He meant both church and seeing her again. And he feared it showed in his eyes.

She smiled softly. No mocking. No challenge. "Until tomorrow then." She reined about and rode from the yard.

He watched her until he could no longer see her. A sigh rose from deep inside him. Then he shook his head. He'd once followed his heart and look where it had landed him. From now on he meant to follow his head and his head said Mercy was a pack of trouble who would turn all their lives upside down and sideways if he wasn't careful.

* * *

Mercy put on her prettiest green taffeta dress. She might be wild and unconventional, or so her friends said, but she wouldn't go to church in pants. She snorted. Despite Ambrose's opinion of her. Not even if church was in a cookhouse on a ranch.

She pulled her hair back into a twist at the back of her head. When she, Jayne and Sybil had spent the weeks on the ship crossing the ocean they had brushed and styled each other's hair. She missed it but her friends were now married. It sure hadn't taken them long. They claimed God had sent their husbands into their lives even though Jayne had accidently shot Seth and Brand had ridden in with his dog to break Eddie's horses.

Maybe God had sent Abel and the children into Mercy's life.

She dismissed the idea before it could light in her thoughts. Abel made it clear as the water in the stream that flowed by the ranch that he didn't approve of her. Not that she cared. Not a whit. She had plans that did not include a man and children…a ready-made family. Nor did she think God concerned Himself with the petty affairs of man.

She looked at the picture of her parents that sat on the dresser. What did family mean? She shook her head, dismissed the question and hurried to meet Linette and Grady.

Grady had recovered from his cold but Linette still looked pale.

"Are you sure you're up to this? And having everyone come for dinner afterward?"

Linette nodded. "I'll have lots of help." She let out

a large sigh. "I'm missing Eddie. I wish they were all back home."

"If Eddie was correct about how long it would take they'll be gone another week."

"I know." She took Mercy's arm as they walked down the hill to church. "It will be the longest week of my life." They had reached the steps to the cookhouse when Abel and the children rode into sight.

"Mercy, Mercy," the twins called, waving madly.

Abel immediately caught Allie's hand and calmed her.

Linette chuckled and withdrew her arm. "Seems your attention is requested."

Mercy smiled and waved at the twins while her gaze went unbidden to their father. The brim of his hat shaded his face so she couldn't make out the expression in his eyes and yet her lungs constricted so sharply she almost stumbled. "The children have accepted my friendship readily enough." Where did that note of regret in her voice come from? Maybe Linette wouldn't notice it.

But the way her friend studied her and patted her hand, Mercy knew she hoped in vain. "I expect their father is glad of your friendship, too."

"I didn't mean that. The last thing I need or want is a rule-bound man."

The twins continued to call out to Mercy.

Linette took Grady's hand and climbed the steps to the cookhouse door. "You best go greet your friends." Laughter rounded her voice.

Mercy opened her mouth to protest that Abel wasn't her friend and found she couldn't force the words out. Were they friends? Or did he simply tolerate her for the sake of the children? She shrugged. What did it matter? Just because he'd hugged her...out of gratitude. Just because her heart broke into a gallop when he smiled... It meant nothing. It only indicated her growing restlessness. She needed to get back to practicing her riding and roping tricks.

They reached her side and Abel handed the children down, then swung off the horse to land at Mercy's side.

"'Morning," he said. "Are we late?"

"No. Right on time." She waited as he tied the horse to a rail. "Come and meet the others."

The children held her hands as she led the way up the stairs. "Cookie will be happy to meet you." She hesitated a moment. Maybe she should warn them of what to expect, but what could she say? She opened the door and stepped inside, the children at her side and Abel bringing up the rear.

Cookie swept across the floor toward them.

Mercy held the twins firmly. "This is Abel Borgard and his children, Allie and Ladd."

Cookie ground to a halt before the twins.

"This is Cookie."

"Welcome, welcome." The big woman opened her arms.

Ladd's grip tightened. Allie shrank against Mercy's leg.

"Shy little things, are you?" Cookie patted their heads and swung her attention to Abel. "I've been wondering when we'd get to meet you."

Abel held out his hand.

Cookie grabbed him and pulled him into a smothering hug, patting his back hard enough that the breath whooshed out of his lungs. After several pats, she released him.

Abel sucked in air and glowered at Mercy. "You could have warned me," he whispered as Cookie returned to the table.

"Would you have believed me?" she whispered back.

Abel grunted. "Likely not."

Mercy grinned.

"You don't need to enjoy it quite so much."

"Sorry." She wasn't and guessed he knew it. She indicated he should step forward and meet the others. "Bertie, Cookie's husband."

"Glad to have you with us." Bertie shook Abel's hand.

Mercy went around the circle. "Cassie and her children, Daisy, Neil, Billy and Pansy. My friends who came from England with me, Jayne and Sybil, and you know Linette." Grace and her sister, Belle, wouldn't join them today. With Ward away at the roundup Grace preferred to stay at their ranch a few miles away.

They made the rounds and found a place to sit. The twins sat on either side of Mercy, and Abel sat by Allie. His bent legs pressed Allie tight to Mercy's side. He rested a hand on the bench behind his daughter and leaned close as if sheltering her. Mercy sat very still, afraid if she shifted, she would bump into his fist or rub against his shoulder. She crossed her ankles and tucked her feet under the bench, holding herself stiff and upright, and focused her attention on Cookie, who rose to lead them in singing a few hymns.

But how could she ignore him when he sang with a clear deep voice that made all the female voices, and indeed even Bertie's, sound mild and weak?

Did he really mean the words as firmly as he sang them?

Then Bertie stood to speak. "I know you're all missing

your men." The women around Mercy murmured agreement. "It brings to mind a time when I was alone and wandering far from God. I had convinced myself that God didn't care about me. I was convinced I had no part in His great plans. It was a mighty lonely place for me to be."

Mercy didn't normally give Bertie's speeches much thought; today she clung to each word in order to stop herself from feeling Abel with every pore.

Bertie continued. "I found shelter in a church one night and happened to overhear the preacher practicing his sermon. 'Thou knowest my downsitting and mine uprising, thou understandest my thoughts afar off.' Unaware that I listened from my bed on one of the pews, the man went on to talk about how God knows and cares about every aspect of our lives. 'Too wonderful,' he said over and over." Bertie sighed deeply. "That was the day I began my journey back to God…a God who cares personally about each of us. Ladies, and Mr. Borgard, rest assured that not only does He know and care about us, He knows and cares about the men on the roundup, too."

Abel nodded.

Allie shifted to lean against her father and Abel wrapped an arm about her shoulders. His hand brushed Mercy's arm as he drew his daughter close and Mercy stiffened. She kept her eyes on Bertie though she longed to glance at Abel and see if he'd been as aware of the touch as she.

As she wondered, the service ended and Cookie invited them to share coffee and cinnamon buns. Mercy bolted to her feet at the invitation and hurried to Cookie's side. "I'll help you."

Cookie laughed. "I can manage. You go enjoy that Mr. Borgard." She leaned close. "My, he's a handsome fellow."

Mercy's cheeks burned and she couldn't look at Abel. Hopefully, he hadn't heard.

"Now go sit with your friends."

Mercy hurried to sit beside Jayne.

Her friend nudged her. "Shouldn't you make Abel feel more welcome?"

Finally she allowed herself to glance at him. He stood before the bench where they had sat together, the children at his side. The three of them looked about at the women and children, then Abel turned toward the door.

"Don't let him leave," Jayne whispered.

Mercy's awkward awareness of him vanished as she bolted to her feet and went to the trio. "Come and join the others for coffee. It's a tradition. And no one should miss out on Cookie's cinnamon rolls. There's nothing like them."

Cookie beamed her approval as Mercy took Allie's hand and urged Abel forward.

He sat across from Linette and Cassie.

Mercy sat beside him. The children crowded in next to them, pushing them shoulder to shoulder.

The sighs of enjoyment verified her claim that the cinnamon rolls shouldn't be missed.

Linette wiped her mouth. "It's also a tradition that we all go to the big house for dinner. I hope you'll consent to join us."

Mercy had been fighting awareness of every move Abel made—lifting a coffee cup to his lips, taking bites from the cinnamon roll. Each movement caused his arm to rub along hers, sending tingles skittering up her nerves. Why was she so conscious of the man? It wasn't as if she even liked him. And certainly he didn't like her. Yet—

She closed her eyes and clamped her teeth together.

But the thought persisted. Yes, she admired certain things about him. The way he showed love for his children. How concerned he was about their welfare. It kind of reminded her of what Bertie had said about God. Abel knew his children and cared about them. Of course, Bertie had meant it about God, but she found it easier to believe about Abel because she saw the evidence.

"I don't know what to say to your kindness," Abel said.

Mercy heard the pending refusal in his voice. "I'm sure the twins would enjoy visiting with the other children," she murmured.

"Please, Papa," Allie whispered.

He shifted. She assumed he looked at Allie and turned to watch, but her gaze collided with his. She was struck by its dark blue intensity. His look went deep and long. What did he seek? Certainly nothing from her. She swallowed hard as he continued to study her. Did he want to know her opinion of him staying? The thought flared through her head. Why would it matter?

"I'm sure you'd all enjoy it," she managed with a tongue as thick as an ax handle.

A smile flickered across his face. He turned back to Linette. "Thank you for the invitation and we accept."

Ladd leaned forward to look past Mercy and grin at his father.

At that moment, little two-year-old Pansy climbed

to the bench across from Abel and stared at him. "You see my papa?"

Abel shook his head. "I'm afraid I haven't."

Pansy's bottom lip trembled. "I miss my papa."

Allie sat forward on the edge of the bench. "You can share my papa if you like."

Pansy turned to study Abel with wide blue eyes.

Mercy held her breath as she waited to see how the toddler would respond. She felt Abel's arm tense, as well.

After a moment Pansy smiled. "Okay." She climbed down, trotted around the table to Abel and held out her arms. "Up."

Abel picked her up and she perched on his knee, as content as imaginable.

He smiled at Mercy and she grinned back, struck to the core by his gentle, easy way with the child. The man certainly knew how to charm little girls. She averted her eyes. Big girls weren't so easily charmed. Especially when big girls knew he didn't approve of them and their activities.

Linette rose. "Shall we go up the hill then? I need to check on the roast."

Abel and the children fell in at her side. Cassie and her children followed. Mercy joined arms with Sybil and Jayne and brought up the rear.

Jayne leaned over to whisper, "What a charming man. You didn't tell us."

Mercy shrugged. "He isn't like that with me."

"Oh, do tell." Sybil shook Mercy's arm. "How is he with you?"

Mercy wished she needn't respond but knew her friends would persist until they had an answer. She shrugged to indicate it didn't matter. "He doesn't approve of me."

They both jerked to a halt and turned to her. Sybil looked concerned. Jayne grinned.

"Why would that be, I wonder?" she asked. "Let me guess. You go out of your way to be wild and unconventional and then wonder why he is disapproving."

"I do no such thing. I am just me."

"That's what I mean." Jayne shook her head. "Always challenging life and conventional behavior." She looked at Sybil. "Why do you think she's like that?"

Sybil shrugged. "We've discussed this before and I still hold that she's trying to get her parents' attention."

Mercy let out a noisy gust of a sigh. "I am not."

"Face it, Mercy. They only notice you when you do something so outrageous they can't ignore it. So you do it again. And again."

Mercy recalled Ambrose had said much the same before he informed her he didn't care for her behavior. "You are so wrong. I simply like adventure. I'm not interested in the ordinary and expected."

Sybil grabbed her arm and clung to her side. "I might believe that if I didn't see the hunger in your eyes as you watch Abel and his children. What he has is what you want even if you won't admit it to yourself."

She ground to a halt. "And what is that, may I ask?"

"A family and a heart of love."

Mercy stared straight ahead. She hadn't expected Sybil to have an answer. Especially not an answer that cut a wide swath through her heart, leaving a trail of... fear. She swallowed hard. Fear? What utter nonsense. "I want a life of adventure. In fact, I am going to practice extra hard so I can join a Wild West show real soon."

She plowed ahead, not giving the others a chance to reply.

Inside the house, she went directly to the kitchen to help Linette. Normally, the men would visit in the front room, but Abel was the only man present so he followed the women into the kitchen.

Mercy tried to ignore his presence but every time she turned around, there he was, big and bright, watching her every move. She bit her tongue to stop from telling him she found him annoying.

"It's ready," Linette announced an hour later, catching Mercy staring into space as she plotted a way to prove she had no interest in Abel apart from his children.

Thinking of the twins brought a smile to her mouth and she allowed herself to be shepherded to the table. Only after she took her place did she realize she sat directly across from Abel. So what? He was just another cowboy and not one had ever intimidated her.

Vowing to act normally, she passed the food and ate and joined in the table conversation. Only when Abel mentioned how much he enjoyed the meal did her thoughts stutter.

"I'd forgotten what good food well served tastes like."

"But, Papa," Ladd said. "Mercy cooked us a nice meal."

Her gaze collided with Abel's. A regretful smile curved his lips. "So she did and I truly appreciated it."

Mercy made a small, disbelieving noise. "I barely know how to cook."

Linette chuckled. "When I arrived here I didn't know how to cook a thing. I learned in a hurry though I made a few mistakes." She regaled them with stories of hard beans and failed bread. "Cookie kept saying baking bread was as easy as falling off a log. I thought I'd never learn."

Neil edged forward. "Can we go play?"

"Of course," Cassie said.

"Can Ladd come?"

Abel studied his son. "Would you like to?"

Ladd nodded, his expression eager.

"Very well."

The boys clattered from the room and their calls could be heard as they ran down the hill.

"Papa?" Allie whispered.

"I'm sorry. You can't join them. You must take it easy."

"She can play with Grady's things," Linette said. "Come along, I'll show you."

Abel pushed to his feet. "I don't know..."

"It's only some carved animals. She can play quietly."

Abel reluctantly agreed. He sank back to the bench as the ladies rose to clear the table and do the dishes.

When Pansy grew fussy, her older sister, Daisy, rose to take her home and put her to bed.

Sitting there alone, Abel rubbed his legs, scratched at the table and looked about restlessly.

"Why don't you show Abel around the place," Linette whispered as she leaned close to Mercy. "Take pity on the poor man. He's uncomfortable surrounded by women."

Mercy sighed deeply. The last thing she wanted was to spend the afternoon entertaining the man, but she could hardly refuse Linette's suggestion. "Shall we?" She waved toward the door.

How could she possibly keep her errant thoughts in line while trailing about the place? She pushed her shoulders back. She could do it. She only had to remember how much he disapproved of her. Called her foolish. Accused her of being careless with his children.

A little wayward voice broke into her arguments. He praised her cooking. Hugged her, his arms warm and protective around her.

She shook her head nearly hard enough to loosen the pins in her hair.

She, Mercy Newell, cared not what Abel Borgard, or any man for that matter, thought of her.

Chapter Six

Abel let Mercy lead him from the house. Grateful as he was to escape the kitchen full of women, he glanced back, reluctant to leave. He'd seen Allie playing quietly in the corner of the living room, but would she stay there? Would the women realize she must not exert herself? Did they know of her fragile condition? Still, Linette had promised to keep her quiet. He had to trust her. He could see Ladd playing tag with the boys. His son deserved a chance for such play.

"What would you like to see?" Mercy asked.

He pulled his thoughts to the promise of the afternoon. How long had it been since he'd been able to enjoy himself without worrying about the children?

"The barn." It seemed a good enough place to start.

They traipsed down the hill and entered it. The interior was dusky and empty.

"Almost all the horses are gone with the men," she said.

"Of course." He nevertheless toured the place. "I'd like to have such a big barn someday and a nice herd of cows. Right now though, I'd be happy to have enough room for my horse and a milk cow. And a decent-sized cabin." He knew he rambled but he couldn't help it. His little rental cabin and meager supply shed seemed laughable in contrast to this ranch.

"Where's your horse?" he asked to turn his mind from such thoughts.

"He's out in the pen behind the barn along with the half-dozen horses Eddie left behind in case we need them."

She led him out the door and around to the back and whistled. Her horse trotted up to her and whinnied. She patted his neck. "He's a real good horse. So easy to train."

He scrubbed at his neck. "Why do you want to join a Wild West show?"

She laughed a little and kept her attention on her horse. "Why not?"

"What would your family say?"

She shrugged. "I doubt they'd care."

Her words stunned him. "Of course they care."

Her gaze bored into him. "I'm sorry but you simply can't say that. You don't know." She headed past the pen.

He followed on her heels. "What makes you think they don't?"

She spun about to face him. "What makes you think they do?"

"I— Well, it just figures. Family cares about family."

"Really?" She moved onward. "What happened to your wife?"

He ground to a halt at her unexpected question. "What's that got to do with anything?"

She faced him, a look of victory on her face. "Seems she's family."

"She was. A reluctant part, I confess. She'd dead. She drowned."

Shock filled her face. "That's awful. I guessed she was gone but I thought—" She lifted one shoulder. "The children said something about her that made me think she'd been ill."

"What did they say?"

She considered his question. "Something about her not looking after them. I took it to mean she wasn't able because of poor health."

He snorted. "Not because of poor health but because of disinterest. She never wanted children. Didn't want to settle down." They fell in side by side and walked along the trail, crossing a wooden bridge over the river and climbing a slight hill as they talked. "When I wanted to settle down and become a family, she accused me of trying to end her fun."

Mercy brushed her palm against his arm. "That must have been difficult."

"Yes, it was. Though I had no one to blame but myself."

"Oh, I'm sure that's not true."

They reached the top of the hill and stopped walking. "I'm afraid it is. You see, when I was sixteen, I rebelled against my parents' rules. Against God's, too. I thought the rules ruined *my* fun. By the time I realized they protected me and those I loved, I was married to Ruby and had twin babies."

She stood so close to him that he felt her stiffen.

"I'm guessing you don't agree. Maybe you think more like Ruby."

"I'm not saying rules ruin my fun, but I guess I don't think they protect me either. That makes it sound like God sees and cares what we do. That He rewards obedience and punishes disobedience."

"I'd say that was true."

"It's what you believe. Seems Bertie does, too. But I'm not convinced it matters that much to God what we do. Oh, I don't think we should hurt others or disobey the ten commandments, but beyond that, do you really think He cares?"

Her voice had grown deep with emotion.

He wondered what triggered such a response. "What happened to make you believe this?"

"Nothing." But she answered too quickly. She looked at the hills beyond them and sighed. "I never stopped to consider why I believe that way. I suppose…" She paused. "I used to have a brother."

"Used to?"

"He died when I was six. He was eight. And the light of my parents' life. When he died, it seems they did, too. Oh, they kept breathing, kept doing their work, but they were never the same."

He felt her pain though he guessed she would deny it. He brushed his knuckles across her cheek. "I'm sorry. Sorry you lost your brother and, in a way, your parents."

Denial flared in her eyes and died before she could voice it. "Sometimes I felt they didn't see me." She walked onward at a pace that forced him to lengthen his strides to keep up.

"I guess that explains the Wild West thing."

She ground to a halt and flung around to confront him. "What do you mean?"

"Performing in such a show would make certain you weren't invisible."

She harrumphed. "I'm never invisible."

He chuckled. "You make sure of that."

She turned on her heel and steamed onward.

He kept pace. "But God is not your parents."

She stopped again. "What are you talking about?"

"You aren't ever invisible to Him. That passage Bertie spoke about this morning says, 'Thou hast beset me behind and before, and laid thine hand upon me.'"

She rolled her head back and forth. "You simply hope that by keeping rules of your own making you can ensure God will take care of you and your family. Like you can buy His protection. I just can't believe God can be controlled by our behavior."

"That's not why I obey rules. Rules give us safe passage."

"So why are you raising the twins alone?"

He ground to a halt and couldn't go on. Did she have any idea how her words hurt? How they stung at his beliefs? How many times had he asked the same question? Yet, what choice did he have except to continue to do what was best and trust God for the rest?

She realized he had fallen behind and turned to study him. A flicker of compassion crossed her face, then disappeared. "If God honors those who honor Him, then why are my brother and your wife dead?" Her words ended in a whisper so filled with pain he reached for her, resting his hand on her shoulder.

"I can't explain pain except to say it should serve to push us toward God, not drive us away from Him."

She shook his hand off. "If you need rules to make

you feel safe, that's fine for you. It doesn't work for me." She faced him, her eyes wide with determination.

He longed to pull her close and pat her back, assure her that rules did keep a person safe, but he knew she would not accept either his physical comfort or his words. "Mercy, I hope and pray that someday you will find out you don't need to get anyone's attention, including God's or maybe especially God's."

"I suppose I will then become ordinary and dull."

He leaned back on his heels and laughed. "I don't think you could ever be either of those."

The fight left her eyes, replaced by uncertainty as she studied him.

He sobered and met her look for look, unblinking before her intensity. His heart hammered and he tried in vain to tell himself he didn't care what she thought, but for some unfathomable reason, he did. Only, he reasoned, because he knew the folly of living a life of flaunting rules. He wouldn't wish that for anyone.

"What have rules ever done for me?" She flung about and headed for the ranch.

He trotted after her, trying to shepherd an argument that would convince her. He sighed heavily and his steps slowed. He'd never been able to make Ruby see the truth. Why should he think he would have any more success with Mercy? She would go her own way regardless of who got hurt in the process.

One thing he'd be certain of. Neither he nor his children would be victims of her wild ways.

They crossed the bridge. The happy screams of children at play filled the air. Thor, the tame fawn, bounced across the yard chasing a crooked-tailed dog. A little girl in a blue dress ran by giggling.

"Allie."

She kidded to a halt. "Hi, Papa."

He glowered at his daughter and then looked around the yard. "Who is supervising you children?"

The happy noise stopped. Half a dozen children stared at him. He felt their fearful waiting. It wasn't their fault. "Where's Linette?"

"She fell asleep," Allie whispered.

He turned on Ladd. "You know your sister isn't supposed to be running."

Ladd hung his head. "I didn't notice her."

Abel glowered at Mercy. "Why is it every time I'm with you my children end up in danger? Children, come here." They hurried to his side, both looking fearful. "We're going home." He turned to Mercy. "Be sure and thank Linette for her hospitality."

He strode to Sam, pulled the children up with him and reined away.

The last thing he saw was the narrowed-eyed look Mercy gave him.

She had every right to wonder at his sanity. How had he gone from living such a careful life, trying to protect his children from all harm to wandering around the country with Mercy, trying to convince her his way was best.

The children were quiet, no doubt afraid he was angry at them. He wasn't. Any more than he was angry at Mercy despite his harsh words. His ire was directed toward himself. He'd allowed a woman to make him forget his duties and responsibilities. Hadn't he learned the lesson well enough already? He scrubbed a hand across his eyes. He really should go back and apologize to Mercy. No, it would have to wait. Right now it was imperative he get Allie home and tend to her. *Please, God, don't let her little lapse damage her heart further.*

As soon as they reached the cabin he took the children inside. "Allie, I want you to go directly to bed." He could only hope that rest would offset the afternoon.

"But, Papa, I'm hungry."

"I'll make something to eat in a bit." He waited as she begrudgingly changed into her nightie and crawled into her bed. "Ladd, you make sure she's okay while I tend to the chores." He hurriedly cared for Sam and gathered an armload of firewood. As he approached the cabin, he heard Ladd talking and paused to listen.

"Allie, please stop. Papa will blame me if something happens to you."

What was she doing? He shoved the door open. If he wasn't mistaken, Allie scrambled into bed as he stepped inside. He eyed her for a full thirty seconds, but she only smiled sweetly.

He shook his head and heated up soup for them.

"Papa, can I sit at the table to eat?" Allie asked as he filled bowls for each of them.

He studied his daughter. Her cheeks were pink. If he didn't know better he would say she looked the picture of health. She squirmed about until her bedcovers were tangled. Perhaps she would be more comfortable at the table. "Yes, you may sit with us."

She bounced from the bed and across the floor, perched on the edge of her chair and wriggled until he feared she'd fall off or make herself sick. But she ate the entire contents of the bowl and finished before Ladd.

Obviously the child was overexcited. "Both of you get into bed and I'll read to you." That bedtime routine usually calmed them like nothing else.

They sat cross-legged on their beds as he pulled a chair close and read. He'd finished one page when Allie started to bounce, sending her bed hopping.

He lowered the book and stared at his daughter. "Allie, what's wrong with you?"

"I don't feel like being sick all the time." Another bounce emphasized her words. "I want to ride a horse like Mercy showed me." She sprang to her feet and pretended to balance as if standing on the back of a horse. "I want to do rope tricks like Mercy." To illustrate, she swung her arms over her head.

Ladd leaped to his feet. "And I want to shoot fancy guns." He twirled pretend guns.

Abel swept Allie into his arms. "You know you can't do that. Your heart won't take it." He held her close. What had he done by exposing his children to Mercy's wild dreams? And how was he going to change it? He still needed help with the children and she'd promised to watch them.

He eventually got the children settled and then cleaned up the supper dishes, his mind twirling with confusion all the while. If he had any other choice—

He could think of no option other than taking them to Linette. And she wasn't feeling well enough, she'd said.

Sleep did not come easily as his thoughts grew more tangled. He couldn't deny he'd enjoyed Mercy's company after church. And, yes, at church, too. She listened so intently. Perhaps only because she didn't agree. Poor Mercy. To be neglected by her parents after her brother's death. Again, he vowed to always put his children first, take care of their interests before his own.

Which meant he needed to accept Mercy's help even if she did leave him confused.

Having resolved the problem, he fell asleep.

But the answer didn't seem as clear the next morning.

He and the children had eaten breakfast and they'd helped him clean up between trips to look out the door to see if Mercy came.

"Papa, maybe she's not coming. You were rude to her yesterday. Why were you so angry with her?" Ladd asked.

"I had my reasons."

"Like Mama always had her reasons for leaving?" Allie whispered.

"Not like that at all." Ruby's reasons were selfish. His were self-preservation. A whole lot of difference.

"What if she isn't going to look after us anymore?" Ladd demanded.

He sighed. He didn't need Ladd pointing out that he might have burned some bridges, an act that might put him in a jam yet again.

It seemed contact with Mercy pushed him into one difficulty after another.

"But she said she'd come." Allie's voice grew strong and certain. "So she will." Then her face crumpled with worry. "Unless something's happened to her." Her eyes widened. "Maybe a bear got her."

He patted Allie's shoulder. "Do you think she'd let a bear catch her?"

Allie's eyes shone as she shook her head. "She'd rope him."

"Or shoot him," Ladd added, and the twins grinned at one another.

But what if that man in the woods had waylaid her? What if a wild animal had pounced on her? Would anyone think to go looking for her? They'd assume she was at his cabin.

"Let's go to the ranch and see what's keeping her."

The twins hurried to pull on coats as he went to saddle Sam.

He rode slowly, scanning the trail and the trees beside them. He strained to catch any unusual sound, all the while being careful not to alert the twins to his concern.

A dark shadow flitted through the trees on his right. He slowed Sam further and watched for another glimpse yet saw nothing more. Had it been the whiskered man? Or his imagination? But he knew he'd seen something beyond the normal shapes and shadows of the woods. His heart clawed at his ribs.

If the man had taken Mercy he would find her. But he wouldn't have the twins with him. He nudged Sam into a faster pace. He must take the twins to the ranch and then he'd go looking for Mercy.

If that man had harmed her…

Mercy swung the loop of rope into a huge circle and held Nugget steady as she tried to keep it swinging over the pair of them. It was harder than it looked and took a great deal of concentration. The loop caught on her shoulder and she sighed as she coiled it back into her hand to try again.

Thanks to Abel's taunts yesterday her concentration wasn't what it should be. *Why is it every time I'm with you, my children end up in danger?* The man had a whole repertoire of insults. Good thing she'd soon be gone…a star in a Wild West show. Maybe she'd even get her picture on a poster. She could imagine herself on Nugget's back as he reared up on his hind legs while she swung a rope around them. But first she had to perfect the trick.

She swung the rope into a circle again.

Would the children miss her? She let the rope fall. She already missed them. But she didn't miss their father.

Ignoring the way her arm had begun to ache, she again swung the rope into a circle.

The hoofbeats of a horse riding into the yard made her forget the trick. Linette had gone back to bed, and Jayne and Sybil had gone for a walk. In the cookhouse Cookie and Bertie might not notice the approach of a rider. She would see who visited. She coiled up the ropes and rode past the barn.

She saw a horse approach, with three riders.

"Mercy," Ladd called. "We've been looking for you."

Abel looked up at her. Surprise shifted to relief before his face darkened with anger.

She held her ground. She'd done nothing to justify such a dark look.

He lifted the children down. "Go to Cassie's house while I talk to Mercy."

The children scampered away. He didn't even bother to tell Allie not to run, a fact that scratched up Mercy's spine.

He swung off his horse and stalked toward her.

She stared down at him, determined not to reveal any hint of trepidation while, inside, she shivered at the way he studied her.

He planted his hand around her waist and lifted her to the ground.

"How dare you?" she sputtered.

"I'm not going to look up at you while I say my piece."

"There's nothing to say." At the way his jaw muscles bunched she wondered if she should have said that.

He planted his hands on his hips and glowered at her. "Why are you here?"

"I live here."

"I suppose you're practicing your fancy tricks." Each word dripped with disapproval.

"So what if I am? I don't see that it's any of your business." She jammed her fists on her hips and met him look for look.

"Right. A strange man is wandering the woods, maybe looking for a pretty young lady to kidnap, and it's none of my business." His breathing grew ragged.

She stared. "You were worried about me?" It didn't make sense. "But you don't even like me."

He narrowed his eyes. "Who says I don't like you?"

"You." She jabbed a finger at his chest. "You call me foolish, a menace, accuse me of being a danger." She delivered every word with a jab.

He caught her hand and held it firm. His eyes darkened. He scrubbed his lips together, then opened his mouth and closed it without uttering a word "I can't afford to like a woman. My children come first. Now and always."

She shook her head. What did that have to do with liking her? Or anyone. Must the two be exclusive? He was too much like her parents. Seeing her as inconsequential. She was tired of being seen that way.

She had to get away from him before she said or did something she'd regret. She grabbed Nugget's reins and led him toward the barn.

"Where are you going?"

She ignored him.

Muttering about stubborn women, he strode after her. "We need to talk."

"I have nothing to say and I certainly don't want to hear what you have to say." She stepped inside the barn and headed down the alley.

He followed her.

She turned and glowered at him, but her anger died at the way he looked at her.

He snagged a strand of her hair and brushed it off her cheek, sending a jolt of sweetness through her veins. Oh, to receive such loving touches. She'd longed for it all her life. But he didn't even like her.

She pulled away and continued walking down the alley.

A deep sigh followed her. "Mercy, it doesn't matter what we think of each other. The children need someone to watch them so I can work. Will you please come?" The words grated as if his throat closed off at having to beg.

Did it matter what they thought of each other? His feelings were adequately clear even though she found it impossible to pull hers into any kind of sense. Of course, she didn't care for him. He was an arrogant, judgmental rule keeper. Nor did she care what he thought of her.

Only trying to convince herself made her ache like a giant festering tooth.

"Please?" He stood in the middle of the alley, his hat in hand.

It hurt to see him beg. Even if he didn't like her and she didn't care about him.

"I didn't think you'd want me back after yesterday."

"I'm sorry. I spoke in haste. I wanted to come back and apologize, but I was concerned about Allie and rushed home. Will you accept my apology now?"

The ache inside her developed a teary feel. When had anyone, apart from Sybil and Jayne, ever apologized for unkind words to her? Mostly they didn't even notice that something they said had hurt her feelings. And she'd learned to hide her reactions.

She swallowed hard and sniffed. Hiding her feelings proved more difficult at the moment than ever before. "Apology accepted, and if you're sure you trust me with the children, I will take care of them."

He struggled to answer, no doubt unable to say he trusted her.

"If you don't, then are you wise to ask me to look after them?" She intended to press the matter.

Finally, he nodded. "So long as you remember Allie's fragile health."

She sighed long and heavy. "Abel, I know the pain of losing someone because of poor health. I lost my brother, remember? I would never put Allie's health at risk."

He closed the distance between them and again brushed his knuckles across her cheek. Again, she experienced a rush of something elemental and needy.

She was not needy.

"I'm sorry about your loss."

"It's in the past."

"Your feelings are not in the past. You're still trying—" He shrugged. "Never mind."

What had he said yesterday? About her wanting to do things so she wasn't invisible. But he was wrong.

That too was in the past. She simply liked adventure. Didn't care for an ordinary life.

"Can you come today?" he finally asked. "I can still get some work done."

"Sure, I'll come now if you like."

"I would." He gave a quick grin that caused her to catch her breath.

A few minutes later they rode toward his cabin, Ladd and Allie chattering happily. As the trail widened they rode side by side and Abel smiled at her.

It didn't matter what he thought of her, but it was pleasant to enjoy a few minutes of approval.

Chapter Seven

Four days later, Abel returned with more logs. The weather had turned cold and damp, so Mercy and the children spent the days indoors. He jogged across the yard to the cabin and ducked inside, met by warmth and the smell of coffee simmering on the back of the stove. The children glanced up and called hello. Mercy had been laughing at something the children said and the smile lingered in her eyes.

He could get used to this sort of welcome.

Scraps of paper covered the floor. He didn't care for the mess, it bringing to mind Ruby's carelessness as a mother. But so long as it was cleaned up at the end of the day he tried to not let it bother him. "What are you doing?"

"Making a treasure map," Ladd said.

"We're going on a 'venture," Allie added.

His daughter's cheeks were slightly flushed thought Mercy had lived up to her word and kept the child playing quietly. Suspicion poked in an ugly thought. Did Mercy let them do rambunctious things when she knew he wouldn't be around? No. He had promised to trust her. Relied on the fact she'd lost a brother due to illness and, because of that, understood the risks for Allie.

"What kind of treasure? And what kind of adventure?" he asked.

Ladd grew serious. "Well, you see that's part of the adventure. We don't know where we're going or what we'll find."

"I see." He quirked any eyebrow at Mercy, guessing Ladd quoted her words. "So how will you know when you're there?"

She gave a little shrug as if to indicate she understood he found their play amusing. "We'll know. First sunny, warm day we're going treasure hunting."

"Not too far, I trust."

"Trust? Hmm."

He understood her disbelief. He'd promised to trust her, so how was he to make her understand his trust only went so far? He would never let someone put his children at risk, even if it meant constant checking and supervising.

He poured himself a cup of coffee and lifted the lid on a syrup bucket that she kept filled with cookies. He snagged a handful. He sure did appreciate the cookies and hot coffee waiting when he returned. And the children were getting lots of attention.

He drank deeply of the coffee, but the warmth that encircled his heart had nothing to do with the heat of the drink and everything to do with all the good things Mercy brought into his life and the lives of his children. Despite her wild ways. He ate the cookies hurriedly. "Thank you," he murmured as he headed for the door.

She rose and followed him outside. "For what?"

He twisted his hat between his fingers. "For looking after the children." The words fell short of what he meant. "For making life good."

She blinked, then widened her eyes.

"I gotta get back to work." He strode away so fast she must wonder what bothered him. And he couldn't explain that although the words were true they scared him, like being treed by a wildcat. Which was mighty close to the truth. Mercy was as close to being a wildcat as any woman he'd met. She would never belong in his life. She meant to join a Wild West show. This was temporary and he best keep that in mind for all their sakes and his sanity. No more women. Especially the kind that didn't care to settle down.

He worked so hard the rest of the afternoon that despite the cold, damp air, he was down to his shirt with the sleeves rolled up.

When he was about ready to head back to the cabin, a snap in the woods jerked him to full attention. Someone was out there. That strange man? The hair on the back of his neck tingled. What did the man want? Was he waiting for a chance to intrude into the cabin? Would he bother Mercy? Did he want something Abel had?

Slowly, he edged around to the horse and removed his rifle. He kept it at the ready as he made his way back to the cabin. He unloaded the logs, unhooked the stoneboat and took Sam to the corral to brush and feed. All the while he secretly scanned the area around the cabin. Had the man followed him? Would he wait for Mercy to leave? His nerves twitched.

How much risk did Mercy face as she rode back and forth? If only she could stay. He snorted. That was impossible. Under any circumstances.

Finally he made his way to the cabin. A couple days ago he'd brought in a deer, and the succulent aroma of roasting venison filled the room. He breathed deeply. "Smells good."

"Everything is ready." She snagged her coat off the hook by the door. "I'll return tomorrow if you need me."

"I do."

She hugged the children goodbye and left, with Abel following her. "Mercy, about that man in the woods…"

She saddled her horse as he continued talking.

"He was watching me again today. I don't know what he's up to and until I do, I can only assume it's not good. So be careful on the ride home. Don't let your guard down for a moment."

She stood before him. "Are you worried about me?" Her words were teasing.

He gripped her shoulders. "I don't mind saying I am. There's something strange about a man hanging about watching others."

Her eyes filled with something he could only explain as longing, which made no sense so he dismissed the idea.

"I'm pretty good at taking care of myself," she said.

He couldn't seem to release her. He wouldn't know if she got back safely until she returned the next day. It was a long time to worry and wonder. "I know you are, but if the man got the drop on you what would you do?"

"Shoot him." She said it so matter-of-factly he laughed.

"What if he pins your arms behind your back?"

She scowled. "In that case he better be prepared for some well-laid blows from my boots."

"Promise me you'll be careful."

Her eyes bored into his, demanding something he couldn't determine. Shoot. What was wrong with him? Only one thing mattered to him—that she get back safely. And she wanted only to be allowed to continue her training for the show. "Promise!"

"I am always careful so you don't need my promise." Her grin seemed a little lopsided.

"Nevertheless, I'd feel better if you give it."

She sighed. "Very well, I promise to be alert, to watch front, back and sideways, to keep my gun at the ready, to check every shadow, to ride like the wind at the first hint of danger…" She chuckled. "And to return tomorrow to put your mind at ease."

He let out the breath he'd been holding. "I know you're jesting but if you do everything you said, I might be able to rest."

She gave his chin a playful tap. "You'll rest just fine."

He caught her hand and pulled it to his chest. "Not everything is a joke, you know."

Her eyes darkened. "So you say. You see that's where you and I differ. I'm content to think life might be for fun while you make it a serious matter."

He pulled her closer. "It is a serious matter." The words growled from his chest. He half joked but only half. Then he kissed her forehead.

She jerked back. "What are you doing?"

Shock raced through his veins. What had he been thinking? "It's what I would have done to one of the twins." Though his concern didn't feel the same. "Now go and be careful. I'll see you tomorrow."

She stared half a second then swung into her saddle and rode from the yard at a gallop. At the edge of the clearing she swung Nugget around and had him rear up on his hind legs. "Until tomorrow," she called, and with a wild whoop disappeared into the trees.

He sighed. So much for leaving quietly so as not to alert the man in the woods. Yet he grinned at the place where he last saw her.

She sure did enjoy life.

He sobered. Where did that leave him and the twins? He knew the answer. He'd lived his wild life and found it unsatisfying. Now he had the children to think of and absolutely no intention of repeating his mistakes.

Thanks to Abel's overly developed sense of caution, Mercy's nerves twitched as she rode through the lengthening shadows. She shivered and not because she was cold. If only she could remember when and where she'd seen that whiskered man. Again she scoured her memories and again came up with nothing but a vague sense of having seen him somewhere. He'd been on the edge of the scene wherever it had been. Sort of a fleeting figure. Much like he was now. She simply couldn't place him.

A rustling in the underbrush sent her thoughts into a frenzy. Her arms tensed, her hand clenched her pistol. Then a rabbit hopped away.

See that's what happens when you let fears control you. You start to see danger when there is none.

But she couldn't deny a sense of relief when she broke into the clearing around the ranch. She shuddered. All those dark shadows had filled her with wild imaginations.

Sighing, she turned toward the sun tipping the top of the mountain peaks. Abel had intentionally stopped work early enough in the afternoon to allow her to ride back before the sun dipped below the mountains. At times like this, she appreciated his caution.

She exercised caution of her own the next morning as she returned to Abel's place, though she saw nothing to make her suspect the whiskered man hung about. Perhaps Abel had been mistaken in thinking he saw him. But she doubted it. Abel was far too careful to make such mistakes.

She rode into the clearing and spotted Abel waiting outside the cabin.

He puffed out his cheeks when he saw her and stepped forward. "I don't mind admitting I worried about you all night."

"Really? So why did I bother to promise I'd be careful? Wasn't that to ensure you wouldn't worry?" She swung off Nugget's back.

Abel did not move away, forcing her to stand toe-to-toe with him. "It didn't work."

"Because you don't trust me."

"No, because I don't trust that crazy man out there." He touched her cheek.

When had he gotten so free with his touches? Of course, he touched his children all the time. Guess it simply got to be habit. But why did she let it make her heart jump with eagerness as if hoping for more? The man out in the woods wasn't the only crazy person here. She seemed to have caught the disease.

"I'm glad you're here safely."

Did she imagine his voice thickened? As if her safety really mattered? Well, of course it did. Who would look after the children if something happened to her? Braced by the thought, she edged past him and made her way to the cabin.

He followed right behind.

She hung her coat and hugged the children then turned to regard Abel. Wasn't he going to work today?

He seemed to realize he stood at the door. "I best be on my way." He jammed his hat on his head and left.

That afternoon Abel exacted another promise for her to be careful, but he did not kiss her forehead in his fatherly way. Good thing. She might have taken objection to continued familiarity. The disappointment edging her heart was only imaginary.

When she arrived the next day, Abel's welcome was full of relief. "I won't rest until I find out who that man is and what he's up to."

She was not prepared to let worry cloud her day. "Like I said before, he's only a lonely old mountain man come down to avoid the early snowfalls." She didn't believe it, though. She'd never been in the mountains and couldn't have seen him there. And she knew she'd seen him somewhere.

"Can we go outside?" Ladd asked after Abel left.

"I'd say so. We wouldn't want to waste such a lovely day. Soon winter will be here." She gave a mock shiver. "In fact, I was thinking we should have our treasure hunt today." She'd let them create a map that would keep them close to the cabin yet allow them to explore as they followed clues.

Despite Abel's opinion of her, she wasn't so foolish as to wander into the woods with two children while a strange man was out there.

For the better part of two hours, they followed clues around the edge of the clearing. Finally they discovered the treasure—a bag Mercy had hidden. Inside was a small lariat for Ladd and a pair of fringed gloves for

Allie. Mercy had also packed a lunch and blanket and they sat down to enjoy their picnic.

Abel whistled as he worked. Another pleasant day. Each one a blessing, allowing him to hope he might achieve all he wanted and needed to do before winter set in.

The only thing marring the day was the knowledge that a crazy man wandered the woods.

He quickly prepared a load of logs and headed back to the cabin, anxious for a cup of strong hot coffee. And a glimpse of Mercy and the children.

He straightened and studied that thought. Of course, he wanted to assure himself they were all safe. No need to picture a welcoming smile from Mercy and a scheme of reasons to touch her, maybe even pull her into his arms. He'd allowed himself one brief kiss of her forehead. It meant nothing.

Shaking his head to clear his thoughts, he dismissed the whole notion. How many times did he have to tell himself that she did not belong in his plans?

So he forced himself to unload the stoneboat before he went to the cabin. And if he crossed the yard with hurried steps it was only because he longed for coffee and cookies.

He flung the door open and ducked inside.

The place echoed with silence. "Hello?" The cabin provided no place to hide. He called out again, louder. "Hello? Where are you?"

He lifted a stove lid and saw glowing coals. Why had she allowed the fire to die down? Because, he reasoned, the day was warm. The pail of cookies beckoned from the shelf but he no longer imagined their sweetness, only a dusty dryness.

Surely he'd overlooked them. He turned full circle. But the cabin remained silent and empty.

"Mercy, Ladd, Allie," he bellowed, his words reverberating in the room. They were gone. He grabbed the back of the nearest chair as his legs buckled. The crazy man in the woods had taken them. Just as he feared.

He raced back to Sam, grabbed his rifle and stared at the trees. Which way would he go? He opened his mouth to yell their names again, then clamped it shut. His call would only alert the man. Best he sneak up and catch him off guard.

If only he knew what direction to go.

He studied the problems for two seconds. Probably he'd head for the mountains. Having made up his mind, he headed west, moving carefully, pausing to look for an indication they had been there. He grinned when he noticed a broken branch. Perhaps Mercy had intentionally left clues.

Another branch led him to the right, as if circling the cabin. Had the man stood here, watched the cabin for hours? Maybe even days? The skin on his arms tightened at the thought.

He slowly made his way forward as he spotted a small footprint in the fallen leaves. Or at least that's what he thought it was. And he needed the encouragement to keep going. As he moved, he prayed. *God, keep them safe. Help me find them before—*

He would not think before what.

Did he hear Allie's voice? He straightened and listened. There it was again.

He crept forward. If he could surprise the crazy man—

There! Through the trees. Ladd and Allie sitting on the edge of a blanket. Where was Mercy? And the crazy man? His mouth dried so sharply he had to hold back a cough. The things the man might do to her…he dared not contemplate them.

He edged forward an inch trying to see her. Should he sweep in and snatch up his children? Would that put Mercy in more danger?

God, please guide me.

Something cold and hard pressed to the side of his head.

"Arms in the air." A low, guttural voice half growled the words.

He raised his arms. How had it come to this? He'd done all he could to protect his children. Gone out of his way to live a careful life so they wouldn't suffer the consequences of his choices. Yet he'd fallen into the hands of a crazy man. Who would look after his children?

"Turn around slowly."

He hesitated, giving his children a farewell look. *Be safe. Know I love you.* Then he slowly turned. And gasped. "You!"

Mercy grinned at him. "You ought to know better than to sneak around the woods when there's a stranger lurking nearby. I might have shot first and asked questions later."

He stared at her. "I thought—" He rubbed at his collarbone. "I thought—" He couldn't talk. His legs turned to weak ropes and he leaned against a tree. "You're safe. You're all safe."

She nodded. "Told you to trust me. I'm not as foolish as you judge me to be."

"I repent of all the times I said anything negative." He closed his eyes and willed his heartbeat to return to normal but it refused. There was only one way to calm it. He planted his hands on Mercy's shoulders and pulled her to his chest. "Just let me hold you for a moment."

She leaned into his embrace with a little chuckle. "If it will make you feel better."

He pressed his chin to her head. "It will." He breathed deeply. She smelled of sunshine and cookies. And horse. A smell he no doubt also wore. "Do you have any idea how frightened I was to return to the cabin and find you all missing?" His arms tightened around her as he recalled the moment.

She sighed. "Someday you will learn to trust me."

"It's not that I don't..." he protested, though he knew his worry seemed to prove otherwise.

"Yes, it is. But never mind." She eased out of his embrace, causing his heart to clench. "Two children are waiting to see what I found."

He nodded. He hadn't forgotten them but now that he knew they were safe, he felt no urgency to join them. The thought made no sense and he pushed himself away from the tree.

She led the way to the clearing. "Look what I found."

The children jumped up and raced to him.

"Mercy made us promise we would sit here and not make a sound until she came back," Allie said.

"She gave me a rope." Ladd showed Abel a coiled lariat. "She said she'd show me how to use it."

"Look at my gloves." Allie lifted the fringed pair for his inspection.

Being run over by a stampede of wild horses wouldn't have made him feel any more confused. Just when he felt overwhelming gratitude for Mercy's care of his children she did something to remind him of who she really was—a woman intent on living a wild life. He stared at the gifts, more than half tempted to order the children to give them back. "What are you doing out here?"

Both children talked at once.

He caught enough to understand they were on a treasure hunt.

"We were about to have a picnic lunch," Mercy added. "Do you care to join us?"

The twins begged him to say yes.

He might have refused Mercy—or so he tried to convince himself—but he couldn't deny his children. "You sure there's enough for me, too?"

"We'll share," the children chorused.

So with more eagerness than he should allow himself, he sat cross-legged on one corner of the blanket while Mercy sat opposite him and the twins sat between them. A sense of peace engulfed him. "I really should get back to work." It was a token protest. He had no intention of leaving them out in the woods even if they were only a few yards from the cabin. Nor did he have the heart to order them all back inside.

He knew he was in trouble when he allowed himself to ignore his sense of caution, but he'd deal with his failure after he'd eaten.

Chapter Eight

Who was this man? Mercy passed around sandwiches and freshly scrubbed carrots recently dug from the garden at Eden Valley Ranch.

Abel obviously did not trust her. Yet he'd hugged her and she'd let him, though she couldn't begin to explain why. One minute he was all business, rules and being careful. The next, he plopped down to share a picnic right in the middle of a sunny day—the perfect sort of day for working in the woods.

Why had he hugged her so tight? And why had she let him?

Because it felt good and made her feel warm and secure and cared for.

She was indeed as foolish as he accused her of being. She didn't need anyone caring for her and hadn't in a very long time.

Except—a memory refused to be dismissed—how many times had she stood in a doorway observing her parents, wondering why they never seemed to see her? One time when she was about ten and far too old to act in such a way, she'd thrown a temper tantrum right in front of them. She only wanted them to acknowledge her.

Instead, the nanny had been summoned and Mercy had been locked in the nursery. After two days she no longer cared for anything but her freedom and had stolen out the door as a maid came to change the bedding. That was the day she discovered the joy of freedom.

She didn't intend to give up that joy for anything or anyone. Though, she allowed herself to confess, she'd discovered a different kind of joy in caring for the twins and seeing Abel's gratitude at the meal she left prepared for him.

The situation was only temporary.

Besides, she'd seen the pained look in his face as he considered her gifts to the children. He didn't approve of riding, roping or anything that seemed out of the ordinary and she had no intention of giving up her joyful freedom.

No sir! She didn't intend to give up anything and if Abel thought a little hugging would change her mind—

Well, she knew how to correct that.

"Ladd, when we're done here we'll go back to the corral and I'll show you how to handle a lariat."

Abel choked back the last of his sandwich and bolted to his feet. "Mercy, can I talk to you private like?"

Taking her agreement for granted he strode into the trees.

She noticed he didn't return to the spot where he'd hugged her and where she'd stuck a gun to his head. Not that he was ever in any danger. She'd heard him coming and gone to investigate. As soon as she saw it was him, she decided she'd show him who needed to be careful.

He stopped several yards from where the children watched with wide-eyed interest. "I don't want Ladd learning silly rope tricks."

She'd known he'd protest. "I didn't have any such thing in mind. But he's nine years old. He lives on a ranch in the West. Likely he'll be around animals a lot. A boy should know how to throw a rope around a cow, wouldn't you say?"

"I'd say he's a bit young for roping cows."

"But not too young to start learning." Her challenge stung her eyes.

He scuffed his boots in the dry leaves. He jammed his fingers in his pockets.

"Surely you wouldn't want the boy to grow up to be a sissy. Would you?"

He closed his eyes as if he was in pain and let out a long-suffering sigh.

She knew it meant he'd given in and forced herself to not smile.

"Nothing fancy, mind you. Just roping a post."

She shrugged. "It's all I had in mind." Though if the boy got it in his head to try something more, she was prepared to turn a blind eye.

"I suppose you have something in mind for Allie with those fancy gloves."

She chuckled at his suspicion. "I thought it would be cute if she and I did trick riding together."

He jerked as if she'd shot him through the heart. "It would not! I warned you—"

She cut him off with a laugh and a playful punch to his shoulder. "You are so gullible. That's what comes of being so suspicious all the time." Not waiting for him to find his voice, she headed back to the picnic site.

"I am not suspicious," he called.

"You most certainly are," she flung over her shoulder. She reached the children, folded the blanket and stuffed everything into the sack. "Come on, you two. We've got roping to do."

Like a merry parade they returned to the clearing.

He went directly to his horse and fiddled with the harness while casting suspicion-filled glances in her direction.

She led the children to the corral. Allie sat by the fence while Mercy showed Ladd how to twirl the rope over his head.

Abel continued to delay his departure.

Mercy glanced at the sky. "The light is wasting." She directed her words at him.

He turned his back to her and left.

She brought her attention back to Ladd. But somehow teaching him to toss a loop had lost some of its joy.

Abel helped the children prepare to attend the Sunday service at the ranch. He would have skipped it except he didn't want the children to think missing church was acceptable. No, he'd face Mercy and never once let her guess how she managed to keep him dancing from one extreme to the other. First, he hugged her, then he was upset with her. What had he been thinking hugging her in the first place? Relief. That was all. He'd prayed for their safety and he'd been overcome by gratitude to see them safe and sound.

How did that indicate suspicion, as Mercy had said? It didn't. Of course, he knew she hadn't referred to that when she called him suspicious. She meant the way he always jumped to the protection of his children. And he always would. It was his job.

"Are you both ready?"

The twins nodded. Both of them looked eager for the visit to the ranch. For their sakes he would try to enjoy the day.

As they approached the ranch, he forced himself to be honest. He would enjoy the day for his sake, too. Seeing Mercy in a different situation filled his mind with possibilities. Perhaps they would take a long walk together.

He lifted the twins down from the horse and threw the reins around the hitching post, then headed for the cookhouse.

Allie grabbed his hand. "There she is." She pointed toward the big house, where Mercy stepped out the door with Linette and Grady.

He didn't need either of the children to point her out. He'd seen her the moment the door opened. Wearing an emerald-green dress, her hair coiled at the back of her head, she had donned a fetching straw-colored bonnet. At the sight of her, his lungs sucked flat. She made the perfect picture of a lady.

The children waved and called her name.

Mercy lifted a gloved hand in response.

Abel's arm came up of its own accord. This Mercy caused his heart to beat faster.

"Let's wait for her," Allie said, tugging at his hand to slow his advance toward the cookhouse.

He allowed Allie to hold him back though she might have noticed it took little effort. Then both she and Ladd broke away and ran toward Mercy.

She laughed as they approached and bent to hug and

kiss them. They clung to her hands as they came to join him.

"Good morning," Linette said as she passed them.

"'Morning, ma'am." He yanked his hat off and then Mercy stood before him, her eyes shining with good humor, her mouth curved in an inviting smile.

He swallowed hard.

"Good morning, Abel. Isn't it a lovely day?"

He managed to find his voice. "It is a fine day. Shall we?" He tipped his elbow toward her, inviting her to put her arm through his.

With a little nod, she did so. The twins marched behind them.

Knowing what to expect from Cookie, he braced himself as the woman hugged him and patted his back hard enough to cleanse his lungs. He held Mercy tight to his side, thinking she needed protection, but she laughed and returned Cookie's hug.

Cookie leaned over to confront the twins.

Abel feared she might break Allie if she hugged the child but instead she straightened and opened her arms to them both. They went to her ample body and let themselves be pressed to her sides.

He sat next to Mercy as Cookie led the little group in singing. It felt good and right to be singing songs of faith with Mercy at his side.

Bertie rose to speak. "I know you ladies were hoping the men would be back by now."

They murmured agreement. Four young wives missing their mates. From what Abel knew, another young woman and her sister lived nearby and her husband was also on the roundup.

Bertie continued. "I could tell you all to be patient, to

trust God to take care of your men, but I figure nothing I say will make you more patient for their return so I'm not going to bother. Instead, I'm going to tell you how I met Cookie. Eliza, as I knew her then."

Cookie waved a hand in protest. "Oh, Bertie. They don't want to know that."

Bertie grinned at his wife. "I think they might enjoy it. Would you?" he asked the audience.

Even Abel nodded.

"There you go." He leaned back, a distant look on his face. "As most of you know, I wandered far from God. But He found me and brought me back. I had a long way to come and it took some time. One Saturday found me in a little town in western Montana. Everyone I knew had gone to the saloon. I no longer had any desire for that kind of life. But what was I supposed to do on a Saturday night? I remember looking up and down the street. Lots of noise and action both inside and outside the saloon. The general store was still open and a few people went in and out. Across the street the door of the hotel opened and closed. Through the windows of the main floor I could see straight into the dining room. Maybe I could find entertainment of a decent sort there. I dusted my clothes off as best I could and strode inside and found a vacant table. I'd barely sat down when this beautiful woman appeared at my side and handed me a menu. Well, I never did get a look at the menu. My Eliza commanded my full attention." He beamed at Cookie, who ducked her head.

"To this day I can't tell you what I ate. Only that it took until closing to finish it. I sat there as she cleaned up. Finally she came to me and said I'd have to leave. I asked her where a man could worship on a Sunday. She told me of the church she attended. I told her I hadn't been in church much in the past few years but I meant to change all that."

Cookie nodded. "You surely did, too."

Bertie and Cookie gave each other such warm looks that Abel felt he intruded into something very personal.

Then Bertie returned to his story. "She invited me to accompany her the next day. Which I did. We spent the afternoon together and learned about each other. And I'm proud to say we have spent the past thirty years together." He faced his wife. "I'm looking forward to the next thirty."

Cookie grinned. "Me, too, my love."

Bertie turned his attention back to his audience. "You might wonder why I'm telling you this. It's because no matter where I wandered or how far I got from God, He had plans for me. He led me to the right town, on the right day to meet Eliza. His love never fails."

Abel nodded as Bertie finished. Hadn't he found the same thing? God had blessed him with the twins and led him here, where he could build a safe and secure life for them all. *Thank you, God. Help me to honor what You have given me.*

They again gathered around the table to share coffee and cinnamon rolls, but he sensed a restlessness in the others. The children finished and moved away to play.

Linette wandered to the window to look out. "It's snowing up higher. I can see it from here."

Sybil went to her side. "I'm sure they're all safe."

Her voice was so strained he wondered if she believed it herself.

"There are so many dangers out there," Linette said. "Snowstorms, wolves, bad men—"

Sybil laughed a little. "And young women accidently shooting innocent cowboys."

Abel turned to stare at Mercy. "Who'd you shoot?"

The others chuckled as Mercy bristled. "I didn't shoot anyone." Her eyes narrowed. "At least not yet, though I've been sorely tempted."

The laughter increased.

Jayne let out a long sigh. "It was me. I wanted to learn to shoot a gun."

Mercy shook her head. "You were supposed to keep your eyes open." She turned back to Abel. "That's how she met Seth. Poor man."

Jayne's expression grew fierce. She looked at Bertie. "I can verify what you say. The circumstances weren't good, but God used them to bring us together. I will never cease to thank Him."

"Me, too," Sybil said. She faced Abel to explain. "Brand rode in to break horses for Eddie. He was aloof and mysterious because his father and brother were part of the Duggan gang and he didn't want anything to do with them." She shuddered. "But God spared him and the Duggan gang was conquered."

Linette withdrew from the window. "I can also say that God turned an unfortunate situation into a blessing. I arrived here thinking Eddie had offered me a marriage of convenience. But he expected his former fiancée to come in answer to his letter." She looked past them, a smile wreathing her face. "He didn't think I was at all suitable but over the winter we learned we were perfect for each other." She drew in a long breath. "God is good to us all."

"Don't leave me out," Cassie said. "Look what God's done in my life. I planned to be independent, but I soon found it was nothing compared to being mother to four lovely children." She nodded toward her family playing across the room. "And a loving husband. But I do miss him. I wish they would ride in this moment." The four ladies crowded to the window looking west, where they hoped to see their men.

"I hope they're safe," Linette said as the cold wind blowing down the valley whistled past the cookhouse.

Mercy snorted softly. "You all talk about how God guided you and then you fret and worry because the men haven't returned."

Linette turned and drew the other women with her. "Mercy is absolutely right. God will protect our loved ones."

Mercy waved her hands. "Enough of this. You'll soon be in tears if you keep it up. Makes me glad I don't have a husband to worry about. Now let's plan something fun."

The women crowded around her, pushing Abel closer to her side.

"What do you have in mind?"

Seems they were all eager for something to divert them.

She lifted her hands. "Nothing specific."

"I know." Linette grew eager. "Let's plan a party for when the men return." Her suggestion was greeted with a chorus of approval and they all began to talk at once.

Before he knew it, Abel had agreed to attend and to add something to the program. "What will I do?"

The women studied him.

Mercy jabbed his ribs. "Now don't you wish you knew some roping tricks?"

"Not really." An idea had formed but he decided to keep it a secret. "I'll think of something."

They turned back to the others and their plans. The talk continued as they climbed the hill to the big house and all throughout dinner. Abel felt a little out of place after the meal. The women washed the dishes, while the children played in the front room. He didn't feel like dragging the twins away yet. Didn't want to return to the tiny cabin and his lonely thoughts.

"I could check on things around the place if you like," he offered to Linette.

"I'd truly appreciate that. Mercy, you go with him."

"Me?"

Did she have to act as if it was an insult? He was about to say he didn't need her company when Jayne shoved her forward.

"You know you're dying to get out of this hot kitchen."

Mercy laughed. "I am, indeed." She grabbed her shawl and hurried from the room.

"Don't shoot him," Jayne called.

"Or rope him like a calf." Sybil giggled.

"Girls, don't tease her," Linette interjected calmly.

Cassie followed them down the hall. "No fighting either. Half the time the two of you look ready to bite the other's head off." She sighed dramatically. "The rest of the time you look like you wish the rest of us would disappear."

Mercy glowered at her. "Can you guess what I'm wishing right now?"

Cassie laughed.

"I think it's time to leave." Abel pulled Mercy's arm though his and walked them to the door. "Let's have a look around and make sure everything is as it should be." The door closed behind them. "Do any of them know about the man in the woods?"

"I've not said anything."

"No need to worry them," he replied, "but let's take a look around."

And so they circled the place, checking for tracks or signs of the man. They reached the hill they had visited the Sunday before and paused to peruse the area.

"It's gotten cold," Mercy said, pulling her shawl tighter around her shoulders. Still she shivered.

He put an arm about her and pulled her to the shelter of his body. "Like Linette said, there is snow up higher."

"I hope it doesn't get down this far." She looked up at him. "What will you do if winter sets in before you're ready?"

He studied her upturned face, gratified to see she cared. "I can keep working unless the snow gets heavy, and I wouldn't expect that this time of year."

"I'd help you if I could."

"You are helping. Having you with the children allows me to be out in the woods."

"I meant I'd like to help you in the woods."

He tightened his arm about her shoulders. "I prefer to think of you at the cabin with the children."

She quirked her eyebrows. "Are you saying you don't think I could handle the work?"

He tipped his head to touch hers. "If I said that it would spur you to prove otherwise, wouldn't it?"

"Of course not. But I could do it."

"Be glad you don't have to."

She squirmed. "Glad?"

"Mercy, why do you have to take objection to

everything I say? I'm trying to be friendly and nice here."

She softened and leaned into him a bit more. "And here I thought you were trying to turn me into your usual type of woman."

"My usual type of woman was a saloon girl. It's not something I wish to repeat."

She pressed her head to his. "I'm sorry. I didn't mean to remind you." She shifted to stare out at the landscape. "Tell me about your parents. Do you have siblings?" She drew in a sharp breath. "Look. Something's moving in the bushes."

He squinted at the spot she meant. Indeed, a shadow shifted and a four point buck slipped into the sunlight.

She chuckled. "I'm getting so I see danger in every little shadow." She told how she'd gotten all nervous at a rabbit. "It's your fault. You're so worried about that man in the woods."

"A person can never be too careful." He drew her to a grassy spot and they sat down. He thought she might withdraw but she shivered and pressed closer. For the time being, he didn't mind the cold weather.

"I have two brothers," he began. "One three years older and the other two years younger. They are both working with my father in a shipbuilding business back in Nova Scotia."

She twisted to look into his face. "Shipbuilding? I'd have never suspected."

"Why not?" Her surprise was a little off-putting.

"I don't know. Shipbuilding seems like the ultimate adventure. Didn't you want to get on one of those ships and sail around the world?"

"Shipbuilders aren't necessarily sailors. Besides—"

He shrugged, at a loss for words. He'd had big ideas but not of sailing away. He couldn't put his finger on the reason he'd been so restless. Nothing he could think of made sense now.

"What?" When he didn't answer right away, she nudged him gently. "Tell me."

"I guess I longed for adventure but I went after it the wrong way. I threw out the rules with the pursuit of excitement."

She studied him a long moment. "You believe you can't have one without the other? It's either rules or excitement?"

"Isn't it?"

"I don't think so. I don't have to enter a wayward way of living in order to enjoy my life."

He squeezed her shoulders, not wanting to argue yet uncomfortable with the direction she meant to take her life. "Frank is my older brother. He's very rigid. Everything by the book. I used to resent him for that but now I understand why he was like that. It was because in the shipbuilding business you can't afford to make mistakes."

"And your younger brother?"

"John." He knew his smile filled the word. "We used to have a lot of fun together." He didn't go on.

"What happened?"

"My father took me into the business and he and Frank made it clear there was no room for fun."

She tsked. "I can understand why you left."

"I was wrong. I needed to grow up and accept responsibility." He sighed. "But I did miss playing with John. We used to play tag, toss a ball back and forth and go on great adventures."

She sat up, allowing his arm to fall to his side. "I remember playing with Butler...that's my brother." She turned and stared at him. "I couldn't remember before now. I always wondered if we did. But we did. We played chase. I suppose it was a form of tag. I remember giggling so hard I couldn't run anymore. I'd fall down on the ground and he would lie beside me and we'd stare at the sky." She looked up as if trying to recapture the feeling. The light caught on her cheeks, revealing silvery tracks of her tears.

With a muffled groan he pulled her into his arms and pressed her face to his shoulder. His heart thumped against his ribs. "Don't cry, Mercy. Please don't cry."

She grabbed his coat front and squeezed the fabric in her fists.

How did he stop her pain? Make it go away? He tipped her head back and kissed each cheek, capturing the still silent tears.

Her eyes grew wide and...dare he think she invited more? Before he could reason a response, he captured her lips, feeling the dampness of tears, feeling her uncertainty. He had started to draw back when her arms came around his neck and she sighed. He captured the sigh and deepened the kiss.

It began as a means of comfort but grew into something more. In the back of his mind he understood he would have to explain this to himself. But he'd do it later. For now, he gave comfort and he also received it.

The kiss ended. She sighed. "I shouldn't have done that."

"Done what?"

"Cried." Relief surged through his heart. He was afraid she might have meant the kiss.

"I'm sorry if what I said was responsible."

She smiled a glorious, glowing smile. "Don't be sorry. I'm grateful for remembering my brother that way. It seems—" She shook her head. "It seems all I could remember was the deathly quiet after he was gone."

"We're more alike than one would think."

"How's that?"

"Seems fun left your life when your brother died. Mine ended when I had to grow up. Unfortunately, it led me to make some dreadful mistakes." He wanted to warn her against making similar mistakes but she bounded to her feet.

"I hear the warning in your voice—don't say it. Don't ruin the moment." She reached down and held her hands out to him.

He let her pull him to his feet and retained her hands, edging her close so he looked down into her dark eyes.

They were so different—she craved adventure; he lived carefully.

But they'd found a special closeness between them today. Though he knew it could only be temporary, he didn't want to spoil it.

Chapter Nine

Mercy's throat clogged with tears. Butler had become a happy memory. She remembered laughing and playing with him. Abel would never understand the beautiful gift he'd given her in causing her to remember Butler this way. Not even his disapproval could mar the joy.

He touched his forehead to hers. "I wouldn't think of spoiling the moment." His voice had grown husky.

She rested against him, so filled with quivering softness she knew she would sob if she tried to talk. The wind tugged at her shawl and he drew it more closely around her shoulders.

"I must take the children home before it gets any colder." But he did not move for two more heartbeats. Then he pulled her to his side…to protect her from the wind, she assured herself.

They went down the hill and got Sam.

She had to say something. Let him know how much she appreciated all he'd done. "Thank you for the nice day." Such inadequate words.

"I made you cry."

"They were good tears."

He touched her cheeks with his cool fingertip. "You're sure?"

"I'm sure." She squeezed his hand and pressed it to her cheek, wanting to plant a kiss in his palm but afraid of her trembling emotions. She had no desire to start crying in earnest.

He pulled her to his side again as they led the horse up the hill. They paused outside the door and as he looked down at her, his gaze drifted across her face, lingered on her lips, then came to her eyes. His smile seemed full of regret.

"I have to go."

She nodded and stepped to the door.

He followed and called the children. "See you tomorrow?"

"Of course."

He and the twins were soon on Sam's back. He wrapped a blanket about the pair and tucked them close to him.

She smiled. One thing about Abel—he would always take care of those he loved. Her eyes stung as she watched them leave. She had not known such loving care from her parents but thanks to Abel, she remembered when life had been kinder.

Cassie shepherded her children out the door. "My goodness, that wind has a nasty bite."

Linette stood at the window, holding Grady's hand. Mercy knew she wouldn't be able to relax until she saw Eddie and hugged him.

Mercy slipped past and went to the kitchen, where Jayne and Sybil visited.

Sybil studied her hard. "You have the look of a woman who's been kissed. Well kissed."

Heat flamed Mercy's cheeks. She would not confess she and Abel had kissed. How would her friends interpret it? *She* didn't even know what to think. "Abel told me how he and his brother played tag and chased each other. It made me recall Butler playing with me." She sucked in air. "I'd forgotten everything but the tiptoeing quiet of his illness and the deathly stillness that followed." She shuddered a sob. "I miss my brother."

Both Jayne and Sybil rushed to her side and wrapped arms about her. They patted her back and made soothing noises as Mercy struggled to contain her emotions. After a few minutes she was able to breathe normally and she gave a tight chuckle. "I'm fine."

The girls pulled chairs close and sat holding her hands.

Jayne spoke. "It's like Bertie said, God brings people into our lives at just the right time. He's sent Abel into yours to help you remember good times."

Sybil chuckled. "I think God might have brought him into Mercy's life for more reason than that."

Mercy made a protesting noise. "He doesn't approve of me."

Jayne drew back, her mouth open in mock surprise. "You don't say!"

Sybil patted Mercy's hands. "There's a difference between not approving of some of your activities and not approving of you." She nodded as if her sage advice should make all the difference in the world when it made little sense to Mercy.

Determined not to rob herself of the comfort Abel had provided as she cried, she refused to analyze why it had felt so good to be in his arms and why she had accepted his kiss.

And even more. Why had she offered a kiss in return?

The questions remained unanswered the next morning as she watched Linette return again and again to look out the window.

The cold wind continued, giving Linette cause to worry about the men.

"Do you want me to stay?" Mercy asked.

"No, no. I'm fine." Linette sighed. "Or at least I will be as soon as I can see and hold Eddie again. I miss that man so much I feel ill."

Mercy wrapped an arm about Linette's waist. "You should rest."

"I know. I'll be okay. Truly." As if to prove it to them both, she sat in her green wingback chair and pulled out a little garment she'd been stitching.

But Mercy knew she could see the trail coming in from the west as clearly from her chair as she could standing at the window.

"You go look after those children. And don't worry about me. There's only one thing that will make me feel better and that's Eddie striding through the door." Linette's voice caught and she ducked her head to concentrate on her sewing.

Mercy guessed she wanted to hide her trembling lips and teary eyes. Staying here would do nothing to ease Linette's lonesomeness. Only Eddie could do that, so Mercy donned a heavy winter coat and headed for the door. "I'll be back before dark. Perhaps the men will return before I do."

Linette nodded. "Be careful."

"I always am."

Sybil and Jayne both stood at the window of their cabins as Mercy rode by. She waved, knowing they didn't watch for her. All the women were so tense. It made her glad she didn't have to worry about a man returning.

Alert to any danger as she rode through the woods, she nevertheless smiled just recalling the previous day. Abel had been so solicitous. Her smile faded and she narrowed her eyes. Did he see her as a responsibility? Like one of his children? She snorted. If so, he would soon enough learn she didn't need looking after, though she acknowledged a tiny argument to the contrary. It had felt good to be sheltered in his arms.

She reached the cabin. Abel must have been watching for her for he strode from the cabin as she swung from Nugget's back. "You came."

"Any reason I wouldn't?" After all, she'd said she would.

"I guess not."

"There you go again. Always so suspicious." Her words were sharp but she didn't care. Must they always circle his lack of trust in her? "You're always certain I'm going to fail or disappoint."

"I am not. It's just that it's cold. I thought you might think you…we…should stay in where it's warm."

She gave him a hard look, not believing his excuse. "What I thought is that I said I would come, so I did. What I thought was you need to get things done while you can, so here I am."

He couldn't quite meet her eyes.

She grabbed his elbow and shook him. "Admit it. You don't trust easily."

He brought his gaze to hers. Dark blue misery. "Mercy," he growled. "I don't trust myself."

"What?"

"I've made such foolish mistakes. I live with the consequences but so do my children." His voice deepened. "So did Ruby." He shook his head. "I can't let my emotions guide my decisions. That's how I get led astray."

She dropped his arm. "Are you saying if you like something it's automatically wrong?"

"Of course not." He shrugged. "Maybe."

"Sounds to me like you think having fun is wrong."

He shuffled his feet. "Maybe not wrong, but risky."

"Guess that includes me." She flung Nugget's saddle over a sawhorse and stomped past him toward the cabin.

He raced after her. "I have to live by rules if I want the twins to be safe."

She paused to give him another hard look. "Safe or overprotected?"

He drew back.

But she wasn't done. "Be careful you don't make them afraid to face life."

His look could have burned a hole in wood. "You forget I have a daughter who must be taught to be very careful or the consequences could be fatal."

"I know that. Though—" She'd wondered a time or two and now that he'd brought it up, she might as well say it. "Could the doctor have been mistaken?"

He jabbed his finger at her. "You will not take it upon yourself to presume to know more than the doctor."

"I could promise I would never put her at risk, but

seeing as you don't trust my promises there isn't much point. However, maybe you should get another opinion. Take her to another doctor. Or are you afraid?"

He snorted and ground about to head back to the corral. Before she closed the door behind her, he thundered from the yard.

She sighed. How had she gone from anticipation at seeing him and being reminded of the closeness she thought they'd enjoyed yesterday and her even being thankful to him, to this churning resentment?

She pushed away her mental turmoil and turned her attention to the eager children.

He didn't return until late afternoon, when it was time for her to leave. She told herself she didn't care. Tried to convince herself she wasn't getting as bad as Linette, glancing out the window every few minutes to see if he rode into the yard.

She slipped on her coat and headed for the corral before he unloaded his logs.

When he saw her intention of leaving before he got to the cabin, he jogged over.

The time had come. She closed her eyes. All day she'd wondered if she'd pushed too far, feared he would ask her to stay away from him and the twins.

"I want to apologize," he said. "You're right. I'm far too suspicious. But it's only because I don't trust my own judgment." He smiled a little. "I can't afford to repeat my mistakes."

She had expected a scolding. Not an apology. Especially when she'd told herself all day she deserved one. "It's my fault. I need to learn to mind my own business."

If she thought her apology would relieve him, his

stubborn expression convinced her otherwise. "I know you care about the children and they care about you, so I can't ask you not to voice your opinion about them."

She blinked. "You're saying you don't mind?" She shook her head. "You're sure?"

He nodded, a little sheepish. "I'm not saying I won't continue to be—"

"Suspicious?" she supplied.

"It's not a nice word but, to my embarrassment, I have to admit it's accurate. I'll try to do better. Can you be patient with me?"

What had happened to this man? Had he spent time out in the woods thinking about her accusations? While she indulged in misery in the cabin thinking she had overstepped the boundaries and he would never forgive her?

He touched her cheek. "Friends?"

"Of course." She nodded, too confused to do otherwise.

He lowered his hand to her shoulder and squeezed. "Thank you."

"You're welcome."

A warm smile curved his lips. His eyes darkened. He leaned toward her to plant a quick kiss on her mouth, then pulled back before she could react. "Now be on your way before it gets dark."

She didn't move, too stunned by this sudden change in him and by the way relief surged through her veins.

He turned her toward Nugget. "Will I see you tomorrow?"

She swung into the saddle and looked down at him. "I'll be back." A little bubble of laughter left her lungs, riding the wind as she headed toward the woods.

* * *

Abel could not explain his actions. She wasn't right for him. She represented all he'd once been and had vowed never to be gain—wild, undisciplined. And yes, he found himself reluctantly attracted to her. But never again would he go down that path and therefore he did his best to drive her away. Except every time he tried to do so, he hated himself for hurting her and missed her before she'd even left.

God, help me. Give me strength to do the right thing.

Not that he could even say what the right thing was anymore.

He made his way to the cabin. The kids played contentedly on the bed with little animals created from folded paper.

Savory hash was ready for his supper.

This side of Mercy he enjoyed and appreciated.

They ate and cleaned up, then he read to them. Allie insisted on taking the fringed gloves to bed with her.

If only Mercy would abandon her plans to join the Western show. Maybe then he could begin to trust his feelings for her. Maybe then he wouldn't have to quell his eagerness for her to return the next morning. He forced himself to sit at the table and wait for her even after he heard her ride into the yard.

Allie and Ladd raced for the door.

"Wait here. It's cold out there."

"But we want to see Mercy," his daughter said. "She said she'd bring us a game."

"Wait." He'd allowed not only himself but the twins to grow too fond of her, too anxious for her return each morning.

Her boots sounded on the wooden step outside. The

twins hovered at the door. It took all his rigid self-control to remain at the table.

She flung the door open, her face wreathed in happy greeting. "Good morning." She hugged the twins before turning her face toward Abel.

"The men returned last night just before dark. You have never seen so much hugging and kissing and crying." She laughed. "What a commotion. The men were as bad as the women."

"They cried?" Ladd sounded incredulous.

Mercy chuckled. "No, but they sure did laugh."

"There were glad to see each other." Allie sighed with the joy of the idea. "I'd be like that, too." She turned to Abel. "Were you and Mama like that?"

Abel's mouth fell open. He'd been thinking of how glad he was to see Mercy come each morning. Ruby had not even entered his thoughts. "I was always glad to get home and see you two." He felt the twins studying him.

Ladd sighed. "Mama and Papa weren't like that."

"Mama never hugged us either. How come?" Allie looked about ready to cry.

"You've just forgotten," Abel said, but the stubborn look on both little faces said otherwise.

Mercy hung her coat and turned back to the room. "Linette says we'll have a great big party on Friday. Everyone is invited. She wants us all to celebrate."

He could have hugged her for diverting the children from regrets about their mother. "We'll certainly be there, won't we?"

The twins nodded.

"Have we ever been to a party?" Ladd asked.

Abel scrubbed at his hair. "Why, I don't know. Didn't Mama take you to any?"

Their two heads shook a negative response.

"Mama went to her parties by herself," Ladd said.

This conversation threatened to take him down paths in his memory he didn't care to travel. His parties had been wild, wicked events. He'd never gone to one after the twins were born, while Ruby had never quit. "I need to get to work." He shrugged into his heavy woolen coat. "Will you be okay?" He looked at Mercy, wondering if she would be able to handle the questions the children would likely voice about their mother.

She grinned at him. "You can trust me. Remember?"

Her teasing reminder lifted his concerns and he grinned back. "I do. Remember?" He scuffed his fist across her chin and walked out the door, singing one of the hymns from the Sunday service as he left.

Mercy's laughter rang out, following him from the yard. It continued in his heart as he worked.

Realizing he had gone from resolving to guard his heart to smiling at a shared few minutes, he bent his back to the work of the day. He must get a cabin built and firewood stacked.

Several hours later, he straightened to wipe his brow and stretch his aching back. He downed half the water in his canteen. As he recapped the container, a crackling noise drew his attention to the right. Was that strange man watching him again?

The crazy man posed danger to himself and those back at the cabin. Every day as Mercy rode back and forth, the risk of who he was and what he wanted haunted her ride. Anger raced up Abel's spine and pooled behind his eyes. "Who are you? What do you want?" He roared the words. "Come out and identify yourself."

Only silence, as heavy as a January snowstorm, answered him. His horse whinnied and shook his head. Sam, too, sensed the strangeness of someone watching them.

"Show yourself," Abel called again. He listened and waited, hearing nothing but his own heartbeat. The man must have left.

Abel returned to his work, his nerves twitching with every real or imagined sound. An hour earlier than normal, he packed it in and headed back to the cabin.

Not until he stepped into the warm interior and counted three happy, surprised occupants did he finally relax.

Sooner or later he was going to track down the man in the woods and confront him. Not until then would he be at ease.

Mercy came to his side. "You're back early. Is something wrong?"

He lowered his voice so the twins wouldn't hear him. "I heard that man in the woods again. I won't feel safe until I find out who he is and what he's doing."

She nodded, though her eyes remained skeptical. "I'll head for home then. Linette will be up to her ears in plans. I can help her. I've left you a pot roast and vegetables cooking. It will be ready whenever you are."

He followed her outside. "I know you don't need the warning—nevertheless, I have to say it. Be careful. There's danger out there."

She grinned at him. "So you are fond of saying. But like I've said time and again, I am always careful. I am not going to live my life in fear." Imitating his action, she brushed her fist across his chin. "Life is too short to waste it worrying about what might happen."

"My experience has given me reasons to worry that people won't get home safely."

"I'm not Ruby."

"I know you're not." There were differences between the two women, significant ones. Mercy loved spending time with the children. She made the cabin smell like home. She had always come when she said she would. But there were similarities, too. That wild streak. Not wanting to settle down and be ordinary.

She began to saddle Nugget. "Tomorrow then?"

"If you can come. I need to get my work done before the snow comes."

She swung into the saddle and rode away.

What he hadn't said was he wanted her to return even if he didn't have logs to get. But soon winter would be here and there'd be no need of it.

The thought shivered through his mind like a cold winter wind.

Chapter Ten

Abel repeatedly told himself he must not care about Mercy, but every time he had himself convinced of this fact she would do something that made him forget his decision.

Like the next day when she had the children draw pictures and post them all over the cabin.

"You remember this, Papa?" Ladd asked, leading him to the picture beside the table.

Abel leaned closer to examine the drawing. It looked like a little house with a brown door and a body of water behind it. "What's this?"

"'Member the house we lived in by the lake?"

He nodded. "I do. You and Allie were five years old. I had to warn you to stay away from the water."

"We learned to swim."

Abel straightened to study his son, then shifted his gaze to Allie. "You did?"

"Mama said we could play in the water when you weren't home."

Abel lifted his gaze to Mercy. He knew his eyes were filled with so many things…regrets, mostly. But also a touch of anger that Ruby had ignored his wishes. Not that he should have been surprised.

Mercy smiled gently. "Learning to swim is a good thing."

"I guess so." That wasn't the point, but he didn't expect her to understand.

Allie tugged at his hand. "I drew this one. It's Mama in her prettiest dress."

A stick woman wore a bright red dress, her yellow hair tied with a matching bow. He wished he could forget that outfit. It had a revealing neckline and whenever Ruby put it on she got a faraway look in her eyes. He knew it meant she would soon be taking one of her trips. "What else do you have?"

Allie pointed to the next picture.

"A ball?" A blue one with white stripes.

"You gave me and Ladd balls for Christmas when we were little."

"So I did." He hugged the pair to his side. "You played with them for days. What happened to them?"

Ladd sighed heavily. "We lost them."

Allie shook her head. "No, we forgot them when we moved. They were in the backyard."

Ladd nodded. "I wonder if someone else found them."

Abel shifted to the next picture. Mercy stood nearby and as he held her gaze, he felt a jolt of sympathy from her. He vowed he would not let his emotions show in his face. She didn't need to know the depth of his hurt at Ruby's failure to be a parent or a wife.

Ladd directed his attention to the picture.

"A plate of cookies?" he guessed.

"Gramma Lee used to live next door and she would bring us cookies for special occasions."

"I didn't know that."

"You weren't home. And Mama was gone a lot."

Silent accusations filled his heart, draining it of everything but regret. He knew Ruby didn't stay home all day every day, but only recently had he realized how frequently she'd been absent.

The twins drew him to the next picture. A stick girl in a bed with a brown cover.

"It's Allie," Ladd said. "When she was sick. I was so scared. Mama was gone. I wished Gramma Lee still lived next door, but we'd moved."

The three of them stared at the picture. If Abel was a child or a woman he might have cried. Instead, he sucked back sorrow as sharp against his throat as steel filings and clamped his teeth together. The air about them seemed fragile. He could hear the twins breathing, and his own breath cut through his lungs.

He couldn't take the memories, the pain and the regrets any longer. He spun around and hurried out the door, closing it quietly behind him.

His emotions drove his legs like pistons as he strode to the edge of the clearing and stared into the trees.

The click of the cabin door informed him someone had come out. Mercy was then at his side, and she brushed his arm.

"I didn't mean for the pictures to upset you. I suggested the children draw things to decorate the cabin. It was meant to be a surprise for you. They wanted to know what to draw. I said draw some of their favorite things or things they remembered…" Her voice trailed off.

"I'm not blaming you. I'm blaming myself. I knew Ruby wasn't taking care of them as she should but I kept hoping things would improve."

She pressed her hand to his arm. "I'm sure you did what you thought best."

He no longer believed it or excused himself. "We moved a lot," he said. "I told myself it was necessary so I could find work, but mostly it was to satisfy Ruby's restlessness." He closed his eyes against the pain of his past. "It was all so futile."

Her hand tightened against his forearm. "There's no value in blaming yourself for the past. Nor in letting regrets cripple you. I'm certain you did what you thought best at the time."

The warmth of her hand slipped up his arm and sent calming blood to his heart. "I suppose I did." It was small comfort considering how everything had turned out, but even small comfort was welcome.

He faced her. "I will never put the children at risk again. Not for anything."

She drew back and dropped her hand from his arm, leaving him cold and alone. "Why do I get the feeling you're saying that as a warning to me?"

"No more to you than myself. I found it far too easy in the past to think my decisions wouldn't affect others. I was so wrong."

"Perhaps you were." She took a step away, then stopped. "But there is a risk of swinging too far in the other direction, don't you think?"

They studied each other. At times like this, Abel realized how far apart their philosophies were. He wished it could be otherwise but unless she changed...

Because he would not.

After she left, he went to the woodpile and lifted his ax. Wood needed to be split for the winter. Chop. Chop. Chop. Bits of yellow, pine-fragrant wood scattered at his feet. He pressed his boot to the length of log and chopped until the log disappeared into a mangled pile of wood chips. He tried to remember how careful he must be but her laughter weakened his defenses, making it difficult to think of her as merely a friend.

Finally spent, he wiped his brow and returned to the cabin and care of the children but the wood chopping had not helped clear his thoughts.

He looked forward to her return tomorrow for more than just the children's sake.

The day of the party arrived. Abel was grateful Mercy wasn't coming to watch the children. The past two days had been a strain for him as he fought an internal battle. Her absence made it possible for him to get his thoughts under control.

Or so he hoped. But the twins couldn't seem to hold a conversation without bringing her name into it.

"Can we go now?" Ladd asked.

"Not yet. Do you want to draw another picture?"

"No. I want to see Mercy." The children spoke the same words at the same time. They got their coats and put them on a chair as if it would make the time go faster.

He couldn't stand to confront their silent demands any more than he could ignore his own impatience to see Mercy. "I'm going to chop wood. You two stay inside. I'll be back soon."

"And then we can go?" Allie asked, rocking back and forth on her feet.

"You're flushed." He pressed a palm to her forehead. "Are you okay?"

"I just want to go."

"Then you better lie down until it's time to leave. We aren't going anywhere if you're sick."

"I'm fine." Her bottom lip came out and she crossed her arms.

"Nevertheless…" He pointed toward the bed.

She looked ready to defy him, then marched over and flung herself on the bed.

"I'll watch her," Ladd offered.

Abel hesitated. He didn't want to disappoint them. He'd been looking forward to the afternoon of fun as much as they, but if Allie—

"Papa, I'm okay." Her voice interrupted his thoughts, ringing with unfamiliar firmness. "Ladd's cheeks get red too when he's excited and you never say anything to him."

Abel studied his son. His cheeks were indeed flushed. Why had he never noticed it before? What kind of parent was he? He knew the answer. He was a father who had made mistakes in the past and seemed destined to continue making them. But, he promised himself, he would not make the same mistakes twice.

"Ladd's never been sick," he explained to Allie. Needing to sort himself out, he left the pair and went outside to chop and stack firewood.

Two hours later, Ladd appeared before him.

Abel slammed the ax into the chopping block. "Is Allie sick?"

"No, Papa. She's hungry. Can we eat now?"

Abel glanced toward the sky. It wasn't noon yet but— "Why not?"

He returned to the cabin. Allie perched on the bed, her innocent expression and flushed cheeks did not convince him she had been resting since he left. He made sandwiches and poured them glasses of water. He hadn't found a milk cow yet.

Another of his many failings.

The children ate their sandwiches so fast he wondered they didn't choke. They cleaned the table before he could drink his coffee.

"We're ready," Ladd said, his coat on. Allie waited impatiently at his side, her coat buttoned to her chin.

"I give up." He hurried out to saddle Sam and was barely finished before the twins were at his side. He insisted on wrapping a blanket around Allie's shoulders and tucked two more in the saddlebags in case it turned cold.

As they rode toward the ranch the twins tried to get him to gallop the horse, requests that he steadfastly refused. "We'll get there soon enough."

Still, their excitement was contagious. At least that's how he explained his growing impatience. When before had six miles seemed so long?

Even though it was too early for them to appear, Mercy's gaze went often toward the trail that would bring Abel and the children. Already people from around the area had arrived. Hands from the OK Ranch and the owner, Sam Stone, his foreman, Ollie Oake, and Ollie's sister, Amanda, were there.

Some of the townspeople from Edendale had ridden in a few minutes ago.

It had been such a strange week. Mercy felt as if she rode a bucking horse every time she and Abel were in the same room. One minute he was warm and welcoming, making her insides fill with sweetness. Then he grew fierce and disapproving. Seeing his reaction to the twins' drawings had made her ache for him. He blamed himself for things he shouldn't feel responsible for. As far as she could tell from what he'd said to her, he'd done his best for his children and even for Ruby. His wife's decisions and choices were beyond his control.

She'd told herself again and again that it didn't matter what Abel thought. The children had drawn the pictures they wanted to draw. So what if they reminded Abel of his wife? Or if they made his jaw muscles tighten visibly? Or if he suddenly grew fierce as if remembering he lived by rules, and squinted at her to remind her she did not?

Yet despite the bucking ride he sent her on, she continued to check the trail.

Ward, Grace and Belle rode into the yard. Billy and Grady raced over to greet their friend Belle.

Linette hugged Grace. "I'm so glad you're here. And isn't it wonderful that the weather turned warm so we can be outdoors for the entertainment and picnic?"

Long tables had been set up, laden with food that Linette and Cookie had been busy cooking for two days, along with Mercy's help. Sybil and Jayne would contribute food, as well as Grace, who had brought a covered dish.

Mercy hugged Grace and Belle after Linette stepped back.

"Do you need anything else?" she asked Linette.

"I think we're ready. Run along."

Mercy glanced toward the trail again.

"Go on and meet them," Linette said.

Jayne and Seth's door opened and in an attempt to persuade Linette she wasn't anxious for Abel to appear Mercy ran toward them.

Jayne took Mercy's arm. Mercy spared a brief glance toward the opening in the trees. Still no one.

"They'll be here," Jayne said.

"Who?"

Jayne laughed. "I won't even answer that."

A horse bearing a man and two children broke into sight.

"Mercy, Mercy," the twins called. Allie shrugged from the blanket covering her. Her golden hair shone from beneath a knit hat. Her blue eyes glistened. Her cheeks glowed with healthy pink excitement.

Ladd leaned around his father, waving. Handsome little lad.

Abel's smile caught her heart and held it captive. The man certainly looked glad to see her. She tried to control the eager leap of her heart and failed.

"Oh my," Jayne whispered. "I don't know which of you has it worse."

"I don't know what you're talking about." She looked away from the welcome she imagined in Abel's smile.

"What don't you know?" Sybil walked over and joined arms with Mercy, as well.

Jayne chuckled. "Look at them. What do you think?"

Sybil gave Mercy her full attention, then studied Abel. She chuckled. "I think I see another wedding coming up."

Mercy shook off their hands. "You are both crazy. The children like me. He does not."

Her friends laughed.

Abel and the children were now close enough to hear them and she gave both her friends a quelling look.

Laughing, they left arm in arm. She faced Abel alone.

He lifted the children down. "Can you watch them while I take care of the horse?"

"Surely." She held her hands out to the twins and led them toward the growing crowd, without—she congratulated herself—glancing back at Abel.

She found a spot on the slope overlooking the open area that had been set up for the program. She made sure to squeeze in between Jayne and Sybil. But if she thought that would save her from sitting beside Abel, she was wrong. As soon as he crossed toward them both Sybil and Jayne moved and waved him over.

He jogged to her side. Ladd shifted to make room for Abel between them. Great. So much for proving to her friends that Abel didn't care for her.

So much for proving to herself she didn't care about him.

Eddie stepped to the center of the stage area. "Welcome, friends. My wife wanted everyone to be able to celebrate the end of the roundup."

"And having you back home," Linette added, bringing laughter from those assembled.

Eddie held out a hand, inviting Linette to join him, pressing her to his side when she did. "We won't have many more opportunities to gather like this before winter sets in, so let's enjoy ourselves."

Linette signaled to Jayne, who stepped forward and recited a poem. One by one, others followed. Buster, the youngest cowboy on the ranch, juggled five balls and earned a roar of approval. There were solos and duets.

Bertie recited Psalm 147 with such conviction Mercy's heart was stirred.

"'He telleth the number of the stars; he calleth them all by their names.'"

She'd never thought of that before. God cared enough about stars to name them. Did that mean He cared for her the same way? Or did He only want her unquestioning obedience?

Two gray-headed cowboys from the OK Ranch limped to the center. One pulled out a mouth organ and started a fast tune. The other danced a jig, so lively and quick Mercy guessed she wasn't the only one who was surprised at the man's grace. Soon everyone clapped along.

Then Linette signaled Abel. He and the children went to the center. He held each child by their hand, grinned down at them and then they faced the audience and began to sing.

Jesus shall reign where'er the sun
Does his successive journeys run;
His kingdom stretch from shore to shore,
Till moons shall wax and wane no more.

Allie's sweet clear voice, Ladd's uncertain one and Abel's deep tones filled the air with conviction. It was the sweetest sound Mercy had ever heard. Jesus did reign across the world. That meant He reigned right here at Eden Valley Ranch. Mercy blinked back tears.

Jayne squeezed her hand on one side, Sybil on the other.

Mercy scrambled to her feet and rushed away. She did not look back to see Abel's reaction.

She hurried to the barn, where she'd left her costume, and ducked into the tack room to change into trousers and a fringed shirt.

A few minutes later, she rode Nugget into the performance ring. She had him rear on his hind legs and waved, the fringes of her gloves fluttering.

The crowd burst into cheers and clapping. Their approval continued as she did some rope tricks, then twirled her pearl-handled guns. To conclude, she had Nugget bow, then she rode back to the barn.

Only once had she glanced toward Abel and the children. The twins cheered and clapped. Abel sat with his hat pulled low and clapped halfheartedly. After that she would not look in his direction. She knew he didn't approve. Just as she knew he would never trust her.

What difference did it make? She knew what she wanted and it wasn't a man full of unbending rules with a ready-made family.

Chapter Eleven

"Oh, Papa," Allie gushed. "Didn't I tell you she was glorious? The most glorious thing I ever saw. Wasn't she?"

"Oh yes," Ladd answered. "The best ever."

The twins turned to him. "Papa, don't you think so?"

Fire and flame. That was what he'd seen when he'd looked at her. Her hair streaming down her back, her face shining with pure joy and excitement.

His gaze went to the barn. Beauty and boldness. It was the final word he focused on. Boldness that overlooked rules and safety. He could not, would not ever go back to that sort of life, or that sort of woman.

"Allie, you're flushed. Calm down or we'll have to leave."

Allie's expression flattened as if he'd slapped her. His heart stung at the joy he'd taken from her, but she must not get overexcited, and watching Mercy perform had already achieved that.

"There she is." Ladd pointed to Mercy as she sauntered over to the crowd. Men and women alike reached out to congratulate her.

Abel held the twins back or they would have run to her side. Instead, he steered them toward the tables where the ladies were still piling mounds of food.

"Mercy," Ladd called. "Over here."

People pressed on either side and at his back, while the table penned him in the front. Abel could not escape. Slowly he faced Mercy.

Thankfully the twins had her attention, giving him time to calm his thoughts.

"Oh, Mercy," Allie said. "You were so glorious."

If Abel heard the word one more time he would leave.

"You will be the best person ever in a Wild West show," Ladd assured her.

Several others clapped her back or shook her hand.

She fairly glowed at their praise. Her gaze claimed his, brown and demanding.

He felt her silent question but he couldn't answer it.

Then the twins claimed her attention again.

"Did you like our song?" Allie asked.

She hugged them both. "It was beautiful." She grabbed a plate and led them by the table, filling her plate and guiding Allie and Ladd in selecting food. He followed the twins, doing the same.

Thankfully, he didn't need to worry about carrying on a conversation with her as others continually stopped to visit with both of them.

He hadn't met Ward before and immediately liked the man and his redheaded wife, Grace. He soon learned their little girl, Belle, was Grace's sister and they lived on a small ranch to the west. "My mother and brothers live there, too, but Mother wasn't feeling well so didn't come. I thought the boys would come but they said something about going to town instead."

Ward told him about the two cabins on his place and gave some advice about construction.

Eddie and Sam Stone talked about a work bee to get the church built and soon everyone offered to help.

Abel hesitated. He had his own building project but a church would be nice, though he had no objection to the meeting held in the cookhouse. He wondered what Bertie and Cookie would think and noticed that they nodded their approval.

Conversation shifted to how to obtain a preacher. Then Eddie said, "I'd like to see a doctor in the area, too. We've certainly had need of one several times in the past."

The Mountie, Constable Allen, was in attendance and offered to send messages to the different forts and towns in hopes of stirring up some interest.

Abel paid close attention to all the discussion, more, he admitted, to avoid facing Mercy and his troubled feelings than because of an overwhelming interest in the proceedings. He figured the others would go ahead with plans with or without his help. His own buildings must be erected first.

Eventually the party ended. The food was whisked away. Wagons and horses departed. He headed for the corral and Sam. If he left soon he could avoid time alone with Mercy.

He should have known he couldn't hope for that. She followed him.

"Abel, aren't you going to say anything about my riding?"

He faced her, knowing his lips were pulled back in disapproval.

Her shoulders sagged. "Of course you don't approve."

To him her performance signified she still wanted to leave. "I'm sorry, but why do you do such…such—"

"Foolish things?"

"I was thinking unpredictable." Among several other things.

She shrugged. "It's who I am. And you live by rules."

"Well, rules keep you safe."

"I tried the rules. Tried to do everything right." Her voice grew harsh. "But only when I did something unpredictable did anyone notice me."

Ahh. So now it became clear. "Are you talking about your parents?" Hadn't she said they didn't see her after her brother died?

She shook her head but her eyes said yes.

"I'm sorry. Sorry you never felt important to them. Sorry you still feel the need to do unusual things before anyone will notice you."

She closed her eyes, but it did not hide the pain in her face.

He didn't want to add to that pain and caught her shoulders and eased her toward him. When she didn't protest, he wrapped his arms about her and held her tight.

"You don't need to get people to notice you anymore. Don't the children appreciate you even when you're ordinary?" Though he couldn't imagine her ever being ordinary. Nor did he think he'd like her any better that way despite all his talk to the contrary. "I know I do."

A twitch shivered through her. He held her tighter, wondering how she'd respond to his words. He hadn't planned them. If he had he wouldn't have said them. Fire and flame. Beauty and boldness. Only she didn't seem so bold now as she clung to him. He liked her this way. Maybe she would believe him that she didn't need to try and get attention from anyone, especially him.

Jayne and Sybil waited for Mercy as she wandered back to the thinning crowd.

"You've gotten really good at riding and roping," Jayne said.

"And handling guns." Sybil shivered. "I will never like guns." She tipped her head to consider Mercy. "Are you still planning to join a Wild West show?"

"Yes." Abel had held her and assured her he liked her just the way she was. "No." Did he mean it or was he trying to convince her to change—maybe abandon her plans. "Maybe." Would she forget about joining a show if he asked her to? "I don't know."

Jayne and Sybil looked at each other and laughed.

"What?" Mercy demanded.

"We both remember that feeling." Jayne's smile seemed condescending.

"What feeling?"

Sybil pressed her hand to Mercy's arm in a soothing gesture. "The feeling that you aren't sure which way is right anymore. You aren't even sure what you want."

Mercy denied it flatly. "I know exactly what I want." But did she?

She tossed the question around throughout the rest of the evening and still mulled it over the next morning as she rode to the cabin.

Maybe, she finally decided, if he came right out and asked her to consider staying, she'd give it serious consideration. She arrived at the cabin and Abel stepped outside. Her breath stuck in the back of her throat. Was he planning to make his wishes clear?

"Good morning," he said, trotting toward the corral.

She headed the same direction and swung off Nugget's back. Sam was already harnessed. Was Abel in a rush to leave? Because of her? Had he said more than he intended? More than he felt?

"The twins are anxious to see you," he said, leading Sam from the enclosure. With a barely there wave, he left the yard.

"At least someone is," she muttered. It certainly wasn't Abel, who couldn't wait to get away from her.

She entered the cabin.

"Mercy, Mercy." Allie rushed to her side. "Do you think I can learn to ride fancy like you?" She dipped her head. "Maybe like you showed me before. You know, standing on Nugget's back?"

"I've been practicing with the lariat," Ladd said, his voice cautious yet hopeful.

Mercy sighed. They both wanted to imitate her. No doubt their eagerness explained Abel's withdrawal. "Allie, you know you can't do those kinds of things."

"What about me?" Ladd asked.

The resignation in his tone bothered Mercy, reminding her of her own childhood. Ladd was often expected to curtail his activities in order to protect Allie. Did anyone ask him if he minded the sacrifice? Or if he felt insignificant?

She pulled them both close and kissed the tops of their heads. "Ladd, I think you can keep swinging your rope. Someday you'll get really good. Now what shall we do?"

"Can we go exploring?" Ladd asked.

The sun had moved over the treetops and sent warmth into the clearing. Like Eddie said yesterday, they wouldn't enjoy too many more nice days. "That's a good idea."

Ladd glowed at her approval.

She vowed she would go out of her way to give him more attention.

They wrapped up in warm coats and hats and ran outside. She chased Ladd through the trees while Allie laughed at them.

"Can you chase me?" she asked when Mercy caught Ladd and held him tight.

Mercy shook her head. "I wouldn't want to make you ill." She wondered if Allie knew her heart might have been damaged. A cold breeze tugged her coat. "We better go indoors. It's getting cold."

She hurried them inside as the wind increased. "Let's make some soup." She always let the twins help even though it took longer and generally made a mess. She'd noticed the pained look on Abel's face when he saw the mess and promised herself to have it cleaned up before he returned.

The soup was ready, the table set, but Abel didn't ride into the yard. She delayed half an hour while the children begged to eat and she finally gave in. They finished and still Abel didn't come.

The children played with the collection of paper animals she'd helped them create, leaving Mercy free to listen to her thoughts. Had she really expected Abel to ask her to stay? Even worse, she'd foolishly allowed herself to think he might want to make this arrangement permanent. It was all because Jayne and Sybil had said they foresaw a wedding. Pshaw. They lived with their vision clouded by their own romances.

The afternoon dragged on, but she had no doubt he'd

return soon. In the meantime she decided to make the place welcoming. "Let's bake cookies."

Two hours later the cookies cooled on a tea towel. She'd cleaned the place so not a bit of flour dusted anything. And she waited. And waited.

Then the truth hit her. Abel hadn't said he liked her just as she was. He'd said he approved of her as ordinary. Huh! Who wanted to be ordinary? A perfect little woman, cooking and cleaning and washing clothes. Not her sort of life at all. He was just like Ambrose.

The children ate cookies and drank milk tea.

Yet wasn't that exactly what she did every day? And she enjoyed it because she cared about the twins. And yes, she cared about Abel. Though she couldn't explain why.

The twins joined her at the window. "Where's Papa?" Allie's voice sounded thin with worry. "Why isn't he back?"

"He'll be along any minute." Already the shadows lengthened enough that it would be dark before she returned to the ranch.

"It's just like Mama." Ladd sounded resigned to the fact.

She drew the pair away from the window. "How is it like your mama?"

"Mama went away and didn't come back."

She nodded. "Your papa will come back."

"Mama would be gone for days." Ladd clung to her hand.

"But now she's never coming back." Allie cuddled close.

Mercy wrapped her arms about them. "Don't worry. Your papa would never leave you."

The three of them sat huddled together as the minutes ticked past with painful slowness.

Mercy slipped away from the pair and returned to the window. Dusk filled the clearing. Abel would never be so late at returning unless something happened. She curled her fingers into her palms as she counted off the many risks. A bear. A wildcat. A crazy, whiskered man. A wandering outlaw. A—

She spun away from the window and hurried to the stove to stick in another piece of wood. She pushed the kettle back and forth and shook the coffeepot. Aware the children watched her every move, she forced herself to smile and act as if everything was perfectly fine. But her insides burned with worry.

Someone should go looking for him. But she was the only adult who knew he should be back by now. Only she could help him. "Children, bundle up. I'm taking you to the ranch."

"You're worried about Papa, aren't you?" Ladd asked.

"He should have been back by now. I need to go see if he needs help." While they dressed in warm clothes, she hurried out to get Nugget. The cold had deepened. If Abel was out there hurt—

She would find him and bring him home.

She grabbed a lantern from inside the little shed and led Nugget to the cabin. The children joined her on the horse and she wrapped them in blankets, knowing if either of them got sick, Abel would hold her personally responsible.

As they rode toward the ranch, she held Allie close and made certain Ladd held on tight. She rode right up to the big house and handed the children down to Linette, who came immediately to the door.

"I need to leave the children here," Mercy said.

"Where's Abel?"

"I don't know but I intend to find out." Ignoring Linette's protests, she rode down the hill and across the yard.

Jayne had seen her ride in and stepped from her cabin as Mercy rode past. She called out something, but Mercy ignored her. She knew they would all try to dissuade her. Advise her to wait for the men to return and one of them would go look for Abel. She didn't intend to wait for anyone.

The growing darkness forced her to make her way slowly back to the cabin. She passed it without stopping and took the trail Abel had created. Her slow pace gave her plenty of time to think. If something had happened to him—

She swallowed a lump so sharp it scratched her throat. The twins would be heartbroken. How would they survive?

She couldn't imagine life without him. Her mind flooded with pictures of him—holding Allie close, stroking Ladd's hair, the three of them singing together.

Being a star in a Wild West show lost its appeal. In comparison to what she'd found with Abel and the children, it seemed a foolish goal. Foolish, just as Abel said.

Ordinary, he liked. He'd said he appreciated her when she was ordinary.

She rode through the trees, pausing often to call his name. But she heard nothing except the rustle of the branches in the wind, the squawk of birds disturbed by her noise and the whistle of her own breath.

She'd show him she could be ordinary. If only she would get another chance. *Please, God, he's a father. Keep him safe for the children's sake.* And mine. But she did not pray the final words. Why would God care for her sake?

She reached a place where he'd chopped down trees and dismounted to look around more closely.

"Abel. Where are you?"

Not a sound indicated his presence. Where could he be? Tension clawed at her throat. What if—

She dare not finish the question

Abel's mind cleared long enough for him to know he was in serious trouble. And so cold he ached. The cold might be responsible for the fact he couldn't feel his legs. He prayed it was so.

He faded. Couldn't tell how much time had passed except to note the sun dipped to the west. How long had he lain out here? He tried to move his legs. Nothing. He reached down to see why they wouldn't respond and felt the log that lay across them.

That's right. The chain had slipped. The tree had rolled and caught him. He recalled falling and his head whacking the ground. Probably explained the pain in his head. How long ago was it? He couldn't remember for certain but it seemed it had been early morning. He squinted at the sky. And now it was late afternoon. Almost dark. Would anyone look for him? Would Mercy? Of course she would. Darkness wouldn't stop her any more than she'd let the man in the woods make her too fearful to search for him.

Mercy would come.

He lay back and tried to relax. Cold seeped into his bones like a disease.

His mind clouded over and he dreamed. In his reverie Mercy stood at his side, a plate of cookies in her hand. Behind her the children beckoned for him to come. He hesitated, wanting Mercy to go with him.

"Mercy." His cry jerked him awake. He shivered. "Mercy," he called again in desperation.

Off to the side, he saw and heard the tall bushes being crushed to one side. He closed his eyes. If a wild animal meant to eat him, he prayed it would be swift.

"Abel?"

Wild animals didn't say his name in Mercy's voice. He looked up. "Mercy?"

"There you are." She broke through the trees. "I would have gone right by you if you hadn't called."

"I'm pinned."

"Let's have a look." She held a lantern up and made her way around him. "Yup. You're pinned. Where's Sam?"

"Haven't seen him since the log broke away. How bad is it?"

She wouldn't look at him.

"Mercy, is it real bad?"

She squatted by his head. "Truthfully I can't tell. Won't be able to until I pull the log off you." She didn't move. "It's likely going to hurt some."

"Just do it."

Still she didn't move.

"What's wrong?" He squeezed the words past his shivers.

"I'm afraid of what I might find when I pull the log off."

He struggled to suck in air. "Me, too, but I don't intend to lie here forever."

She chuckled though he thought the sound rather strained. Then she touched his brow. "Then let's do it." She rose. "I need to find Sam. Nugget isn't strong enough to move this log. Don't go anywhere."

He clamped his teeth together to stop shivering. And to stop himself from calling at her not to leave. He unclenched them long enough to say, "I'll be right here when you get back."

"Sam, Sam." She whistled and called, beat her way through the underbrush.

He strained to hear her, and caught enough rustling and grunts to be comforted that she hadn't left him. A few minutes later—or what seemed so, but his mind faded in and out so he couldn't be sure—he heard the rattle of a chain. She'd found Sam.

Then the light of her lantern flickered. "You're back." He couldn't say for certain if he spoke the words aloud or only in his mind. It didn't matter. She'd returned. She'd get him out of this predicament.

She returned to his side, tucked two blankets in around his body. "As soon as I get you home, I'll get you warm."

"Where are the twins?"

"I took them to the ranch. Linette is watching them."

He wanted to ask why she hadn't gotten Eddie or one of the cowboys to look for him, but he couldn't quell the relief he felt as seeing her. He would trust his life to her hands.

She led Sam to the butt end of the log and hooked

the chain around it. She picked up a smaller log and wedged it under the downward side of the one pinning him to the ground. "I don't want it to roll back on you if Sam slips or something."

Good to know.

"I'm going to put a log on this side, too. I want the one on your legs to roll off without doing more damage." She adjusted the chain, checked the wedge, then squatted at his side. "It could hurt."

"Just do it."

She brushed her knuckles across his cheek. He caught her hand and pressed it to his face. Brought it to his mouth and kissed the palm. She wore gloves so he was unable to feel her flesh. Nevertheless, he found strength and courage in holding her hand close for a moment.

She withdrew, leaving him cold and alone. "I'll holler when I start to pull."

He grunted a reply, not trusting himself to speak calmly.

She skirted around the log. "Ready? Here we go." She guided Sam forward. The chain snapped into place. He could imagine Sam leaning into the harness. The log pressed harder into his legs. He stifled a moan. And then it eased off as it rode up on the logs she'd put in place.

And as the pressure eased, the pain began, sharp as a deep knife cut, digging into his shin until he wished she'd put the log back in place.

The pain grew, swelled, until it consumed him. He squeezed his lips tight, determined not to cry out, but a moan welled up from someplace deep inside, a reservoir of pain he'd never before uncovered. It escaped past his clamped teeth and rent the air.

"Almost done," she called.

A moment later she hurried back to his side. "I have to look at your legs and see what kind of damage you've done."

He grabbed her hand and held on like a drowning man.

She seemed to know what he needed and squeezed back, stroked his forehead and made comforting noises. "I need to check your legs in case you're bleeding."

He forced his hands to release her.

She moved to his feet. Cold touched his flesh as she exposed his legs. But he *felt* the cold, which surely was a good sign.

She grunted. "No bleeding." She straightened and looked about. "I have to get you out of here. I'll get Nugget."

"I'll ride Sam." His voice squeaked, giving away the depth of his pain.

She stood over him. "I don't know how you'll get on his back."

"I'll do it."

"Very well." She brought Sam forward, then leaned down to offer him a hand.

He wanted to refuse. To do it himself. He managed to sit up fine despite the pain clawing at his brain. "My head." He would have pressed his hands to the back of his head but needed them to keep himself upright.

"Let's have a look." She held the lantern behind him and ran gentle fingers against his scalp.

He grunted when she touched the bruise.

"There's a nasty lump here but no bleeding. You must have banged your head."

He heard the worry in her voice and could offer little in the way of assurance. Truth be told, his head felt like someone had attacked him with an ax handle.

Her soft touch lingered a moment more, smoothed his hair, then left him hurting more than he had before.

He pulled his blurry thoughts back to the need to get home. Which meant getting to Sam's back. He tried to put his feet under him, but his muscles turned to pudding.

"Put your arms around my neck and I'll pull you to your feet."

With little option except to obey, he put his arms about her, breathing in her comforting warmth. To his embarrassment, he clung to her like a baby.

She wrapped her arms about his waist. "On the count of three. One, two, three." She leaned back and he did what he could to help. Somehow she managed to right herself despite his weight, and steady him. "Grab the horse."

He gritted his teeth and forced himself to release her even though he wanted nothing more than to hold her tight and feel her strength and determination. But he must get home.

Gathering together every remaining ounce of his waning strength, he pulled himself upward, clawing his way to Sam's back while she lifted his legs. Somehow they managed to get him on the horse. The exertion was so intense he swayed.

She grabbed him and steadied him. "Can you stay there?"

"I'll stay here."

"Then let's go." She led him through the trees back to the trail, where Nugget waited patiently. She called him to follow, then swung up behind Abel. "I'll hold you." Her arms came around him and took the reins. He buried his fingers in Sam's mane and hung on.

"We'll soon be home." Her voice carried a sharpness that jerked his head up. Had he fallen asleep? Passed out? He righted himself and blinked his eyes hard.

"I'll be okay." How far did they have to go? He didn't recall having gone such a distance from the cabin.

The trail was dark. He shivered and not just from being cold. A thousand dangers hovered in the dark trees. Like that crazy mountain man. "I hope you're praying," he croaked.

"I have been since I set out to find you."

"Guess God answered your prayers."

"Yup. I have to say I am as surprised as you."

"Who said I was surprised?" Talking helped keep him alert.

She chuckled, the sound reverberating up his spine. "You didn't have to say it."

"Are we almost there?" He didn't care that he sounded like Ladd.

"We're here." She guided Sam to the door and slipped to the ground. "Let's get you inside."

How did she figure to do that? He doubted he could stand and she couldn't carry him.

She helped him swing one leg over the horse until he sat sideways. "I'm braced against the door," she said. "I can hold you. Come on, get down."

Knowing he would crash to the ground but not seeing any alternative, he reached for the door frame, held it as tight as he could and launched himself off Sam.

He fell into her with a barely muffed groan.

Grunting under his weight, she grabbed him about the waist and steadied him. Once she had him fairly well balanced, she reached for the doorknob and they staggered inside.

The narrow space of the cabin seemed to yawn before him. But somehow, between the two of them, he dragged himself across the room and fell on the bed.

Home sweet home.

Chapter Twelve

Mercy tucked blankets around Abel, who shivered like a wind-struck leaf. His skin was icy. She hurried to add wood to the fire and to fill the kettle, then turned back to Abel. His boots needed to come off.

Explaining what she meant to do, she began to ease off the first boot. His groan shivered up her spine. She closed her eyes, gritted her teeth and would not allow herself to look at him as she removed one boot and then the other and dropped them to the floor. "Done." She breathed hard, swiped at beads of sweat on her brow. She set the lamp on a shelf above the bed. "I want to have a better look at your legs." In the woods, she'd worried about bleeding and how she'd stop it. Now she meant to check for broken bones. She picked up the edge of the blanket and bent closer, touching each shinbone, moving each foot. Her guess was his legs were badly bruised but not broken. "God watched over you."

She recalled a verse Bertie had recited the day before…was it only a day ago? She felt she'd lived several days in the past few hours. He'd said it was Psalm 147. *God delights not in the strength of the horse, nor is His pleasure in the legs of a man.* She repeated the words to Abel. "Seems God cared enough about your legs to keep you safe."

Abel grunted.

Mercy moved closer to his head. His eyes were dark with pain. "Where do you hurt most?"

"My head." His words were thick, almost garbled.

She tried to remember what Linette had said about the time Eddie had been unconscious with a head wound. Was there anything special she did? Or—her brain froze—had she said all they could do was wait and see?

Abel's eyes closed.

"Abel? Are you okay?"

He didn't open his eyes. Didn't respond.

"Abel." She shook him a little.

His eyes cracked open so briefly she would have missed it if she hadn't been straining to see some response. After that he slept. Or was he unconscious? She couldn't tell.

What if something happened to him?

She fell on her knees beside the bed. "Abel, don't you die. You've got Allie and Ladd to think about." Why had she thought adventure was so important? All she wanted now fit into this small cabin. Abel alive and standing on his feet, the twins clinging to his hands as the three of them smiled at her.

"Lord God, I've never been one to call on You much. I've always figured I could take care of everything myself. But now I can't. Abel's head is hurt. I don't know how bad it is or what to do. Please, let him be okay."

She remained on her knees half praying as she

watched Abel's chest rise and fall. The *clop clop* of horse hooves jolted her to her feet. She was alone except for an injured man. She grabbed Abel's rifle and faced the door. No one would be allowed to harm him.

"Mercy," a familiar voice called from the other side of the door.

"Jayne?" She rushed over and flung the door open. "What are you doing here?"

"Seth brought me. He'll be here as soon as he tends the horses. Abel's horse and Nugget were wandering about the yard."

She'd completely forgotten the horses. "Come in." A cold wind shivered across the floor. "Why are you here?"

"Because you need us. Linette told us about Abel being missing. As soon as he heard, Seth saddled horses for us both and here we are."

Seth stepped into the room. "Are you okay?"

She nodded. "I don't know about Abel though." She explained how she'd found him trapped by a log. As she recalled those anxious moments when she couldn't find him and then when she wondered what she'd discover when she pulled the log off, her legs refused to hold her weight and she sank into a chair.

Jayne wrapped an arm about her shoulders.

Mercy sucked in air and held it until her strength returned. "I think his legs are okay but he hurt his head." She led them to Abel's bedside and showed them his legs.

"I don't think there's any reason to be concerned about his legs," Seth said, after examining them. "How long has he been unresponsive?"

"He's not." She shook him and called his name.

But Abel didn't open his eyes.

Mercy grabbed the edge of the bed to hold herself upright. "Is he—?" She would not give words to her worries.

"He can't be left alone," Jayne said.

Mercy had no intention of leaving his side until she saw him standing and his mind clear.

"We'll stay with you," Jayne added.

"We'll pray." Seth bowed his head. "God in heaven, You care about sparrows but we know You care about us a lot more. Because You love us, we humbly ask that You heal Abel's wounds. Amen."

Seth and Jayne looked at each other, eyes so full of trust and assurance that Mercy straightened her legs. Abel would recover. He had to.

"Have you eaten?" Jayne asked.

Mercy shook her head. "I'm not hungry."

Jayne made tea and sandwiches and insisted Mercy leave Abel's bedside and sit with them at the table. To placate her friend, Mercy nibbled at a sandwich and drank a cup of tea. Then she pulled her chair to Abel's bedside. "Abel, if you can hear me, I want you to know you have to get better. For Ladd and Allie." She repeated the words again and again. Inside her head, she added, *And for me. I have so much I need to tell you. Changes I need to make. But I need a chance to make them.*

Jayne and Seth moved about the room almost soundlessly, pausing often to glance down at Abel, then returning to the table where they spoke quietly. Mercy didn't listen to them. Every thought, every word, every breath concentrated on willing Abel to get better. Silent prayer followed every lungful of air. *God, please heal him. Make him as good as new.*

"We brought bedrolls," Jayne whispered. "We'll sleep by the table. Why don't you pull out the trundle bed and put it against the wall and try and get some rest?"

"I'll stay here." She meant to stay at his bedside until he opened his eyes and recognized her. "You can have Allie's bed."

Jayne chuckled softly. "It's too small for Seth, and I intend to sleep with him. There's nothing you can do except wait. You'll hear him if he calls out." Jayne pulled her from the chair and tugged out the bed. She shifted it away from Abel's side and pushed it against the wall. "You need to rest."

Rather than argue, Mercy stretched out on the tiny bed, but as soon as she heard Jayne's and Seth's breathing deepen she slipped from the bed and returned to Abel's side, where she sat in a chair to guard him. She watched his face in the lowered lamplight, waiting and praying for him to wake up.

"Mercy." A hoarse voice jerked her alert. Had she fallen asleep? How long since she'd last checked on Abel?

She blinked to focus and looked at him. His eyes were open and he looked at her.

"Mercy." The word whispered from his lips into her heart.

She leaned close and spoke softly so as to not disturb Seth and Jayne. "How are you feeling?"

"My head hurts and my legs ache, but I am grateful to be here." He swallowed hard. "Can I have a drink?"

She hurried to fill a cup with water and hold it to his lips.

He drank eagerly then settled against the pillow.

For a moment she wondered if he'd fallen asleep or drifted into unconsciousness, but then his eyelids came up. "I am grateful to be alive."

She squeezed his hand. "Me, too."

His grip on her fingers was surprisingly strong. The fact filled her with encouragement. Surely it meant he was going to be just fine.

"Thank you for coming to find me."

She grinned. "You must have known I would."

He smiled softly. "I counted on it."

She stroked his brow with her free hand. "You've given me enough adventure to last a lifetime." Would he understand what she meant?

"I'm tired," he murmured as he pressed her hand to his chest. In no time his breathing deepened. He'd fallen asleep. But when she tried to remove her hand, his eyes jerked open. "Don't go," he whispered.

"I won't."

A few hours later, daylight crept into the window. Seth and Jayne scrambled to their feet. Jayne rushed to Mercy's side. "How is he?"

Mercy had tried several times to slip her hand away, but he held it firm even in his sleep. "He woke and was clear in his head. I think he's just sleeping."

Jayne patted her shoulder. "He's lucid enough to know to hang on to the person who rescued him."

Seth rolled up the bedding, built a fire and joined them at Abel's bedside. "His color is good. His breathing is even."

Abel opened his eyes. "I'm fine."

Mercy tugged her hand away lest her friends read more into the way Abel held it than they should. She couldn't say what it meant. And until she could...

Abel pushed himself to a sitting position. The color left his face.

"You need to take it easy," Seth said.

"I'll be fine." Every breath Abel took rasped into his lungs.

Mercy's lungs felt impossibly tight before they released with a whoosh as his color returned. She'd never seen anything so beautiful in her life as the way his eyes focused, clear as a cloudless sky. He smiled at each of them in turn. Mercy thought he looked at her several seconds longer and it wasn't imagination or gratitude that made her think his smile was wider as he regarded her.

"Are you hungry?" Jayne asked.

"A cup of coffee would be mighty nice."

She slipped away to make some. Seth followed his wife, leaving Mercy alone with Abel.

Her smile felt too wide for her face, but she couldn't help it. He was alive and well.

Life felt wonderful and exciting and promising all at once.

Despite the pounding of a cattle stampede in his head, Abel couldn't stop looking at Mercy, afraid she'd disappear if he blinked. How many times had he wakened shaking with the fear of being alone and each time he'd found her at his side? She'd rescued him just as he knew she would.

"Thank God," he murmured.

"Amen," she whispered back.

He wondered at the way she blinked until he realized she'd been up all night. Most likely she had a hard time keeping her eyes open.

He shifted, preparing to put his legs over the side of the bed, but the movement sent a stabbing pain into his head. He leaned against the wall and waited for it to end.

"I have coffee ready." Jayne held a cup toward him.

"I'll sit at the table." He had to get back on his feet.

Seth appeared at his side. "Don't you think you should take it easy for a day or two?"

"I can't. The twins will be worried about me." He knew from the way Mercy dipped her head and avoided his eyes that she agreed with him.

Seth patted Abel's shoulder. "I suppose they will. How about if I ride back and get them after we've eaten?"

Abel tried to nod but it hurt too much. "I have to get up. I don't want them to see me like this."

Mercy leaned forward. "Why not leave them at the ranch until you feel stronger? As long as they know you're all right they'll enjoy it."

He settled back. His arguments had all been dealt with. "So long as they aren't worried. Especially Allie."

"We'll look after them," Seth promised. "You rest and get strong so you can take care of them."

His lungs spasmed. His ears ached from the noise inside his head. He grabbed at his chest.

"Abel, what's wrong?" Mercy asked, her voice strained.

"The children." The words grated from his throat. He grabbed Mercy's hands, his eyes stinging. "Promise me you will take care of them if something happens to me."

Mercy drew her lips together. Either her eyes filled with tears or he only saw through his own tears.

"Of course I will, but you're fine. Nothing is going to happen to you."

He nodded and fell back, weakened by his surging emotions. "Thank you."

"Come on, Mercy." Jayne drew her toward the table.

Abel drank his coffee and lay back on the bed, shivering from that little bit of exertion.

"I'll ride to the ranch and tell the children." Seth's voice came to him as if through a long tunnel. "Jayne will stay here with you."

He heard Mercy's familiar voice like a wordless lullaby answer her friend before sleep claimed him.

When he wakened, he blinked to drive back the pain behind his eyeballs. He shifted to his side and that's when he saw Mercy asleep in the trundle bed against the far wall. Her dark lashes fanned across her porcelain cheeks. Her mahogany curls spread across the pillow in wild disarray. His heart filled with a hundred different emotions, all of which made him smile. He remembered her strength as she had held him on the back of the horse, her steadying presence at his bedside, how he'd clung to her hand. His smile widened. He saw her dusted in flour as she'd helped the children, recalled their eagerness as they watched her return every morning. Eagerness that matched his own.

Her eyelids fluttered open. Their gazes connected in a steady, unblinking look. He opened his heart to her and let her look deep. Felt her silent search. He wanted her to know how grateful he was for her, how much he admired her and trusted her.

"Hi," he murmured.

She jerked to a sitting position and rubbed her eyes. "What time is it?"

"Midafternoon." Jayne sat at the table and answered the question.

Abel sat up, as well. His head protested with a sharp stab, which he ignored as he looked about the cabin. He'd forgotten about Jayne and Seth. Seth wasn't there. Then he recalled Seth had ridden back to the ranch to tell the children Abel was okay. How long ago was that? He couldn't say. "Has Seth returned?"

"Not yet. I expect him soon." She rose and went to the stove. "Can I get you something to eat or drink?"

"Water would be nice."

She brought him a cupful and stood at his side as he drank it. Over the rim of the cup he watched Mercy as she rose and smoothed her riding skirt. She ran her fingers over her curls trying to tame them, he supposed. She straightened the bedding and shoved the bed back under his, then faced him. "How are you? How are your head and legs?"

"Better, I think." He handed the cup to Jayne. "I'd like to try getting up."

Jayne shook her head. "Not until Seth is here to help."

Abel leaned back against the wall. He could wait a few more minutes.

A little later a horse rode into the yard and Seth called out a greeting before he strode into the cabin. He didn't wait for questions. "The children are just fine. Enjoying their time at the ranch. They wanted to come and see you for themselves—I said you were tired and needed to rest. I promised them I'd let them know when you were ready to have them come home."

Abel shifted his legs over the edge of the bed. "I'm going to get up."

Seth tossed his coat and hat on a hook and hurried to Abel's side.

Abel waved him away. "Let me do it on my own." Dizziness filled his head, but he willed it away and took a step. His legs hurt, though the pain was nothing he couldn't deal with. Finally the dizziness lessened. "The twins need to see for themselves that I'm fine. And I need to have them with me." He made it to the table and sank into a chair. Mercy sat across from him, her gaze following his every move. He guessed at her concern and sent her a reassuring smile that he knew drew his lips narrow as he concentrated on his breathing.

Jayne poured them all tea and set a plate of cookies in the middle of the table.

He didn't feel up to eating, but the tea felt good going down.

"How was church?" Jayne asked.

Abel had forgotten it was Sunday. By the way Mercy jerked back he guessed she'd forgotten, as well.

"When Bertie heard about your accident he changed his mind about what he meant to say and reminded us all of how God watches over even sparrows who are sold two for a penny. 'How much more are we worth?' he said." Seth turned to Jayne. "My wife told me the same thing. She made me see how much God values me." The two of them smiled at each other in a way that filled Abel with a thousand regrets. This couple had what he wanted from a marriage. Not the regrets and accusations he'd experienced with Ruby. Nor the loneliness.

Seth spoke again, bringing Abel's thoughts from that regretful place. "Bertie prayed a very nice prayer for you though he was careful not to say anything to alarm the children. Everyone sends their prayers."

"It could have been so much worse." Abel's words were soft. "Thank God it wasn't."

"Amen," the three said.

"Belle said to tell you that it was God who made sure everyone was in the right place at the right time."

"Belle? But she's only a little girl." She was a year younger than the twins.

"A little girl who has experienced a whole lot of sorrow and trouble." Jayne and Seth told him how Ward had rescued Belle and Grace from a man who held them captive. How afraid Belle was of everyone to begin with but how she soon learned not every man was bad. "She fell in love with Ward before Grace did. Or at least before she would admit it." Jayne reached for Seth's hand. "God has brought so many people together at the ranch. First Linette and Eddie, then Cassie and Roper, then Ward and Grace, us, and more recently, Sybil and Brand." She chuckled.

Jayne fixed Mercy with a wide smile. "And now you."

Mercy bolted to her feet. "I'm going to make soup for supper." She hurried to the stove.

Laughing, Jayne and Seth regarded each other and nodded as if they shared a secret.

Abel shifted to watch Mercy. Did Jayne and Seth think he should marry her? Right now he could think of nothing he'd like better, but despite his thumping head he wasn't about to let his emotions rule his actions.

He remained sitting at the table as Jayne and Mercy made soup. He listened halfheartedly to Seth's talk about a work bee for the church in Edendale.

A little later, he accepted a bowl of soup and ate it. Not because he had any appetite but to prove to the three watching him so carefully that he was fine. He finished his bowl and pushed it aside. The others were done before him.

"Are you going to bring the children home?" He addressed Seth.

"If you're sure you're up to it."

Abel nodded.

"Right then." Seth grabbed his hat. "I'll get them."

"I'll stay with Mercy," Jayne said.

Seth kissed his wife and left.

Mercy waited until the door closed behind Seth. "Abel, I know you want to prove to us that you're fit as a fiddle, but I can tell your head hurts. Why don't you rest until the children return?"

He shook his head, the movement making his eyes hurt.

"Come on." She took his hand and urged him toward his bed. "Just until they get here."

He must have dozed off, because he roused when Mercy tapped his shoulder. "Abel, Seth is back." She stayed at his side as he sat up.

He barely made it to his feet before the door burst open and the twins ran to him.

"Papa," Allie shouted. "What happened?" They both clung to him as he hugged them.

Ladd let go first. "Are you okay?"

"I'm fine. Very glad to see the pair of you."

"Tell us what happened."

He led them to the bed, glad to sit on the edge as he told them. "A log fell and pinned me to the ground. I couldn't free myself, but Mercy found me and got Sam to pull the log off. Then she brought me home safe and sound." He hugged them both again. Nothing mattered half as much as staying safe so he could take care of them.

Allie sighed. "She's glorious. Didn't I tell you?"

At the moment, Abel had no argument to the contrary.

Glorious and brave.

A warning flashed in his brain. Wasn't it simply the flip side of wild and free? But tonight he didn't care.

Chapter Thirteen

Mercy glanced over her shoulder half a dozen times as they left the yard. She didn't want to leave Abel and the children, knowing she would worry about him all night. But he assured them he was fine. And he squeezed her hand secretly before she left. She wished for a few minutes alone with him.

For what? she chided herself. Did she think he would thank her with a kiss?

Well, if he didn't, she'd kiss him just because she was so grateful he had survived his accident.

She didn't care what differences they had. Those no longer held any significance. The only thing that mattered was he was safe and sound. She'd never been so grateful for anything in her life.

Her gratitude made her take more time than normal the next morning. She pulled on a dark blue woolen skirt and demure white blouse. She looked through her jewelry until she found a brooch her mother had given her one Christmas. At the time it had been much too heavy and grown-up for Mercy and she knew her mother had given little thought to the gift, but now the purple amethyst set in a gold setting and surrounded by natural pearls said Mercy was grown-up and serious.

She drew her hair into a roll at the back of her head and pinned it in place, securing it firmly with a plain and ordinary tortoiseshell comb.

She stepped back to study herself in the looking glass. Yes, indeed, she looked exactly right. Serious. Mature. Ready to be ordinary.

A strand of hair escaped and she tucked it back in place. Only a bonnet would hold it secure on the ride and she chose a plain one.

If Linette and Eddie thought anything unusual about her outfit, they refrained from saying so.

Perhaps because they were excited about their own news.

"We've decided to help Abel with his cabin before we work on the church," Eddie said.

"It's a fine idea." Linette glowed with approval. "He's been trying so hard to do it on his own, but the accident will slow him down." She turned to Mercy. "Don't tell him. We want it to be a surprise."

"It's a lovely idea." Of course it was. He'd get his cabin ready before winter. He and the children would be safe and warm. So why did a protest sting her tongue so hard that she had to cool it with a gulp of cold water?

How much time would she have to show him her change if his cabin was built? She gathered up a few things and went out to saddle Nugget. She might wear skirts and pin her hair up, but she refused to ride sidesaddle.

She arrived at the clearing and waited. The cool air was so still she could hear tumbling water in the distant river. A twist of smoke came from the chimney. Sam stood at the corral fence. It looked like he hadn't even been fed yet.

No one opened the door to greet her.

Her heart tumbled against her ribs. Was Abel...? She turned Nugget loose in the corral without bothering to unsaddle him and, lifting her skirts, ran for the door. Why had she decided to wear all these petticoats today? If Abel had gotten worse, he wouldn't even notice.

She flung back the door and stepped inside.

Three pairs of eyes looked up from the table.

Abel skidded his chair back. "Is there something wrong?"

"No." Her breath jerked in and out of her lungs. "But when no one came to greet me—" She slammed her mouth closed before she could give her fears a voice. "I just wanted to make sure you were okay. All of you."

Their surprise overcome, the twins ran over and hugged her. "Papa was telling us how God answered his prayer and sent you."

She lifted her gaze to Abel. Did he really mean that? Of course he meant when she'd found him in the dark. Not, as her overactive imagination first thought, in a general, everyday way.

"I prayed, too," she said, her gaze still holding his. Both surprise and welcome filled his eyes. She shook her head, chastising her overactive imagination again. She took her long coat off and hung it on the nearby hook.

"You're wearing a dress."

Did he sound approving or only surprised? She couldn't tell and untied her bonnet and hung it over the coat.

He studied her hair and opened his mouth to speak, then closed it without uttering a word.

What had he been about to say? That he liked her hair up? Or did he wonder what it meant? She hoped he'd soon figure it out on his own.

From now on she meant to be ordinary.

The dishes still sat on the table, thick porridge lining the edges of the white bowls. Glasses stood before the twins' bowls and a blue porcelain mug before Abel. "Are you finished with your breakfast?"

Three heads nodded.

"I'll clean up." She gathered the dishes into a pile and checked the kettle. Finding it empty, she filled it and set it to boil. She glanced around. Today she meant to begin proving how well she managed as a housewife. *Wife.* The word echoed through her head even though she mentally denied she had such hope.

She made the two beds, pushed the trundle bed away and picked the children's clothing off the floor. All stuff they normally did themselves, but there was no need for them to do it anymore. She would take care of them and their needs. She took the paper animals off the shelf and arranged them on the bed for the children to play with.

"Mercy."

Abel's soft words stopped her. She turned to face him. He sat alone at the table and she joined him.

"How are you? Did you have a good night?" She kept her voice low so the children wouldn't hear and worry.

"Apart from a bruise or two, I'm fine. How are you? You seem different this morning."

So he'd noticed. But she couldn't tell what he thought about the change. It was on the tip of her tongue to ask but she wouldn't. Let him see that she could be the sort of woman he needed—ordinary.

The kettle hissed and she bounded to her feet, poured the water in the dishpan and tackled the dishes.

He rose and reached for his coat. "I still have that log to get home."

Her hands stilled, her lungs stopped and her heart blasted against her ribs and clung there. "You can't." The words crackled from her lips. She shook her head. She'd worry about him every minute. "You might... You aren't..." Swallowing hard, she dried her hands and followed him to the door. "Couldn't you rest one more day?" Just then she recalled that Eddie and the men would soon arrive to help him. Let one of them get the log and any more logs they needed. "Please."

He stood with his hand on the latch. "Winter will soon be upon us."

All sorts of arguments sprang to her mind. Winter would come whether or not he was ready. If he hurt himself he would never be ready. And if his injuries were serious—

She couldn't finish the thought.

"Hello, the house." The call made them both jump.

"Who can that be?" he asked.

She pretended innocence. "It sounds like Eddie. You better see what he wants."

He stepped outside and she followed. There stood Eddie, Seth, Brand, Roper, Slim and half a dozen cowboys from Eden Valley Ranch, along with Ward and, if she wasn't mistaken, some hands from the OK Ranch.

"What is this?" Abel sounded confused.

"I believe it's a work bee," she replied from behind him.

Abel jerked back, forcing Mercy to sidestep. He grabbed her arm. "Whose idea is this?"

"I think it's Eddie's. Why?"

"I can't accept all this help."

She grinned at him. "Try telling that to all those men. They've come to help because they know you need it and deserve it."

"But they hardly know me."

"You're a friend and a neighbor. That's all that matters. I've learned that out west people pull together. It's one of the best things about this country." That, and the freedom allowed woman.

Abel stared at the men, who were now dismounting. "I don't know what to do."

"I'd suggest you go out there and welcome them and thank them." She shoved him in the right direction.

He glanced at her over his shoulder. "Did anyone ever tell you you're bossy?"

"Nope. Not a soul. Best if you don't either."

Chuckling, he crossed to Eddie's side.

The sun shone warm and bright. The light breeze stirred the treetops. The air sang with the smell of autumn leaves and woodsmoke.

Mercy watched the men with a smile on her face. It was going to be a fine day.

Eddie clapped Abel on the back and indicated the men. Each carried an ax or saw or hammer or sometimes two or three tools.

The children joined Mercy and she explained the men had come to put up a new cabin for them.

"Like Papa wants?" Ladd asked.

"Exactly like your papa wants."

They asked to watch. "Put on your coats and stay close. I don't want you getting in their way."

She would like to watch, too, but she had work to do.

She browned meat and peeled vegetables for a stew. Linette had informed her the men would bring their own lunches, but she meant for Abel and the children to have a hot, nourishing dinner.

As the stew simmered, she slipped outside to check on the twins. They sat against the cabin watching the beehive of activity. Some of the men shaped logs, chips of wood flying in every direction as the axes rose and fell. The aroma of new wood filled the air.

Others peeled new logs, the bark peeling off in long strands.

A crew laid logs into place. Already she could see the shape of the cabin. It would be considerably larger than the current one. Roomy enough for a family.

Families had needs. She turned back inside and set to work wiping the logs of the old cabin. Even if it wouldn't be a home for them much longer, they deserved the cleanest, warmest, best-run home in the country.

But again and again, she was drawn to the door to see how the building progressed.

She looked for Abel. He stood by Eddie discussing something. She nodded her satisfaction. Knowing about Abel's injuries, especially the blow to his head, Eddie would somehow divert Abel from doing anything heavy.

Returning indoors, she glanced around. What did a person—a housewife—do in such small quarters? Normally Monday meant laundry, but the morning had flown by. It was too late to start washing clothes. However, she could prepare to do it tomorrow and she went outside to retrieve the copper boiler hanging on the side of the cabin. Still, if she put it on the stove now, the water would half boil away before morning. With a sigh, she hung it back on the nail.

"What are you doing?"

Abel's voice came unexpectedly from behind her, sending her blood to her heart in such a hurry she gasped. She turned slowly. "I was thinking about laundry."

"You seem restless. It's not necessary for you to be here. I can watch the children."

Was the man blind? How could he have so completely misinterpreted the change in her? "Oh, no. I've no place else to be. Nothing else I want to do."

He didn't speak. Didn't nod or shake his head. He simply studied her, his eyes revealing nothing more than confusion. "Why have you been avoiding looking at the new cabin?"

She rubbed a spot on her nose and slowed her breath. All the while she'd been trying to prove she could be a good and efficient housewife, he'd been thinking she wasn't interested in the construction work. "I've been busy. That's all."

"In that case, why don't you come over now and have a look." He crooked his elbow toward her as if she needed assistance crossing the yard. Let him think so. She tucked her hand about his arm and let him lead her.

"It's much bigger and will be sounder than the little cabin. There will be a bedroom, kitchen and living room." He pointed out where each would be. "The loft will have two rooms for the twins."

She could see it all. The table and chairs there. A wide bed there. The cupboards and stove over there.

Little beds with bright quilts in the loft. In fact, she saw it much too clearly. She saw herself at the table rolling out biscuits, at the stove stirring a pot, smoothing the bedding on all three beds. She even pictured herself making the quilts for each of the twins' beds.

She shouldn't have come with him. Shouldn't have listened to his description of the rooms.

"I can't quite decide where to put the window in the kitchen." He stared at the area meant for that room. "Is it better by the door, do you think?"

She saw it over the table. But before she could answer, he spoke again.

"I'm sorry. I know it doesn't matter to you. You'll soon be on your way to join a show." He patted her hand as it lay on his arm. "I just—"

"Abel," Slim called. "Show me where the wall will go."

"Be right there." He removed his arm so her hand fell to her side. "Feel free to look around."

But her thoughts burned within her. How much clearer could he be than to remind her that she'd said she planned to be a trick roper and rider? Had he even realized she'd changed her mind?

It was up to her to make him see it. She glanced at the shape of the future cabin, then returned to the present one.

She stepped inside and leaned against the door. As she reviewed what had just happened, she groaned. She hadn't even asked him how he felt. How did that prove anything but selfishness?

Straightening, she squared her shoulders. She could change and she would. He'd soon be able to see it clearly.

* * *

Although Abel paid attention to each word Slim spoke, he knew every step Mercy took back to the cabin. His thoughts moved a little slower today because of his headache, but Mercy was different. She'd worn a dress for one thing and pulled her hair back into a roll. Not that she hadn't done so before, but only on Sundays. Normally he would have expected to see her watching the construction work. Or amusing the children with games and pretend play. But today she stayed inside the little cabin. Why? He wished he knew what it meant.

Or maybe he didn't want to know.

After she'd rescued him and stayed at his side until she thought he was no longer in danger, he believed a new understanding, a closeness of sorts, had developed between them.

Obviously he only imagined it because of his vulnerable state. Something that no longer existed. He must guard his thoughts and actions lest he make another mistake.

But an hour later, he wished she would come outside and offer a few suggestions. He could use a woman's point of view on some of the decisions.

"Let's have dinner," Eddie called.

The men threw down their tools and jogged to their saddlebags to pull out the lunches they'd brought with them.

Abel didn't have a prepared lunch so he strode toward the cabin, his steps slowing as he neared the place. He could hear the twins talking inside, could hear Mercy respond though he could not make out her words.

He would soon have a new cabin. There would be no

need for her to come and watch the children. He almost wished Eddie would take his crew and go home.

Realizing how foolish a thought that was, he put it down to his headache. Of course, he was grateful. He and the twins would have a safe, warm, solid home for the winter...for those long cold days and even colder nights when he would lie alone in his bed while the children slept in the loft. He'd rise to a cold room. The loneliness of the prospect scratched at him. But he had the twins. That's all that mattered.

If only he believed it... But having had Mercy's company for these past three weeks, he knew he'd wish every day for more than safe and warm.

There must be a solution. One that would satisfy them both.

But she wanted to leave. And he wanted a woman who would stay.

He stepped inside and breathed in the savory aroma of stew. "I feel guilty eating a hot meal while everyone else eats cold sandwiches."

"You aren't everyone else." Mercy filled four bowls and then sat across the table from him.

What did she mean?

"You need extra nourishment after your accident."

Oh. Only that. He dipped his head to hide his disappointment. "I'll say grace." He took a moment to collect his thoughts before he prayed. After his amen, he silently asked God to guard his heart and mind. But an inadmissible thought followed. *God, could You make it possible for Mercy to stay a little longer?* Maybe until it would be too late for her to join a crazy show. Maybe until she changed her mind.

The children plied him with questions throughout

the meal. Good thing, as Mercy seemed interested only in her bowl of food. He thanked her for the meal and thanked her again when she filled his coffee cup for the third time. She smiled nice enough but seemed to be faraway in her thoughts.

His coffee grew bitter and he pushed the half-empty cup away. No doubt she wondered when she'd be able to fulfill her commitment to help with the children so she could pursue her own activities. A Wild West show. What did he have to offer to compare with that? Nothing but two children who needed lots of attention, a cabin under construction and his own demands...food, coffee, laundry. No wonder she grew restless and distant.

Yet he couldn't imagine her leaving. Would she stay if he asked?

He bolted to his feet. "I hear the men back at work." He fled the cabin. But, despite the blow of ax against wood, the pound of hammers, the shrill of saws, his thoughts circled the same question over and over.

He could ask her to stay until the new cabin was finished. That meant windows in, partitions up, the floor finished, the chimney built. It would mean her riding back and forth every day. How long could he reasonably consider that feasible? Once the cabin was finished, then what?

He picked up a saw that leaned against a log and examined it, ran his finger along the teeth. Then what? The question rattled against the inside of his head. Then what?

Eventually he had to say goodbye. Let her go.

Because the only alternative wasn't something he dared think about. Mercy was too much like Ruby. Unprepared to settle down.

Someone called him and he set aside the saw and went to see what was wanted.

Would she stay if he asked her? If only until the new cabin was finished and ready to live in?

He could offer neither of them any longer than that.

By late afternoon, the cabin walls were halfway up.

Eddie called a halt to the work. "We'll be back in the morning. I'll escort Mercy home."

"I truly appreciate your help," Abel replied. But he couldn't help feeling disappointed that he would not get a chance to ask Mercy to consider returning every day until the new cabin was livable.

As she rode away with Eddie, he realized he didn't know if she meant to return in the morning.

Why hadn't he thought to ask?

The question plagued him throughout the evening as he served the children more of the stew that grew more flavorful the longer it simmered.

He tried to stay awake after the children went to bed to figure out what he wanted to do about Mercy, but his body demanded otherwise and he crawled between the covers and fell instantly asleep.

The children woke him the next morning. Not often did he sleep longer than they did. Every bone in his body felt the effects of his accident and he groaned as he got up.

Allie watched him carefully. "Are you okay, Papa?"

He straightened and hid his pain. "I'm fine." It was later than he usually got up. "We better hurry with breakfast or the men will be here. They'll think we do nothing but sleep."

Ladd poured water in the kettle. "The fire is going."

Abel stared at his son. When had he grown so independent?

"Mercy showed us what to do and said it was okay so long as there was an adult present."

He guessed being asleep while Ladd tended the stove qualified as having an adult present. But he didn't know if he should be concerned or pleased at Ladd's ability.

One thing he knew for certain, if he didn't get moving the men would be back before he did his chores. He sliced bread and set out syrup to spread on it. Knowing it would never get him through the morning, he opened a can of beans and another of peaches.

Allie sighed. "I wish Mercy would make breakfast for us."

"Well, she can't be here in time. Eat up. I have chores to do." He downed his food and rushed outside to feed Sam while the twins still ate.

He was returning to the cabin with an armload of firewood when Eddie rode in with a crew. Abel's lungs sucked in air laden with the smell of wood and fall leaves and warm sunshine when he saw Mercy riding at Eddie's side. She'd come back.

She swung down and handed her horse to Eddie, then followed Abel to the house. "How are you?" She studied him. "Seems to me you're limping a little."

"It's only bruises. I'm fine." Even the remnants of his headache had vanished with her arrival.

She paused to take the copper boiler from the hook and carried it to the stove. "I'll get the water heating." She headed to the well with two buckets.

Why would she do the laundry? She'd never done it before. He'd managed on his own, scrubbing a few things as they were needed. But before he could ask her, Eddie called and he had to leave.

So many things about Mercy had changed. She again wore a dress and had her hair pinned up. She seemed set on remaining indoors despite the brilliant sunshine. What was wrong with her? Was this her way of preparing to say a final goodbye?

The walls of the new cabin rose steadily.

"We'll get the basic shell up today," Eddie predicted. "Tomorrow we'll put on a roof."

"I can manage the shakes on my own," Abel said. "And the inside finishing."

"Good, because I assured Linette we'd get the church up this fall."

"I'll help with the church."

"Not until you're ready." Eddie clapped Abel's shoulder. "There'll be lots of people at the church raising. It will be a major community event if Linette has her way."

As Abel watched the walls go up, he made up his mind. He would ask Mercy to watch the children until they moved into the new cabin. It was the most he could allow himself. Even that might be beyond his reach if she had her heart set on joining a Wild West show before winter. Any show in this part of the country would soon be heading south to miss the bad weather. Unless… He smiled. He might need her so long she missed joining before they'd left.

He shook his head. He knew the folly of hoping a person would give up their dreams because of contrary circumstances. Hadn't he learned his lesson with Ruby? And his own choices?

But a delay was acceptable.

Having made up his mind, he discovered how difficult it was to find an opportunity to ask the question. He'd insisted he should join the men eating sandwiches outdoors at dinnertime. Mercy and the children ate indoors. He'd expected her to join the men. The fact she hadn't had him half convinced she was ill.

But she rushed about hanging wet clothes on a line she'd suspended between the cabin and a nearby tree. Later, she took each item off the line and carried it indoors showing no sign of illness.

Then, before he knew it, Eddie called out, "That's it, boys. The walls are up."

Abel went from man to man shaking hands and thanking them. "I appreciate everything."

When he turned to speak to Mercy, she was already sitting on Nugget's back at Eddie's side, waiting to leave.

"I'll bring a crew tomorrow to do the roof," Eddie called as they rode away.

Abel stared after until Ladd asked, "Papa, what's the matter?"

He turned away. "Nothing wrong, son. I'm just thinking how grateful I am for the help. We'll soon be in a big, warm cabin."

"This cabin is warm," Ladd said.

"Except when the wind blows, then the roof rattles and the cold shrieks through the chinks in the wall." It would be plenty hard to stay warm come winter, but now he could get the new cabin ready, fill in every space between the logs so tightly no wind would ever sneak through.

Tomorrow, he vowed, he'd ask Mercy to keep coming.

If she didn't return tomorrow, he'd go to the ranch and ask her.

That night he lay awake after the twins fell asleep and he prayed. He prayed for things he knew were in the children's best interests, like safety and love. But he also wished for things he doubted were in any of their best interests.

Wishes were harmless enough so long as he didn't let them rule his choices.

He was up early the next day and put coffee to boil. The sun had not yet appeared over the eastern horizon but the sky turned steely gray, indicating it would soon appear. Abel opened the door, on the excuse of getting more wood. He paused to listen. No thud of approaching horses. He lingered, straining for a sound. Sighing, he returned inside. The coffee boiled over and he reached for it, remembered just in time to wrap a cloth around his hand. He shook the pot and stared at the mess on the stove.

The children crawled out of bed and dressed, then they sat at the table.

"Papa, are we going to eat?" Allie asked.

He jerked his attention from the coffeepot. How long had he been staring at it, wondering?

"Of course, we'll eat." He dragged out a fry pan, threw in a spoonful of bacon fat and sliced in leftover potatoes before he began another pot of coffee.

Ladd rushed to the stove and pushed the pan aside.

"Ladd, stay away from the stove."

"Papa, the potatoes are burning."

"Sorry. I got distracted." And his lack of concentration wouldn't end until he knew if Mercy would come this morning. Maybe not then even. Not until he asked her to stay and got the response he wanted.

A short time later, horses rode into the yard.

Abel hurried for the door and flung it open. His lungs filled with ease for the first time all morning at the sight of Mercy beside Eddie. Half a dozen men accompanied them, but he didn't even look at them. He couldn't have said who they were.

He and Mercy smiled and said hello. They passed each other as he joined the men and she went inside the cabin. It took almost more self-discipline than he could muster not to follow her and ask her on the spot. Perhaps, at the same time, he'd ask why she'd been acting so differently if he ever got a chance to speak to her without cowboys or the twins or both hanging over his shoulder, listening to every word.

By midmorning, he could wait no longer and, murmuring some excuse, he climbed from the roof and headed for the cabin. He opened the door. Mercy sat with a basket of mending on her lap and a needle and thread in her hand.

On the floor before her sat Allie, also with a needle and thread. She held a piece of fabric in her hand. A handkerchief. She took stitches to hem it.

Ladd sat beside her cutting pictures from a magazine.

Abel's heart threatened to melt out the soles of his boots. This was what he'd wanted since the twins were born. A welcoming home. A happy family. A woman who glanced at him and smiled.

Then reality slammed into his thoughts and he swallowed hard. He had no more room for useless dreams. All he wanted, all he could allow himself, was a few more days of pretending.

Chapter Fourteen

Mercy sewed a button on a pair of Ladd's trousers. She'd done laundry, ironed the clothes. She now worked on the mending. Wasn't she being ordinary? But Abel only said she seemed different.

Different as night from day, if he cared to notice.

The door opened and he stared at the three of them. She couldn't read his expression. Did he approve? Did he even notice?

"Ladd, Allie," he said. "Run outside and play for a bit. Mind you don't bother the men."

The twins set aside their projects and dashed outside without arguing. Mercy watched them go. They were such good children. What did Abel have to say that couldn't be said in front of them? She kept her head bent over the button. The new cabin was almost finished. Likely he'd come to tell her he no longer needed her to come. She would not let him guess how desperately she wished he could see the change in her and understand what it meant.

He remained just inside the door and twisted his hat

round and round. "I know you've got your heart set on joining a Wild West show."

"That's been my plan. I haven't minded delaying though." *I could be persuaded to change my mind if you offered an alternative.*

The hat went round and round. Then paused. "You're good at it."

He meant her trick riding, she supposed. "Thank you." He'd had little enough to say at the time. Why now? She tied off the thread and shook out Ladd's shirt. One more garment mended.

Abel shifted from one foot to the other. "The new cabin is looking good."

"Indeed." The subject she'd been expecting and dreading.

"Of course, I still have a lot of work to do. More firewood to get in. The inside of the cabin to finish. The cracks to fill."

"Mmm-hmm." She selected one of Allie's dark pinafores whose seam needed repairing. She cut off a length of navy thread. The little girl needed someone to dress her up and do her hair, she thought absently. Not that Abel didn't do the best he could.

He jerked a chair from the table and plunked it in front of her, his knees only inches from hers. He leaned forward until she felt him with every breath.

She lifted her head and met his eyes, blinked before his demanding look. She lowered her hands to her lap, scrubbed her lips together. Had she done something wrong? Something to earn his displeasure? But she couldn't think of what it could be. Why, these past few days she'd been so perfectly behaved she thought she'd perish of boredom. How did Linette, and Jayne and

Grace manage? Sybil, she could understand. All Sybil had ever wanted was to live by rules.

"Mercy." Abel's voice jerked her nerves like a taut rope. "What I'm about to say…ask…is big. I know it is. But I hope you'll consider it carefully before you give a response." He scratched at a snag on his trouser's leg. If he kept it up there'd be another mending job.

"Of course." He was certainly being mysterious and her nerves began to twitch in time to his scratching.

He pressed his hand against his leg as if realizing the damage he did. "I would like to ask you to consider coming a bit longer." He sprang to his feet. "There, I've said it." He crossed to the stove, picked up the coffeepot and set it down again, then returned to the chair, swinging it around and straddling the seat. He leaned over the back. "I could get my work done so much faster if I didn't have to watch the twins and they really enjoy having you here."

That she knew to be true. But what did he think of her presence? She dared not ask. "I enjoy keeping them company."

"So you'll think about it?"

It was a beginning. More time would allow him to see how ordinary she could be. "I don't need to. My answer is yes."

He jumped to his feet and stood by her chair. "That's great."

She took her time inserting the threaded needle into the fabric she held. Carefully, she folded it, keeping the needle visible on top, and set it on the basket of other items to be mended. Only then did she lift her gaze to him.

He grinned widely. She wondered if his eyes revealed approval or only relief.

Drawn by the look in his gaze, she rose to face him.

"I'm glad." He smiled at her.

"Me, too." She returned his smile.

The air shimmered between them until she had to blink to keep her eyes from tearing. If only she could read his thoughts. Was he grateful only for the sake of the children? Or did that gleam in his eyes say he was happy for his sake, as well? He scrubbed his lips together. Shifted on his feet. His gaze dipped to her mouth.

Her breath stuck midway up her throat. Without forethought, she leaned toward him.

He leaned in...then he blinked, patted her shoulder and headed for the door.

She lifted a hand, thinking to call him back. For a moment she'd thought he meant to kiss her.

She pressed her fingers to her mouth as he ducked out the door. Next time she'd make sure he followed through on that thought.

The next morning Abel sat at the table pretending he wasn't as anxious to see Mercy as were the twins. Wearing their coats, they waited at the door for the sound of her horse. The morning air was chilly, and he'd insisted they keep the door closed until she arrived.

"I hear her," Ladd yelled, and the pair rushed outside.

Abel slipped into his coat and followed.

"Mercy," Allie called. "Papa made us wait until you got here before we could look inside the new cabin." They trooped after her to the corral, where she unsaddled Nugget and turned him loose.

"He did, did he?" She took Allie's hand on one side and Ladd's on the other, and the three of them waited for Abel to catch up. "Now why would you do that?"

"It was as much their idea to wait as mine."

"I see."

If only he knew what she saw. She'd agreed readily enough to help for a few more days. Would it be long enough for him to provide reason for her to…

What? Make it permanent?

He'd wasted enough of his life chasing after dreams and he saw how that had turned out. All his life he'd wanted…

He couldn't even say. Only that he hadn't found it at home building ships; nor had he found the elusive something living a wild and free life. He certainly hadn't found it in his marriage to Ruby.

The only thing that had ever given him satisfaction was the twins. He loved them and vowed to devote his life to them.

Yet his insides ached for more.

When they reached the cabin, he opened the door and waved them in with a wide sweep of his arm.

The twins dashed in and circled the room at a run. Mercy entered more slowly and stood at Abel's side. "Eddie insisted on putting up the walls for the bedroom and the loft floor. I have yet to put in the chimney and get glass for the windows." He took her arm and led her forward. "I plan to put the stove here. And the table will go beneath the window so we can see out as we eat." Thankfully, she didn't seem to notice his use of the word "we" or she assumed he meant himself and the twins. But he'd been picturing Mercy at the table across from him, enjoying a cup of coffee as the sun shone through the glass.

Ladd and Allie faced them. "Papa, where is Mercy going to sleep?"

"Me?" He noticed a jolt run up her arm. She touched the two little heads. "I am only coming to help until your papa doesn't need me."

Confusion crowded their faces and then disappointment. Ladd led Allie away. Just before the door closed behind them, Abel caught Allie's whispered words. "She doesn't want to stay with us. Just like Mama."

Had Mercy heard the words? He slanted a look at her. If she'd heard she gave no indication.

"It will be a very nice home," she said.

"It's missing only one thing." He hadn't meant to say the words aloud but now that he had, he didn't regret it. Now he would get a chance to say what was in his heart.

He ignored the little warning voice in the back of his brain telling him to listen to his head not his heart.

She turned to face him. "What's it missing?" Her eyes were watchful and, dare he believe, hopeful?

"A mother."

She raised her eyebrows and her eyes filled with disbelief. "Wouldn't that mean you'd have to take a wife?" She stepped away as if to check the view out the window. "And as I recall, you've decided you would never marry again."

He crossed to her side, struggling to find words to express both his desire and his uncertainty. "I think what I said, or at least what I meant, is I would never marry a woman who wasn't devoted to the twins." Suddenly a rush of words flooded his mouth. "Ruby found them a nuisance. It didn't matter to her if they were properly supervised or even adequately fed and clothed. I'll never put them through that again. Never."

"Nor should you."

Her silent waiting sucked at his thoughts. Did she mean—

"Papa!" Ladd's fear-filled yell jerked Abel toward the door. He rushed outside to discover the twins between the cabin and the corrals, staring into the woods. Allie gripped Ladd's hand, her face white and drawn.

"What's wrong?" he asked as he reached them, Mercy hard on his heels.

Ladd answered, "There's something out there."

Abel and Mercy glanced at each other. In her eyes was the acknowledgment of the same thing he feared. The man in the woods.

"You two go to the old cabin and stay inside with Mercy." He shepherded them toward the door.

"Papa," Allie's voice was a thin whisper. "It was a kitty cat."

No kitty cats wandered about the woods, but he'd let her believe it rather than frighten her. Inside, he grabbed his rifle and turned to Mercy. "Do you have your gun?"

She shook her head and avoided meeting his gaze.

How strange. Wasn't she afraid of the man out there? "Where is it? I'll get it for you." He turned on his heel, expecting she'd say he'd find her gun on her saddle.

"I quit carrying it."

His jaw fell lax. He blinked at her. "I must have misunderstood. I thought you said you didn't carry a gun anymore."

"That's what I said."

"What a time to be without a gun." Especially with

a wild man in the woods. "Keep the children with you. Don't wander about in the woods. Call if you need help."

He closed the door behind him and skirted the woods around the cabin, but he saw nothing that made him think either a man or a kitty cat had been there. Perhaps the twins had been mistaken.

The tension slipped from his shoulders. Why would Mercy stop carrying a gun? His shoulders tightened again. Didn't she realize the dangers of riding back and forth through the woods without protection? Kitty cat or crazy man, it was but a fraction of the dangers that faced her.

If something were to happen to her—

It would be partially his fault for asking her to make the journey twice a day.

Assured no wild animals or wild men stalked his family, Abel went to the new cabin. It was time to start on the chimney. Time to get his new home ready for the winter.

He'd been about to ask Mercy to stay on. In the back of his mind, he supposed he meant to ask her to marry him. But he understood a man with two kids and a desire to live a calm, ordinary life held no appeal to her. It was a good thing Allie and Ladd had interrupted their conversation.

He would not think of the long, lonely days. His only concern had to be the welfare of the twins.

The next day Mercy came prepared to give the children school lessons. She'd used every opportunity to teach them math and reading skills. When they helped with a recipe she had them measure, add and subtract the ingredients. When they had a treasure hunt or played sailing on a ship, she let them read from one of the many books she borrowed from Eddie's large library.

But now she needed to be more purposeful about it. She meant to show Abel she could be a responsible mother figure. He'd said he wanted a mother for his children. Well, he'd soon learn she could be that. Would she be willing to settle for nothing more? Of course. Who needed more? Lots of women had loveless marriages and lived for their children. Wasn't Abel satisfied with being a father and nothing more? Yet her answer failed to satisfy an ache deep inside, in a forbidden place behind her heart. A place with solid steel doors for which she'd thrown away the key. Yet somehow the doors managed to creak open a bit each time she thought of Abel.

As soon as the cabin was clean and soup simmered on the back of the stove, she brought out pencils and paper for the children. Linette had supplied her with texts suitable for the twins. "Allie, Ladd, today we are going to start school lessons."

Ladd stared at the books. "I don't like school."

"The others make fun of us because we can't read as good as they do," Allie said, with a tremble in her voice.

No doubt they had missed much school if they moved around as often as Abel said and if Ruby hadn't made sure they attended. Mercy wanted to gather the children in her arms and assure them she would never neglect them. But she didn't have the right.

"Then why don't we work to catch up?"

They reluctantly sat at the table. She explained the lesson to them and guided them to answer the questions. She knew they had the skills for basic arithmetic, but they stalled at completing the work.

Ladd dropped his pencil and chased it across the floor.

Allie followed his lead.

Mercy tried to corral them back to the table, but Ladd climbed on the bed and pulled down their collection of paper animals.

It gave Mercy an idea. Perhaps they weren't ready for formal lessons, but that didn't mean she would give up.

"Ladd, if each of us made three more animals, how many more would we have?"

The twins looked at her as if she'd asked them to number the stars.

"Look. There's three of us and if we each make three animals..." She laid out three piles of three. "How many more would you have?"

"Nine," Allie shouted.

"Right. Now how many all together if you add nine?"

Ladd answered first, pleased at figuring it out.

She went around the house, naming objects. "How many legs in total do four chairs have? How many cans of beans in half a dozen cases?"

Soon the children were asking each other and shouting out answers.

She guided them back to the table. "Let's see how fast you can come up with the answers on your worksheets."

At first she thought they would balk, but when Allie bent over her page, so did Ladd. They finished within seconds of each other.

Mercy checked the answers. "A hundred percent for both of you. Good job." Now to shift to writing. "Let's practice handwriting."

Two bottom lips came out.

"How can you send letters if you can't write?"

Ladd gave her a look of disbelief. "Who would we send letters to?"

"Why don't you write to your grandparents?" She had no idea if Abel was in contact with them, but he'd never said anything to lead her to suspect otherwise.

So she helped them pen simple little letters, suggesting they tell about the new cabin.

"I want to tell about you riding in a Wild West show," Allie said.

"Let's leave that for another day." If the grandparents were anything like Abel, they would be shocked he had a woman like her—someone who had taught the twins about trick riding—caring for the children.

The twins did not like her answer.

"Why don't you write pretend stories about whatever you want? We could put them in a scrapbook and save them? Wouldn't it be fun to read them to your own children?"

Ladd and Allie laughed so hard they almost fell off their chairs.

She chuckled, too. "I'm sure your papa would like to keep your stories."

They nodded and bent over the sheets of paper she gave them. She had to spell many words for them and show them how to shape some of their letters. Half an hour later they had finished their stories.

Just in time as Abel came through the door. "What's going on here?"

"We're having school," Ladd said.

"We wrote to Grandma and Grandpa," Allie added.

"You did?"

Mercy watched his expression, saw it go from

curious to surprised to pleased and she hugged her success to herself.

"We wrote stories, too," Ladd said.

"Do you want to read mine?" Allie held out her piece of paper.

Mercy's heart clenched. Allie had written about a young girl who was the star in a Wild West show.

Abel took the piece of paper. His jaw tightened as he read. It tightened further when he read Ladd's story about a boy who roped a wild horse and tamed it.

Mercy crossed her arms about her. Her success had been swallowed up in defeat.

"Very adventuresome," Abel said as he crossed to the stove.

By adventuresome he meant foolish. Risky. He didn't have to explain; she knew.

"Dinner is ready." She gathered the school supplies together, careful with the pages the twins had written. If he didn't want to save them, she would. And maybe now that they knew how to write a letter they'd write her once she left.

She pressed a hand to her middle and stifled a groan. She did not want to leave them. Any of them. Still, it seemed less and less possible Abel would ever see how much she'd changed.

But as she served soup and then cleaned up, she made up her mind. She wasn't prepared to give up yet.

She decided to seek counsel from her friends. Later, when she returned home, she took care of Nugget and looked up the hill toward the big house. But rather than head in that direction she crossed to Jayne's cabin.

Jayne welcomed her. "I see so little of you lately. How are Abel and the children?"

"They're fine." She crossed to the window and glanced out without seeing past the glass, then spun around and went to the table to run her finger along the surface.

"How is the new cabin coming?" Jayne asked, watching her from her chair.

Mercy shrugged. "They'll soon be moving in." She dropped to a chair facing Jayne. "Are you happy?"

Showing no surprise at the change in conversation, Jayne smiled. "Supremely. Seth is wonderful."

Mercy shook her head. "I don't mean Seth. I mean this." She waved her hand around the room.

"This cabin is only temporary. We'll have something bigger. Not that we need it right now."

Mercy couldn't deny the serenity of both Jayne's smile and words. "I don't mean the cabin. I mean this life. You hardly leave the cabin. You spend most of your days cooking and sewing. Is it enough?"

"It is for me because it's who I am."

Mercy studied her hands as they twisted together in her lap. Realizing Jayne might read more into the gesture than she cared to explain, she folded her hands together and forced them to be still. "I don't know who I am."

"I think you do. I've watched you these past few days. You've changed. That might be good. You've been far too adventuresome, as if trying to fill up a need in your life. But remember, you can't be what you think someone else wants you to be. You will only be happy if you are true to who you are, who God meant for you to be."

"I expect you're right." She stayed and visited a few more minutes then left. She wanted to change so Abel would approve of her. Did that mean she was trying to be someone she wasn't? Or was she trying to become the person she was meant to be?

It was all so confusing. She trotted the last few yards to the house and rushed indoors to see Linette and Grady.

Linette seemed content. So much so that Mercy envied her. But hadn't she had to change to fit into ranch life? Mercy had heard tales of how Linette struggled to learn how to bake bread, make meals and prove to Eddie that she could be a proper ranch wife. That had worked out well. Both of them were so happy.

She drew in a long, slow breath. She would prove her ability to change, as well.

Would Abel then notice and approve?

Would he grow to love her?

Chapter Fifteen

Abel brushed Allie's hair and fixed a bow on it. Over the past few days Mercy had spent time on the child's hair. It made him think he should give the chore a little more thought. At least with Ladd all he had to do was make sure the boy washed behind his ears. And did his wrists. He smiled as he recalled his own mother checking those very places.

His smile flattened and his brow tightened. Mercy had changed. And he didn't mean solely that she had worn a dress every day of the past week and had done her best to keep her hair pinned up. He chuckled softly as he thought how the curls escaped long before she left each day.

"What's so funny, Papa?" Allie asked.

"I was just thinking."

"Of Mercy?"

"Now why would you think that?"

"I was thinking of her and how she braided my hair after she washed it. Do you like it all crimpy like this?"

"It's beautiful. Just like you."

"Oh, Papa." But Allie smiled, pleased at the compliment.

He straightened and shifted to look out the window. Was Mercy acting differently to get his approval? Just as she did wild things to get attention?

He wished he knew what the change in her meant. He wasn't sure how he felt about it. He had spoken his disapproval of her adventuresome nature because he feared the children would be hurt.

And, he silently acknowledged, because it reminded him painfully of Ruby.

But the new Mercy didn't quite fit.

Fit what? asked an inner voice.

"Are we going, Papa?" Ladd asked, cutting into his thoughts.

The twins stood at the door waiting to go to the ranch for church.

Grateful to be pulled from his musings, his answerless questions and his vague sense of disappointment, he lifted them to Sam's back and turned to the trail.

They arrived at the ranch just as Mercy headed down the hill ahead of Linette and Eddie and young Grady.

The twins slipped to the ground and raced to greet her. Abel took his time, tending Sam and trying to sort out his feelings. This was Mercy, who had tended the children and cooked welcome meals for several weeks now. Mercy, who rode like a man, roped better than many and twirled guns like they were toys. Mercy, who taught his children their sums and letters, who made him aware of the emptiness of his heart in a way that sucked reason from his thoughts time after time.

He shifted to study the scene around him. Without forethought, his gaze followed the direction he and

Mercy had gone so many days ago, up the hill to the crown of trees. He'd kissed her there. To comfort her, he assured himself. But despite his reservations and internal words of caution, he was drawn to her. He continued to be drawn. But things had changed. And he didn't mean only Mercy.

Until he could sort everything out, he must guard his heart.

"Papa?"

He turned at Allie's call and came face-to-face with Mercy, a twin clinging to each hand. "'Morning."

She smiled. "Yes, it is."

Her simple mocking observation eased his troubled mind and he grinned.

"A nice day for church."

She chuckled. "A nice day for anything."

They crossed to the cookhouse and climbed the steps. He braced himself for Cookie's exuberant greeting then led the children to one of the benches.

Mercy hung back.

He tipped his head to indicate she should join them.

She nodded, a smile lighting her eyes.

The smile landed in his heart with a gentle plop. Whatever else was going on, he did enjoy sharing Sunday services with her.

As Cookie led them in several hymns, her voice joined his, with the children singing loud and clear. Bertie spoke about the joy of obedience to God. Abel nodded. Obedience provided a safe route. Then those in attendance gathered round the tables for the usual cinnamon rolls and coffee.

The talk immediately shifted to plans for a building bee for the church in Edendale.

"So we're agreed, next Saturday?" Eddie said. "I'll let others in the area know."

"We women will bring plenty of food," Linette said. "It will be a great community gathering." She gave Eddie an adoring look. "I've been waiting a long time for this day."

He pulled her close. "I'm sorry you had to wait so long."

"I'm not complaining."

The children ran out to play.

"Papa, can I go, too?" Allie asked, her eyes big with pleading.

"You can watch but not run."

She sighed softly and shuffled to the door.

Mercy watched her leave, her eyes dipping down at the corners. She glanced at him.

He knew from her look and from things she'd said that she felt sorry for Allie always being excluded from the joyful play of the other children.

If only he knew whether her heart had been damaged. But the doctor had warned him not to take chances.

When proffered, he accepted Linette's invitation to dinner.

"It will be ready in a couple of hours. In the meantime, why doesn't everyone enjoy the beautiful weather?"

"I'll help." Mercy started to follow Linette.

"No need."

She halted.

Abel could feel her uncertainty across the room and blamed himself. He'd been so tense around her the past few days that he'd made her nervous. He went to her side. "Would you care to go for a walk?" The others made enough noise they wouldn't hear his question.

She nodded and they left, retracing their steps of a few weeks ago. They reached the top of the hill and stood side by side, looking out on the landscape.

"The leaves are almost gone." Was that the best he could do? But everything else he thought of offered far more than he knew he could give.

"Winter will soon be here. You'll have a nice warm home. Soon you'll be moving in. The twins will sleep upstairs in the loft."

She spoke quickly, sharply, saying things she was aware he already knew. Was she nervous, too?

"I would like to make quilts for their beds if you have no objection."

He didn't get a chance to say one way or the other as she rushed on.

"Linette says she has scraps I can use. She offered to help me. It would be nice for them to have something to remember—" She swallowed hard. "For them to have something warm and cozy on their new beds." She crossed her arms and stared at the distant mountaintops.

"I think it would be very nice if you made quilts for them." He couldn't help wondering if she would have time to finish them before she rode off to join a show. A thought slammed into his brain. Did the changes in her mean she might have decided against that?

He pulled her around to face him, keeping his hands on her arms. "Remember last time we were here?"

She studied the front of his shirt. "I believe I cried a little."

He chuckled. "I believe you did." He urged her closer. "And I believe I kissed the tears away."

She nodded, her gaze still chest level.

"And if I'm not mistaken, you kissed me back."

Her head jerked up. Her gaze riveted him, full of hot denial. She opened her mouth, closed it without speaking as the protest fled. A tiny smile curved her mouth. "Maybe."

"Maybe? Hmm. That needs a little clarification, I'd say." He bent closer, giving her plenty of time to withdraw. When she didn't, he claimed her lips. Felt their cool resistance that melted like a sudden spring thaw. Her hands came up and caught his shoulders.

He splayed his hands across her back and held her to him. She melted into his embrace. His heart swelled with joy until he wondered how his ribs contained it.

Reluctantly he withdrew.

She eased back without leaving the shelter of his arms.

They studied each other. He guessed she would see both eagerness and caution in his eyes. Even as he saw it in hers.

He dropped his hands to her arms. The kiss had been fine and good. But he could not allow it to mean all he wanted. Not so long as she was set on joining a Wild West show.

"We should go," Mercy said, stepping out of his arms. "Dinner will be ready soon."

Questions tangled in Mercy's thoughts as they sauntered down the hill. Exactly what did his kiss mean?

Neither of them seemed to be in a hurry. Was he analyzing the situation, as well? She gave a silent chuckle. Abel was far more likely to be trying to figure out what it meant and where it fit in his plans than she.

They arrived at the big house and joined the others around the table. She continued to push aside her inner turmoil enough to listen to and respond to the conversation.

Would he ask her to walk with him again after the meal? But the dishes were barely done when he thanked Linette and Eddie for their hospitality. "I don't like how flushed Allie is. I better take her home."

Mercy hugged the twins goodbye. She stepped back before she lifted her gaze to Abel. He nodded, whether as goodbye or to inform her he shared her confusion, she couldn't say.

Ladd waved as they entered the trees but Abel didn't turn. She stared after them until they disappeared from sight.

Her limbs twitched. Her brain churned. Restlessness filled her. She turned and rushed to her bedroom, changed into her riding trousers and shirt. "I'm going riding," she announced to the women lingering in the kitchen.

She trotted down the hill and caught up Nugget. "It is going to be so good to ride like the wind and practice all our tricks again." No one but the horse heard her words. Within minutes she galloped out of the yard.

But half an hour later she reined to a halt. The questions she'd been ignoring had followed her.

Why had Abel kissed her? Did it mean he had begun to see how much she'd changed and he approved? What next? Would he ask her to stay on? Or, like Ambrose, did he find her too unsettling despite her attempt to be otherwise?

She swallowed hard and stared straight ahead though she saw nothing. She'd once thought she could marry him to be a mother to his children.

She no longer believed it. She wanted more. The

depth of her longing twisted inside her, making her squeeze her hands until her gloves threatened to split at the seams. The longing felt frightening, like how she'd felt as she watched her parents and wished they would notice her. She'd outgrown such neediness and had no desire to substitute another situation that made her feel that way.

She had Nugget rear back. She swung a rope over his head and circled it around them both. They practiced his bowing. She twirled her pearl-handled guns.

But nothing she did drove away the restless ache of her heart.

"Papa, I'm not sick." Allie said it several times as they rode toward the cabin.

"Maybe you aren't. But I don't intend to take chances." Not with her health and not with his heart, Abel silently added. He'd almost welcomed the excuse to leave Eden Valley Ranch early. Why did he let himself kiss Mercy when he knew she didn't fit in his world?

Or was she saying with the changes he'd recently seen that she did?

If he hadn't been so distracted by his thoughts he would have paid more attention to his surroundings. He might have noticed the clues before he rode into the clearing and saw the man from the woods standing near the new cabin.

The man looked at him, then darted to the trees.

Abel didn't say anything, not wanting to frighten the children. But he pulled Sam to a stop and watched to see if the man would reappear or simply melt into the woods as he usually did.

When he didn't see him again, Abel took the children with him to the corral as he tended Sam. He carried Allie to the cabin, every sense alert to any sign of danger. Inside, he didn't put her down immediately. "Ladd, stay right there." He pointed to the door. Not until he could be certain there was nothing to be concerned about would he let them go in.

He looked about slowly. The bed was unruffled. The clothing on the hooks undisturbed. The supplies on the shelves appeared exactly as he'd left them. Even his used coffee cup stood on the cupboard exactly where he'd left it.

He put Allie on her feet. She stared up at him.

"Papa, what's the matter?"

"Nothing." At least indoors. "I'm going to do a few things outside. You two stay here. Don't go outside. Don't open the door."

Ladd and Allie exchanged glances. "Something's wrong, isn't it?" Ladd said.

Abel didn't want to alarm them but he couldn't lie to them, either. "I thought I saw something when we rode up. I'll check around to make sure there's nothing out there. Stay here." He left before they could pepper him with questions.

Slowly, methodically, he circled both cabins. He examined every inch of the clearing before entering the new cabin. Apart from a few barely distinguishable footprints that surely belonged to the intruder, he saw nothing to alarm him.

This couldn't continue. He would not live in fear wondering about that crazy wild man.

Tomorrow he would track him down, confront him

and put an end to his lurking about. Only then would he feel his family was safe.

True to his word, the next morning, he packed enough supplies to last the day. This mystery man had vanished in the woods at the blink of an eye. Abel anticipated needing the whole day to track him down.

When they heard Mercy ride up, he told the children to stay inside. "I need to talk to Mercy alone for a moment."

Ladd rolled his eyes and Allie clasped her hands and looked dreamy.

He groaned. "I'm only going to tell her my plans for the day." He ducked out before either of them could reply, and joined Mercy at the corral, where she tended her horse.

He told her about discovering the wild man in the yard when he returned Sunday. "I'm going to find him and see what he's doing here. I might suggest he find somewhere else to hang around."

She kept her attention on putting her horse away. "Be sure to give him the benefit of the doubt."

"I won't shoot first and ask questions later, but I can't think what good reason the man could have for hanging around. It's downright spooky. I feel I need to check around every corner and constantly watch over my shoulder."

She straightened and faced him. "Just because he's different doesn't mean he's dangerous."

He recognized her protest for what it was—a defense of her own behavior—and touched her cool cheek. "I know and I promise I will bear it in mind."

A smile lit her eyes. "See that you do."

As he rode away he contemplated the conversations.

Was it possible that though she was different, she wasn't a danger to his family? But could he believe that thought, or trust it? Because whatever he did affected his children. He could not simply follow his heart.

Leaving Sam behind so he could more effectively follow the tracks, he searched the woods surrounding the cabins, starting at the uncertain footprint he'd found the day before. The man surely wore moccasins because he left little in the way of tracks. He checked the branches and the leaves. There was little for Abel to follow, but he found a bent branch in a couple of places and an old log with moss brushed off it. The work was time consuming and slow, but he climbed to thicker trees. He paused to stretch his back and wipe sweat from his brow. The day had grown unseasonably warm now that the sun hung at its zenith.

He pulled sandwiches from his pack and swilled back some water. Then he moved on. No telling how far the man had gone since yesterday and Abel wanted to find him and return early enough for Mercy to get home before dark.

He tracked for two more hours, finding more evidence, and guessed the man had spent a good deal of time in that area. He straightened and listened, hoping for a sound to indicate the man's presence even though he knew the man was too smart to reveal himself in any way.

The skin on the back of his neck tingled. Someone watched him. He lifted his rifle for easy access and slowly looked around. At first he saw nothing, then he heard a deep-throated growl and the hair on his arms rose. He jerked back. Not twenty feet away, on a branch above his head, a mountain lion snarled, revealing fangs that could rip him to pieces in a matter of minutes.

He edged the rifle upward.

The big cat crouched and snarled.

His fingers twitched. He held his breath to steady his muscles. He had two children at home who needed him. A wild animal would not rob them of a father. Nor rob him of a chance to have a real family. Could he hope to get a shot off before the animal sprang? He sucked in air and forced every move to be slow and steady, but it happened before he could get a shot off.

Chapter Sixteen

Mercy squeezed her fingers together until they hurt. She pressed her knees tight to stop her legs from bouncing. Somehow she must remain in her chair talking about sums when all the while she wanted to rush to the window for a glimpse of Abel. In fact, if she could follow her instincts, she would swing to Nugget's back and ride out to find him.

Although he'd said he would be gone most of the day, every hour that passed wound her nerves more taut. She didn't even have to close her eyes to picture him pinned under a log. And this time he'd gone carrying a rifle to look for a wild man who lived in the woods. Abel must be crazy. And she as well for not stopping him.

She bounced to her feet. The wide-eyed twins watched her. Crossing to the stove, she shifted the coffeepot six inches to the right and then back to its original spot.

"Where's Papa?" Allie asked.

"Gone to the woods." Mercy and Abel had agreed not to give the children any details of his plan.

Ladd pushed from his chair. "When will he be back?"

Realizing the twins had picked up on her restlessness, Mercy pushed aside her worries. "It's early. He won't be back for another hour or so."

She took one quick glance out the window and returned to the table. "If you're done your sums, let's do some reading." She'd brought some easy reading books and listened with a fraction of her hearing as the twins took turns reading aloud.

Did she hear something outside? She jumped to her feet and dashed to the door. Before she opened it she thought of the man in the woods and stopped. She went to the window but saw nothing. The sound came again, jerking her attention to the corral. Only Nugget and Sam chasing each other around. Mercy sighed.

"Why are you so scared?" Ladd asked.

"I'm not." But her skin felt too tight for her arms and she rubbed to loosen it. If only Abel would return. If something happened to him...

She closed her eyes and pressed her palm to her chest, unable to contemplate the possibility.

Did she hear a thud outside? She would not jerk the way she had before. Instead, she edged closer to the window so she could sneak a look. A movement in the trees caught her attention and she raced for the door.

"Stay here," she told the twins. If Abel was hurt she didn't want them seeing it.

Picking up her annoying skirts, she ran from the cabin, across the yard.

Abel waited at the edge of the clearing. He opened his arms and she went straight to him, pausing only long enough to run her gaze over him. Seeing no sign of blood or injury she caught his face in her hands.

"Are you okay?"

"I'm fine." He pulled her into his arms and rested his cheek on her head. "Just fine."

She wrapped her arms around his waist and clung to him. "I was so worried. What if that crazy man attacked you?"

His chuckle reverberated in his chest and echoed in hers. "What happened to assuming the man was harmless?"

"It's easy enough to say that when he's far away." And Abel was close at hand.

"Are the twins okay?"

"They've been wondering why I kept looking out the window so often." She rested her head against his chest, not eager to let him go. He kept his arms tight about her as if he might feel the same way.

"I found the man."

"You did?" She looked into his face, surprised at the way he smiled.

"Rightfully you could say he found me."

Her arms tightened around him. "What happened?"

"I was tracking him when something made me aware I was being watched. I turned slowly but it wasn't a man I saw. It was a mountain lion overhead ready to pounce."

Her mouth dried so abruptly she couldn't swallow.

He smiled down at her. "Before I could even lift my rifle, a shot rang out and the cat fell to the ground." He brushed a strand of hair off her cheek. "I spun around and saw the man I sought. All whiskered and wild looking, but his eyes were calm and kind. He nodded once and slipped into the trees. I called out. 'Who are you?' but he never turned." Abel brushed his knuckles along her jawline, sending happy little dances up and down her nerves.

"He saved your life."

"Yes, he did. I wish I could do something for him."

"Like what?"

He shrugged. "I don't know. But I hate to think of him out there alone."

"Might be he prefers it that way."

"Could be."

"I wish I could remember where I've seen him before." In her memory, she had fleeting images that she could never pin down to a certain place and time.

Abel's gaze swept across her face and lingered on her lips.

Her heart hammered against her ribs and she lifted her face, meeting him halfway. Their lips touched lightly. Then his arms tightened and he claimed her mouth. She leaned into his embrace. He was back safe and sound and she returned his kiss with a heart full of gratitude.

He lifted his head and looked deep into her eyes, searching her thoughts, her heart, her very soul.

She opened herself to him, allowing the steel doors to her heart to swing wider.

"That's a very nice welcome home."

She grinned. "Glad you enjoyed it."

He chuckled. "No more or less than you, I think."

"The twins are waiting."

He laughed and pulled her to his side. "Then by all means, let's go see them."

She stayed at his side until they reached the cabin, then slipped away, not ready to let the children see their father and her together. They'd ask questions she couldn't answer because she didn't know what the kiss meant.

Gratitude for his safe return?

On his part, reaction to being spared an attack by the big cat?

"Do you suppose that's what Allie meant when she said she saw a cat?" she asked him.

"I figure it is. I had a look around and saw some cat tracks. I wonder if the man in the woods has been chasing the cat away from us. I think we owe him a lot."

As he shoved open the door, the twins rushed to him.

"Mercy's been worried about you," Ladd said.

"Is that a fact? Well, it's nice someone cares." Abel sent her a teasing grin.

"We care." Allie insisted Abel pick her up. He sat down and pulled Ladd to his knee.

"So what have you being doing all day?"

"We did sums."

"We read a story."

The twins told him the details of their day.

Mercy hung back. She should be on her way, but Abel had just returned and she didn't want to leave. She wanted to stay and share supper with them, help tuck the children into bed and later, after they were settled, talk to Abel about his day and hers.

Did he want it, too? He seemed focused on the children.

She turned to put on her coat.

Abel set the twins to one side. "You two stay here while I go to the corral with Mercy."

She turned to face the door as a grin widened her lips. He'd never wanted to accompany her before.

He fell in at her side. "I'm glad you can get home before dark. Be careful."

"I thought you'd decided that whiskered man was friendly."

He grabbed her hand and pulled her to face him. "There might be another mountain lion out there or a bear." He shuddered. "I sure wouldn't want you to run into anything like that."

"Nor would I."

"Do you have a gun with you?"

She wanted him to think she'd changed. That she no longer wanted to live a wild, undisciplined life. From now on she meant to be ordinary. But she'd felt naked and vulnerable without a firearm and stuck a pistol in her saddlebag. "I might have a gun with me."

"From now on, be sure you have a rifle at the very least."

She didn't say anything, surprised by his change of opinion.

He shook her a little. "Promise me you will."

She searched his eyes. Did the claiming way he looked at her signify a special kind of caring...or simply responsibility like he'd feel if the twins did something risky?

She couldn't tell and afraid of how desperately she wished it was the former, she said, "Very well. I promise." Then she continued her walk to the corral.

He kept in step with her. As she put the bridle on Nugget, he lifted the blanket and saddle to the horse's back.

She watched him tighten the cinch. "I can do that, you know."

He grinned over his shoulder. "I know you can." He finished and straightened. "Do you object to me helping?"

"No. But why do you want to?"

He closed the distance between them. "It seemed the right thing to do."

"Why?" She'd been coming for weeks and he'd never offered before.

"I thought of doing it before but figured you'd kick up a protest. But lately you seem different." He searched her face, his look again going much deeper.

He'd realized she'd changed exactly as she'd hoped. She shivered. She'd have to be careful not to do anything to make him question it.

He quirked his eyebrows. "Or maybe it's me who is different. Looking at a snarling cat and knowing he could rip you to pieces makes a person value life even more."

She nodded. "I expect it does."

He caught her shoulders, planted a quick kiss on her mouth, then stepped back so she could mount up and ride away.

She stopped at the edge of the clearing and turned around to wave at him. A smile tugged at her heart at the grin blazing on his face.

Her smile remained all the way home.

For the next week she anticipated his welcome smile when she returned to his cabin every morning. Often she'd look at him and find his gaze on her mouth. Each time her heart would lurch like a wild horse ride. She wanted to jump on Nugget's back and do some crazy tricks, swing her rope in a big loop and dance in and out of the circle.

He stayed close by, working on the cabin. "It will soon be done," he said.

Shouldn't he have been happier at the idea? She would no longer come. There'd be no need. Unless—

But he'd given no indication of wanting more. Said nothing to make her think anything other than that this would end when the new cabin was finished.

"I'll be joining the church work bee on Saturday," he said over dinner one day.

"Are you taking the twins?"

They leaned forward, anxious for his answer. "Are you wanting to go to the bee?" he asked her.

"Linette says everyone is going to be there."

"Then by all means, you should go. I'll take the children."

Ladd and Allie cheered.

Abel shifted his attention to his daughter. "You'll have to play quietly."

She hung her head. "I know."

"I'll watch her." Mercy decided then and there she would make sure Allie had fun despite her restrictions. She kept her gaze on her empty dish. She'd do her best to show Abel they could all have fun together with her being an ordinary person.

"Are we almost there?" Allie asked Abel yet again.

"Soon." Edendale was not far away, but Allie and Ladd were excited about going to town and spending the day with friends and neighbors. Abel hid it much better, though he looked forward to the day, as well. Yes, he would enjoy meeting more of the community, but mostly he longed to see Mercy in a different situation. Apart from a few Sundays and one event at Eden Valley Ranch that left him struggling to decide if it had been a good experience or a disappointment, he'd only seen her at meal times and a bit in between at the ranch.

This work bee would give him a chance to spend time with her in a social setting.

Town came into sight and in his excitement to see everything, Ladd leaned over so far Abel had to grab him by the back of his coat to keep him from falling off the horse and tumbling to the ground. Thankfully Mercy had offered to watch Allie because he didn't figure Ladd would do a good job today. He was too anxious to run and play.

He studied those already assembled. Many came from Eden Valley Ranch. He recognized a few from OK Ranch, Macpherson from the store, the Mortons who ran the stopping house and a handful of others. But he didn't see Mercy. His heart battered his ribs. Had he misunderstood her intention to attend?

As the circle of women shifted, his breath whooshed out. There she was. Wearing a pretty, dark red dress, her hair coiled about her head. No trousers. No fringed shirt. When was the last time he'd seen her dressed in such a fashion? She'd dressed in her fanciest riding duds for the celebration at the ranch when she'd done her showy riding and roping tricks.

Since then? He nodded. He hadn't seen her dressed in her outlandish outfits since before the night she'd rescued him. He couldn't say what she wore that night. Were the two facts connected? He couldn't see how they were and yet, for some reason, he felt they were. Would she explain if he asked her?

As always, the children slipped to the ground and raced to her side. She hugged them, then followed the direction Ladd pointed and waved at Abel. He gave a little salute before he went to join the men around a stack of lumber. It was a pretty spot. The mountains to the west were crowned with fresh snow. A few golden leaves clung to the deciduous trees. Darker pine and spruce covered much of the hills. The flash of running water indicated the river behind the store.

Eddie made introductions. "How many of you have experience with a building this size?"

Two men put up their hands. Several said they hadn't built anything bigger than a shack.

"I've worked on ships," Abel said.

"That's good news," Eddie said. "We'll be needing your expertise."

But Eddie was the foreman and soon had the crowd of men organized. Abel readily saw that the man knew how to get a job done and get others to help.

He glanced around to check on the twins. A crowd of children chased each other up and down the street. He straightened. Where was Allie? He scanned the area. Because he couldn't see her, he laid down his hammer to search for her. Then he saw the red of Mercy's dress and beside her, Allie, sitting and watching the children. Mercy pointed at something and they laughed.

He wished he could hear what Mercy said but at least Allie was safe with her. He picked up his hammer and returned to work.

By noon they had made significant progress. "All we can hope for today is to get the shell up."

Eddie nodded. "Once it's that far we can work on it bit by bit, one or two men at a time."

The women had set out piles of food on a long table made of sawhorses and lengths of wood.

When the men joined their womenfolk and children for the meal, Abel went to Mercy's side, the twins beside them.

Eddie stood at the end of the table. He removed his hat. The other men did likewise. "I'd like to say a few words."

The crowd grew quiet.

"As most of you know, this church is Linette's idea. And what Linette wants, she gets. I'm proof of that." He pulled his wife to his side as those assembled chuckled. "However, by the good turnout today, I'd say all of us agree with getting a church built for the community."

A round of applause signaled agreement.

"We are truly becoming a solid community. When I came out here there were people at the Eden Valley Ranch, those at OK and Macpherson here. Now look at us. We're a growing, thriving community."

"Eddie," someone called. "Don't we need a preacher?"

"Constable Allen said he'd ask at the fort. Said he'd ask about a doctor, too." Eddie glanced at Linette and Abel guessed he wished for a doctor nearby should anything go wrong with the birth of their little one.

Miss Oake from the OK Ranch waved to get Eddie's attention. "I recently heard from a cousin from back east who is a doctor. He's on his way to visit us. I don't know if he plans to set up practice here or just visit but he'll be here for a while."

More applause, then Eddie said grace. "Let's enjoy the abundance."

Mercy supplied Abel and the children with plates and they filed past the food.

"There's so much," Allie said, her eyes wide. "How can I taste everything?"

Mercy chuckled. "You might have to make some choices."

"But I want to try it all."

Mercy and Abel looked at each and laughed. Something sweet filled his heart at the shared joy over his daughter.

When they reached the end of the table, Allie eyed the desserts and sighed loudly.

Abel laughed. "I remember when she was ill and I couldn't get her to take more than a spoonful of broth," he said to Mercy.

"I'm all better now," Allie assured him.

Ladd asked if he could sit with Billy and Neil, and Abel gave him permission. Allie sighed again and didn't even ask though she looked longingly at a circle of little girls.

As they sat and ate, Abel glanced about. And felt something deep inside him unfurl. He'd always longed for this sort of thing—community, acceptance and belonging. Many times throughout the morning men had asked his advice regarding the building and he had given it. They'd accepted him. His family belonged here.

Family. He truly felt like family for the first time in his adult life. Even though it was temporary.

Unless he made it permanent.

He studied Mercy out of the corner of his eyes. She certainly seemed to care about the twins. Did she feel anything for him? Fondness at least? He examined his own feelings. Yes, he was fond of her. Very fond. His insides tightened and his fingers clenched the edge of the plate. He'd been fond of Ruby and married her—and that had been a mistake.

He didn't intend to make any more mistakes. No matter what he felt, how fond he was of her.

But hadn't Mercy changed for the better?

Then again, why had she changed? Was it for real or simply a reaction to something? He needed to ask her. He needed to know what she felt about him. About family life. About settling down.

This community gathering would not give him a chance to speak privately with her.

He needed to make such an opportunity.

By the next morning, he had a plan. Because it was Sunday, he would take the children to the ranch. The day would be consumed with eating and visiting. Yes, he and Mercy might get a few minutes alone, but not enough. He had something more than that in mind. At the first opportunity he would ask Linette to watch the children and then take Mercy on a picnic.

He'd tell her all that was in his heart.

But first, he must bring in some more firewood before snow came and found him unprepared.

At church, Abel tried to concentrate on the talk Bertie gave and then later on the conversation about the new church, but with Mercy at his side and the knowledge of his plan, he continually had to shepherd his thoughts back from chasing after the idea of a picnic alone with her.

He accepted Linette's invitation to join them for dinner then wished he hadn't because several times Eddie gave him a studying look and Abel realized he had missed a question.

He could not keep his mind on the conversation. All he wanted to do was arrange a picnic for himself and Mercy.

But the day passed without allowing him a chance to speak privately to either Linette or Mercy.

He would have delayed his departure, but he noted a heightened color in Allie's cheeks. The twins' needs must come first. He had to get them home before Allie got overexcited.

Chapter Seventeen

Mercy tried to think why Abel had been in such a hurry to leave Sunday but couldn't. Had she done something to disappoint him? She reviewed the past few days. She'd been as ordinary as milk. She'd watched Allie, though that was certainly no hardship. She only wished the child could be allowed to join the others at play. Maybe this doctor cousin of Miss Oake could look at Allie and say whether or not there was any damage to her heart.

Consumed by restlessness, she changed into her riding costume and took Nugget out for a long run. She came to a small lake, where she noticed a great honking flock of birds lifting off the water—geese and cranes. Majestic birds. They circled overhead, then returned to the water. She tied Nugget in the trees and sat to observe them. These birds were not ordinary though what they only did was natural for them.

A strange restlessness filled her, peppered through and through with a contrasting peace. Was she the Mercy she tried to be for Abel or the one she pretended to be to get her parents' attention? *God, creator of all this beauty, who have You created me to be?*

Peace swallowed up the restlessness and she sat watching the birds for a long time. Somehow she knew that God, who guided birds from north to south and back each year, would guide her on her own journey. She had only to follow directions—if she could only find them.

Finally, she slipped away, quietly so as not to disturb the flock.

At home she studied herself from every angle in her looking glass. She appeared to be an ordinary woman about to embark on an ordinary day.

Inside, her heart fluttered like a nervous bird. Would Abel look at her with dark blue interest and see how she longed to be accepted?

She shook her head. That wasn't what she meant. It sounded needy and immature. She only wanted—

"To be seen as a person of value," she said to her reflection. But even that didn't sound right and she spun away. Perhaps if Abel would accompany her to see the birds, they could, together, find the answers she sought. The peace she craved. But when she arrived at his cabin the next morning, she knew before she dismounted that he wouldn't. His horse was already harnessed to the stoneboat and Abel rushed from the cabin as soon as he heard her.

"Good morning." He slowed his steps, veered from his path toward the horse and headed in her direction. He looked into her face, his gaze lingering on her mouth. Did he see the woman he wanted her to be, she wondered? He brushed her cheek with his bare hand. "I

want to get a load of wood in while the weather holds."
With a fleeting smile he resumed his original direction.

Did he wish he could spend the day with her and
the twins?

She watched until he disappeared into the trees, then
went inside. Ladd and Allie rushed over to hug her.

"How are you feeling?" She studied Allie. The child
looked fit and eager for life.

"I'm not sick even if Papa thinks I am."

Mercy had thought the same thing many times.
"Nevertheless, you can't afford to take chances. We
wouldn't want anything to happen to you." She hugged
the little girl and tickled her, eliciting crazy giggles.

Together they washed the dishes and tidied the cabin.
Mercy brought out books and schoolwork but had more
trouble concentrating than the twins. The four walls
pressed too close. The stove overheated the small area.

She crossed to the window. The sky held only a
few gray clouds. The calm she'd felt watching the wild
birds on the little mountain lake had dissipated. How
much longer would the flock remain? If only she could
see them again and recapture the peace and assurance
she'd experienced. Why not? It was warm. The children
would enjoy the outing. "Let's go on a picnic."

"Yah!" They both bounced off their chairs and
hurried to her side.

"Help me get a lunch ready to take."

They did so eagerly and a few minutes later the three
of them rode from the yard on Nugget's back.

"Where are we going?" Ladd asked.

"It's a surprise." Despite their frequent asking, she
wouldn't tell them more. "Look around and enjoy the
journey," she said, pointing out moss on the north side of

the trees, a blue jay scolding from a branch nearby. They paused once to watch a V of geese honking overhead.

A little later they stopped and dismounted. "You have to be very quiet now." She held her finger to her lips and guided them silently through the trees. The trees opened up to reveal the lake. Fewer birds were there this time of day, and none of the huge cranes.

"Let's sit here and watch them," she whispered as she indicated a tree.

Their eyes sparkled with excitement and she knew they found the sight of so many birds as awesome as she.

They watched the birds take off and land. Allie covered her mouth to muffle her giggles as a duck skidded into the water.

And then a flock of the majestic cranes approached. Both twins sucked in air as the huge birds settled onto the water. When Mercy had described the birds—their size, the black tips on their wings and red crown—Eddie had said they were whooping cranes.

She whispered the information to the twins.

Mesmerized by the beauty of the birds and the noise coming from the lake, the three of them watched for a long time.

Ladd leaned closer to whisper, "I'm hungry."

Mercy nodded and led them back to Nugget. She found a grassy clearing and they shared the lunch.

"Can we watch them again?" Allie asked.

"Did you enjoy that?"

She nodded, eyes sparkling. "They're fun to watch."

So they tiptoed back to the lake. Mercy warned herself to be aware of the passing time. They must make it back before Abel. He would worry if he returned and they were missing.

After a while, she signaled the children to follow her back to Nugget. "It's time to leave."

As they rode away, the twins chattered nonstop about the birds.

They had only reached the trail when Mercy shivered as a cold wind suddenly blew in and whipped around them. She stopped and pulled a blanket from her bag and wrapped it around Allie. "Ladd, do up your coat and keep tight to me."

A glance at the sky revealed low-hanging black clouds. Rain clouds. If she hurried she might beat the storm back. But they hadn't gone five paces when the heavens opened.

She reined Nugget under the shelter of a tree and pulled the children down to the ground, wrapping them in a big black slicker she'd started carrying after Eddie said she ought to be prepared for bad weather. She silently thanked him for his advice as she held the twins close. At least they'd be dry. She leaned out to glance upward. Would the storm pass quickly or had it settled in for a long visit? She couldn't see enough of the sky to guess. She leaned back. How long could she stay here? The light would fade early if the clouds stayed.

She considered her options, which were limited to two—stay and hope the storm ended or endure the cold rain and get the children home.

The second seemed the most appropriate, though not the most pleasant for her.

She wiped the saddle with her sleeve and lifted Ladd then Allie to it. Ladd put his arms around his sister and held on. He would do everything he could to protect her. Mercy meant to do the same. She wrapped the slicker around them tightly. "Is any rain getting in?"

"No," came Ladd's muffled reply. "It's dry in here."

"It smells funny," Allie said.

Mercy laughed. "You'll get used to it." She swung up behind the pair, pushed her wet hair out of her eyes and hunkered down for a long cold ride.

At least the twins were safe and dry. If Abel happened to return before they got back he would see how careful she was with the children.

She ventured a prayer. *God, could You please make sure we get back first?*

Abel shook the water from his coat. He had continued to work after the rain began but water dripped from his hat, trailed down his nose, ran under his collar. The stoneboat had a decent load. He better get it home before traction became a problem.

As he navigated the trail he thought of what lay ahead. He'd ask Mercy to wait out the storm. A picnic was out of the question, but he could leave the twins in the old cabin and take Mercy to the new one. Actually talking to her about the future in the place where his future would take place made perfect sense.

He rehearsed the words he would say as he made his way home. He arrived in the yard, unhitched the stoneboat and took Sam to the corral. Strange that Nugget wasn't there. Had she tied him in the trees to keep him out of the rain? It seemed like something she would think to do. He smiled as he pictured her running outside, unmindful of the rain, to take care of her horse.

Shaking off as much moisture as he could, he ducked into the cabin and put his hat on a hook. He turned.

"Mercy? Ladd? Allie?" Had they gone to the new cabin? He plopped his wet hat back on his head and jogged across the yard. He called them again. Nothing. He looked around the partitions, climbed to the loft and looked in the corners. Was this some kind of game?

He saw none of the three but searched the cabin again just to be sure. Finally convinced they weren't there, he jogged back to the other one. But they weren't in that cabin, either.

He went to the door and stared out at the pelting rain. Had they ventured outside and been caught unawares? "Mercy, Ladd, Allie," he roared at the top of his lungs.

Nothing but the sound of rain on the roof and water dripping from the trees.

Then it hit him. Nugget missing. The twins missing. Mercy must have taken them on one of her foolish adventures. His fists curled so tightly his knuckles creaked. He thought she'd changed. Just went to prove he didn't dare listen to his foolish heart. If this hadn't happened he might have asked her to—

Marry him.

The idea mocked him. Seems he had this unconscious wish to make his life miserable.

Thank God above he'd discovered his mistake before it was too late.

He circled the cabin, straining through the wet air for a glimpse of them.

Allie would surely catch a chill out there. He pressed a fist to his forehead. If something happened to her or Ladd...

He circled the cabin several times. Not until they were home safely would he go inside and shed his wet clothes. He deserved to be chilled to the bone for trusting his children to the care of a woman like Mercy.

As the minutes trudged by, his insides grew hotter.

Would he have to ride to the ranch and ask for help searching for them? Wait. The ranch. Had she taken them there? Were they safe and dry?

He considered riding there, but he couldn't leave the cabin. What if one of them stumbled in needing help? The woods were full of dangers—mountain lions, bears, strange men. He couldn't be sure the man who shot the mountain lion posed no danger to his children.

He waited in the open doorway, his arms crossed over his chest, but his muscles twitched and he walked around the cabin again. Then he saw a shadow moving through the trees. Reaching for his rifle, he strained forward.

The shadow drew closer, materialized into a horse carrying a dark object.

He rubbed his eyes and blinked. Then he saw Mercy, her dress wet and limp, her hair a springy tangle. He bolted forward. "Where are my children?"

"Here." She indicated the dark shape.

He flipped back the slicker. Two pairs of eyes watched him. He grabbed them and set them inside the door. "Get into something dry and wrap up in blankets. I'll be right there." He had to spare a moment to speak to Mercy.

"Have you no regard for anyone but yourself?" Words spewed from his mouth. Words expressing his anger and fear. Even as he spoke them, he knew they were unreasonable. She wouldn't put his children as risk. He'd been as worried about her as them. His worry had grown until it was completely out of proportion. He needed time to get his emotions under control. "I suggest you leave immediately."

The look she gave him could only be described as

wounded. "You've never trusted me. And never will."
She rode away without a backward look.

He swiped the moisture from his face before he
hurried in to take care of the children.

The twins faced him as he closed the door.

"Papa, why did you yell at her?" Allie's voice rang
with accusation.

"She shouldn't have taken you out in the rain."

"It didn't start raining until we were on our way
home." Ladd crossed his arms and fixed Abel with a
hard look. "Why did you say you didn't trust her?"

"It doesn't matter. Let's get you out of those wet
things."

"We're dry." Ladd's stance suggested disapproval.
"Mercy wrapped us up and looked after us." Ladd and
Allie exchanged looks.

"And you sent her away wet and cold." Allie turned
her back. She reached for Ladd's hand and they retreated
to the bed. He wondered if they wished they could get
farther away, but the small cabin made it impossible.

He touched Allie's cheeks, ignoring the way she
drew back. She was warm and dry.

"You were rude to her." Ladd's look said quite plainly
that he held his father in contempt.

Abel went to the window and looked out. He'd
jumped to a wrong conclusion. Let his anger fuel hurtful
words. "I made a mistake," he said.

"Then best you tell her." Allie was right. He had to
tell her.

But the rain continued to sputter. He couldn't take the
children out and do exactly what he'd accused Mercy
of—putting his interests ahead of their well-being.

* * *

Ice encased her heart, more numbing and invasive than the cold rain soaking Mercy as she rode home. She'd tried. Tried to be an ordinary person, tried to show Abel how responsible she was, tried and failed.

He didn't trust her enough to even stop and look at the evidence before he'd said exactly what he thought of her. Plain and simple, he didn't trust her. Never would. What was the use in her even trying?

She reached the ranch and took care of Nugget before she headed up the hill to the house.

Linette saw her coming and greeted her with an armload of dry towels. "You get out of those wet things immediately before you get pneumonia." She hurried Mercy to her bedroom and threatened to personally undress her if she didn't get it done in what Linette deemed a "reasonable amount of time."

"Put on your warmest bedclothes," Linette added.

Mercy slipped out of her clothes and into a warm nightdress and dressing gown. She began to gather up the wet items. With uncanny timing, Linette stepped into the room.

"Leave it. I'll see to them as soon as I've looked after you."

She drew Mercy back to the kitchen and eased her into a chair close to the stove. She wrapped a warmed woolen blanket about Mercy's shoulders, then prepared a cup of hot, sweet tea.

With a throat choked by unshed tears, Mercy thanked Linette. It was nice to have someone care that she was cold and wet. And bleeding inside as if a sword had been run through her several times.

Linette made clucking noises. "I can't believe Abel let you leave in this rain. What was he thinking?"

Mercy shrugged. She pulled the blanket tightly around her shoulders wishing she could likewise tighten a cover for her heart. She should have never opened the steel doors, but she had, and closing them would take some time and a great deal of emotional strength that she lacked at the moment.

Linette edged the cup of tea closer.

Mercy slipped one hand from under the blanket and picked up the cup and sipped slowly. The warm liquid stole down her throat. It began to melt the ice in the pit of her stomach, but did nothing to thaw the ice encasing her heart. That might never happen.

"Eddie brought home the mail. I had a letter from Grady's father. He sounded more interested in the boy than he has in the past. Oh, I almost forgot. There is a letter from your parents." Linette found it and handed it to Mercy.

Mercy tucked it into her pocket. She knew what it would say. "We trust you are enjoying your trip. We have had rain. Your father and I are well."

She didn't know why they bothered to write. Obligation, she supposed. Just as she replied out of duty.

A newspaper lay on the table and an advertisement caught her eye. The Greatest Little Wild West Show in the West Will Appear. She pulled the paper closer and read the entire piece. The show was coming to a rough frontier town to the north and east.

"The troupe will be heading south for the winter after their final show here."

She flicked the paper toward Linette. "I'm going there."

Linette read the news, then lifted worried eyes to Mercy. "I thought…" She shrugged. "What about Abel and the children?"

"His cabin is about ready to move into." Each word scratched her throat as if it came out sideways. She coughed but it did little to help. She did not attempt to say more.

"I see." Linette's quiet study made Mercy think she probably did see without further explanation.

Linette checked the date on the advertisement. "The show might already be gone."

"No. They were scheduled to do their last show on Saturday. I don't expect they'd pack up on Sunday. I might catch them before they leave. Or catch up to them. They won't have gone far. They won't go fast."

"I don't like the idea."

Mercy shrugged. "Everyone has been clear about that. Nevertheless, I intend to find them and join the show."

Linette slipped away. She must have informed Jayne and Sybil, for they both appeared within the hour and tried to persuade her to change her mind, but Mercy had already started packing. "I'll be off at daylight."

In the end, neither her friends nor Eddie could convince her to change her mind. She had to get away and this was the perfect escape.

When she saddled up the next morning, Slim rode to her side. "I'm to make sure you get there safe and sound."

"I'll be fine on my own."

"I have my orders."

"Very well." She would never admit that she welcomed his presence. This way she couldn't change her mind and ride to Abel's cabin, instead, demanding he look at her. Really look at her and see her for what she was.

Though she no longer knew for certain who that was.

Chapter Eighteen

Mercy stood in her stirrups and strained to see the town ahead. "They're still there." She pointed to the circle of tents and bunkhouses on wheels and horses penned nearby.

Relief surged through her and she sank back into her saddle. With no doubt but that she'd be accepted into the show, she could now face a future full of adventure and excitement, though her heart did not leap with anticipation. It sat heavy and unresponsive in her chest.

"You can still change your mind," Slim said as they turned in the direction of the gathering.

Only one thing would cause her to change her mind—Abel seeing her as someone he could trust. But he'd made it clear that wasn't going to happen. "My heart is set on this." She said the words as much for her benefit as his.

"I'll see that you're settled before I leave."

She started to protest but he cut her off. "Linette will demand to know all the details."

"Fine."

When they reached the area, Mercy reined in to

listen and watch. A man worked with a pen of horses, waving a whip to direct them to do all sorts of tricks. Another man brushed a huge Clydesdale horse. Was he used to pull the wagons and movable bunkhouses, she wondered, or did he perform, as well? She watched for a few minutes, but the man simply kept brushing the animal.

The sharp scent of horse droppings mingled with the smell of canvas tents and wood smoke. And excitement.

This was what she'd wanted since she'd set foot in the West.

A woman in fringed leather strolled by.

"Hello," Mercy called, getting her attention. "Can you tell me who's in charge?"

"That would be Gus. Why? Who's asking?"

Mercy smiled at the woman's soft drawl and at her outfit and simply because she had arrived at her dreams. She quietly and firmly ignored the truth that she did this only to escape the pain of Abel's disapproval.

"I'd like to talk to him. Can you tell me where he is?"

The woman eyed her up and down, then shifted her gaze to Slim and studied him with such bold eyes that Slim shifted in his saddle.

"I suppose you want to join the show."

"I can ride and rope and do all sorts of Wild West tricks."

The woman gave a little laugh. "No doubt you can. And Gus is always on the lookout for performers to add to the show. You'll find him at that bunkhouse." She pointed toward one on the right. Then she held out her hand. "They call me Angel."

Before Mercy could ask if that was her real name or a stage name, the girl left.

Mercy turned toward the bunkhouse Angel had indicated. Slim followed, muttering about how unsuitable the place was. She ignored him and climbed the steps to knock on the door.

"Enter," a deep voice called.

Mercy hesitated.

"I'll wait right here," Slim said.

She opened the door and stepped inside. The room she entered held a desk covered with papers, two wooden chairs, a stove and cupboard and, at the back, a rumpled bed.

Her cheeks heated at the sight, but she drew herself tall. People must forgo certain rules of conduct living in such tight quarters. Not that it mattered to her. Rules were only made by fearful people and she wasn't afraid.

"How can I help you?"

She introduced herself. "I'd like to join your show."

His head jerked up, and she noticed his bold black eyes, an overlarge nose and a heavy mustache. He smiled, revealing a gold tooth. "I see. And what can you offer me?"

"Why don't I show you?"

He pushed to his full impressive height. "Show me."

She stepped aside and let him lead the way. Slim, still on horseback, followed.

Gus tipped a head Slim's direction. "Your husband?"

"No, he only escorted me here at a friend's insistence."

"So he'll be leaving?"

She nodded, her thoughts on the tricks she and Nugget would do. "You have to bear in mind that my horse has been on the road since morning."

"Let's see what you can do." He opened the corral

gate for her to enter, then leaned against the fence to watch.

She did rope tricks, gun-handling tricks and had Nugget do a number of the tricks she'd taught him. Then she halted in front of Gus and waited for his verdict.

He seemed in deep thought, his fingers stroking his mustache. Finally he nodded. "I do believe there is room in the program for you. You're hired. Can you be ready to join us today? We pull out tomorrow."

"I'm here to stay."

"Good to know. I'm Gus Seymor, the boss of this outfit."

She leaned over to shake the hand he offered. He held on a moment too long, forcing her to withdraw.

"Angel," he bellowed, causing several horses to neigh.

Angel trotted over.

"Take Mercy to your quarters. She'll be joining the show."

Something flickered through Angel's eyes. Mercy wondered if she resented Gus hiring another woman. But then Angel smiled and indicated Mercy should follow her. "Leave your horse here."

Mercy paused beside Slim. "You can leave now. Tell Linette that I'm okay."

Slim nodded but, rather than head for the trail, he dismounted. "Don't mind if I look around, do you?" he asked Gus. "Never been to one of these shows. It looks mighty interesting."

Gus gave him a hard look then waved his hand. "Go ahead. Have yourself a look."

Mercy followed Angel to one of the wooden structures on wheels and entered. Bunks for four took up most of the interior, crowded in with a wood heater, wash table and a wardrobe.

"Hang your things in there." Angel watched as Mercy did. "You got some mighty fancy clothes." Mercy had only brought two dresses. "You sure you're gonna fit in here?"

"I mean to."

"Even if you're asked to do things you don't want?"

Mercy stared at the other woman. "Like what?"

Angel shrugged. "Gus has certain expectations."

The skin on Mercy's spine did a snakelike crawl. She hoped Angel didn't mean anything other than shoveling manure.

"Never mind," Angel said. "Come on. I'll show you around."

They went from tent to tent meeting the others. Some were friendly. Others not so much. Several men leered at her and ran their hands along Angel as they passed.

Mercy couldn't tell if Angel liked it or not, but she vowed she'd make it clear she wouldn't tolerate such inappropriate behavior. At one tent two men made lewd suggestions.

Angel dragged her away. "Best you keep your distance from them."

Mercy glanced around for Slim. "Looking for your friend?" Gus asked, startling her with his sudden appearance. "He left a while ago. Said to tell you goodbye."

A little later the performers gathered round a table in a big tent and ate a meal. A man who'd been introduced as Bull squeezed in between herself and Angel. The four other women giggled as he patted Mercy's leg.

"Nice to have a new face in our midst."

A red-haired woman laughed raucously. "Bull, since

when have you been interested in faces?" She winked at Mercy. "He's more interested in your body, if you know what I mean."

Mercy feared she did and her skin felt two sizes too small. "But I'm not that kind of woman."

Everyone except Angel laughed. Later, Angel pulled her aside. "Look, kid. You really aren't going to fit in here."

"Why? Just because I'm not interested in what Bull wants?"

"He's not your only concern." She looked about as if afraid someone would overhear her. "Mercy, you better think hard about this, because we pull out tomorrow and then there'll be no turning back."

"I'll be fine." But she vowed she would carry a loaded pistol with her day and night.

Gus invited her to his place later in the afternoon. "We need to discuss your performance."

Mercy glanced about. Angel had disappeared. She had no choice but to follow Gus up the steps. He closed the door behind him and ran his finger along her jaw. Funny how when Abel did the same thing, her insides got sweet like honey but when Gus did it, she felt like glass shattering on hard ground.

She shrugged away from his touch. "I'm not interested in that sort of thing."

Gus laughed. "All the girls say that to start with." He waggled his eyebrows and grinned as if she should appreciate his behavior.

"Did you want to discuss my act?"

He waved her question away. "Time enough for that. Why don't you sit down and tell me about yourself."

She reluctantly perched on a chair. He pulled the other one close enough to press his knees to hers.

"Tell me about your family."

She considered what she should say. Certainly not that she had no family in Canada. Nor that her parents wouldn't likely miss her if she disappeared. "Eddie Gardiner of Eden Valley Ranch is my guardian." Close enough.

"Never heard of the man. Is he rich?"

Again Mercy considered her answer carefully. "I couldn't say. I've never felt the need to ask regarding his financial status. He's a very important, powerful man though."

Gus laughed. And if the increased pressure from his knees was intentional or not, it made Mercy draw back. She slipped from the chair. "I better check on my horse. He's a valuable part of my act."

He didn't look happy but allowed her to leave. She found Nugget in a tiny corral, his hooves buried in wet manure. She poured some feed into a food bag for him but stopped when she saw the poor quality oats. It was the last straw.

She'd made a mistake. She didn't belong here. It was nothing like she'd imagined. The crowded conditions, the poor food…all of that she could tolerate. The advances by Gus and Bull she would not accept. She headed for the bunkhouse she shared with Angel and threw her things into her bag, then trotted back to Nugget. Several people watched her but no one said anything. She saddled Nugget and went to open the gate. Bull stood there, holding it closed.

"No one comes or goes without Gus's permission." His voice made it clear he would not let her by.

"I've changed my mind. I'm leaving."

He chuckled—a mean sound. "Like I said. You need Gus's permission."

"Then I shall get it." She stomped across to Gus's quarters and knocked. No one answered though she suspected the man was inside. She knocked for several minutes and called his name.

Angel found her there. "He's not going to answer. If he doesn't want you to leave, you won't."

She followed Angel back to their place. "He can't keep me here against my will."

"You came freely."

"Did you?"

Angel shrugged. "I guess I did. I had a cruel stepfather and joining a Wild West show got me away from him. You could do worse, you know. Gus won't beat you."

"I'm not staying." She opened the door. Bull sat nearby, watching. He touched the gun on his hip as if to warn her and she had a feeling he'd use it if necessary. She closed the door again. She would wait until after dark and slip away.

She pretended to be very busy coiling and uncoiling her rope. All the while, her mind raced. She had her guns. She could shoot at Bull but how far would she get? Likely all of the men were of the same mind. A shiver snaked up her arms. What had she gotten herself into?

Abel had to wait a full day for the rain to go from a downpour to a drizzle to nothing. He dressed the children warmly and then the three of them headed for Eden Valley Ranch.

"Are you gonna tell her you're sorry?" Allie asked, for the umpteenth time.

"When I get there, you two can stay with Mrs. Gardiner while I talk privately to Mercy." He'd about had it with their dark accusing looks and the way they shifted away from him every time he drew near. Even more daunting were his own thoughts, accusing and berating him. Why had he been so quick to judge her?

He did not like the answer.

Because he couldn't forgive himself for the mistake he'd made in marrying Ruby and his guilt made him see every woman as too much like her. Mercy wasn't. Even if she thrived on adventure. That was another thing. In his reaction to where his choices had taken him, he'd denied himself the things he enjoyed. He could afford to enjoy life a bit more, have some fun times with the children and Mercy. The picnic that had never occurred would just be the beginning once he'd apologized and told her how he felt about her.

Would she return his feelings?

They rode up to the big house and Linette came out to greet them. After the usual greetings he looked past her. "Can I speak to Mercy? Is she about?"

"I wish she was, but she's gone."

"Gone?" He'd never considered the possibility.

"Do the children want to come in and play with Grady?"

He recognized her subtle hint that she'd like to speak to him privately and lowered the twins to the ground, then dismounted.

She waited for them to go indoors and pulled the door shut behind them. "Mercy left to join a Wild West show." She told him where the Mercy intended to catch up to the show. "We tried to stop her, but the best we could do was send Slim as an escort. I don't mind telling you I'm worried about her."

Abel reeled back on his heels. So this was her answer. She'd always wanted to do this. Nothing had changed.

Except it had. He couldn't let her go without telling her what was in his heart.

He loved her.

He wanted a chance to prove it to her. To win her heart in return.

"When did they leave? Is Slim back yet?"

They'd left yesterday, Linette told him, and Slim wasn't back.

"I don't know what happened between the two of you," she added, "but whatever it is, surely it's not so bad it can't be mended."

"How is it to be mended when she's left?"

She smiled gently. "Go after her. Persuade her to return. I'll keep the children."

He hesitated ten seconds as his head and heart warred over what to do. Couldn't he trust both? Hadn't she proved herself trustworthy? Fun yet responsible. "I'll go." He swung up to the saddle.

Linette caught her arm. "God go with you. I'll be praying."

"Tell the children I'll be back when I find her." He knew they'd approve of his decision.

"I'll let them know."

He rode from the yard and headed away at a gallop, then realized he needed to slow down. He had a long trip ahead of him.

As the miles pounded away under Sam's hooves, Abel prayed. He prayed for forgiveness for the wild life he had chosen for a time, for the heartache he had caused his parents. One thing he meant to do as soon as he brought Mercy back was write his parents and tell them how sorry he was. He prayed that God would free him of guilt. *You've given me life to enjoy and I've been attempting to turn it into drudgery.* Most of all, he prayed Mercy would listen to him and accept his apology and his love.

The sun was high overhead when he reached the town where the Wild West show was supposed to be. But he saw no sign of it—no tents. Nothing. He saw a man crossing the street and rode up to him. "Say, did I hear there was a Wild West show around here?"

"Sorry, mister. You missed it. They pulled out this morning."

"Pulled out. What direction?"

"South. Along that road." The man pointed.

Abel sank back in his saddle. He'd missed her. But surely he could catch up to them. "Thanks." He headed down the street toward the road indicated. The smell of food slowed him. He should eat before he continued, but he couldn't spare the time. He must find Mercy.

The first night at the show, Mercy knew she'd made a mistake. She'd waited until after dark to crack open the door. She saw no one and quietly tiptoed out. Angel knew her plans and tried to dissuade her but promised she would not interfere.

One foot had reached the ground when a hand clamped to her shoulder. Her breath caught in her throat. She tried and failed to control the jolt that shook her body.

"Gus thought you might be foolish enough to wander

about," Bull ground out. "Says to warn you it isn't safe out there. It's my job to make sure everyone is safe, especially you pretty ladies. So be a good girl and go to bed." There was no mistaking the warning in his voice or the pressure of his hand meant to convey the same message.

She spun around and went back inside.

"I tried to warn you," Angel said. "Give it up and go to sleep."

But Mercy did not go to bed. She sat on a chair facing the door. Darkness made it impossible to see anything as she strained for any sound. Maybe Bull would leave. If he did, she'd be prepared.

What a fool she'd been to think she needed excitement and adventure. She didn't want either. She'd found all she needed in caring for Abel and his family. All she really wanted, all she'd really ever wanted, was someone to care about her. If only Abel had shown he did.

Did God care?

What had Bertie said? God sees us wherever we are. We could never go so far away that God wasn't with us.

God, are You here right now? Do You see me? She knew He did. *Can You help me?* She didn't know how He could but she trusted He would. Trust. Maybe that was the heart of her problem. She didn't trust her parents to love her. Maybe Butler's death had destroyed something in them so they couldn't. But she'd used the same measuring stick with everyone, including God. Just as Abel used Ruby as the measuring stick for his life. She held back a chuckle. They were both so foolish.

God, please rescue me. All I want is a chance to show Abel I'm not Ruby. All I want is a chance to give the twins and him the love that I've longed for all my life.

Even if it took a long time, she would not give up.

The night hours slipped away. At times her trust in God faltered. But each time it did, she reminded herself that God was not like her parents to stop loving her.

She jerked to full attention. Had she fallen asleep? What time was it? What had wakened her? She strained to catch any sound. Then she heard it. A scratching at the door.

She bolted to her feet.

Did Bull or Gus intend to take advantage of her? Her hands shaking so badly her teeth rattled, she palmed her pistol. They'd have to deal with that before they touched her.

Chapter Nineteen

The doorknob rattled. *Help me, God. Protect me.* Mercy could barely make out shapes in the darkness. Couldn't be certain but it looked like the door cracked open.

"Miss?" The whisper was kindly enough, but Mercy didn't mean to take any chances.

"Don't come any closer or I'll shoot."

"Miss, I'm here to help you."

Help? Surely it was a trick. "I don't need any help."

"I think you do. You don't know my name so I won't give it but you've seen me plenty of times in the woods around Eden Valley Ranch. I shot a mountain lion that was about to attack your friend, Abel Borgard."

The man in the woods!

"You need to hurry. I don't think Bull will sleep very long."

Still Mercy hesitated, uncertain whom she could trust.

"Miss, your horse is waiting down the street."

Nugget. She could trust him. And God. Was this an answer to her prayer? Tucking her pistol in the waistband of her trousers, she grabbed the bags she had prepared earlier. "I'm coming."

"Be very quiet."

She stepped outside. A thin moon made it possible to see dark shapes. That bulky form near her door must be Bull. The loud snore made her jump but confirmed he slept. She tiptoed past him, following the shadowy figure ahead of her. Filling her mind were a thousand questions that would have to wait until it was safe to talk.

They crossed the yard. She sucked in air and stilled her anger and fear as they passed Gus's quarters. Her attention momentarily diverted, she stepped on a stick. The crack shot into the still air and she halted, holding her breath. When nothing happened she continued after the man from the woods.

They left behind the circle of tents and bunkhouses and stepped into the dark street. Still they hurried along as silently as possible. They turned a corner. Dawn streaked the sky, making it possible to see shapes.

A horse whinnied. Nugget. He stood at the hitching rail down the street and she ran to him and buried her face against his neck, choking back tears.

As soon as she could speak, she turned to her rescuer. "Thank you for helping me, but who are you? How did you know I was here?" She stared at the whiskered face as the elusive memory tugged at her brain. "Where have I seen you before?"

"You do remember me." He grinned. "I wondered."

She snapped her fingers. "I know where. I saw you at Fort Benton at the Wild West show." He'd been one of those grooming a big Clydesdale and then had raced a team of them pulling a careening wagon around the arena.

"Clay Morgan at your service, ma'am." He touched the brim of his hat.

"Pleased to meet you. But how did you end up at the Eden Valley Ranch? How did you know I was here?"

"I left the show at Fort Benton. Got tired of the stuff that goes on after the shows."

She had an inkling of what he meant.

"So I headed for the Northwest. Heard a man could find solitude and peace there."

She wondered if he'd found it.

"I saw you riding in the woods and recognized you. Watched you practice your riding and roping tricks. You got pretty good."

"Thanks." In hindsight it seemed foolish.

"I saw you ride home soaking wet the other day. Later, I started to worry about you and went to the ranch to see if you got back safely and were okay. A cowboy there told me you'd left to join this show." He grunted and stroked his beard. "I know this outfit. Didn't figure you'd find it to your liking."

"How right you were." She held her hand out. "I thank you. I believe God sent you in answer to my desperate prayers."

Their hands were still clasped so she felt the jolt in his arm.

"Miss, you think God can use an old reprobate like me?"

She heard the underlying question because it echoed her own of only a few hours ago. "God loves you. He loves me." The words filled her mouth with sweetness.

Clay pulled his hand to his side. "That's something to think on. Now you best be on your way." He scratched his chin through the mass of whiskers. "I suggest you avoid the roads for a while in case Gus decides to try and track you down."

Her insides tightened again. "Where can I hide?"

He grinned. "Best place to hide is in plain sight. Tie your horse behind the hotel and go to the lobby."

"I will. Thank you." But she didn't leave. "Will I see you again?"

"Could be. I've got a camp set up near the ranch." He sketched a wave and strode down the street.

She took up Nugget's reins and led him around to the alley behind the hotel, intending to stay out of sight in plain view until Gus and his show were a long way from town.

Now that she had escaped her foolish dreams, the enormity of what she'd done slammed into her and, with a moan, she bent over her knees. She had to get back to the ranch. If they'd let her back. Once Abel heard where she'd been and what she'd experienced he might never want her around the children again. He would be right. Her foolishness put not only herself but others in danger.

A question that had hammered relentlessly at the back of her mind insisted on attention. Were Ladd and Allie okay after their cold, wet adventure? Oh, how she ached to know they were both safe.

Would she ever see them again? Ever get a chance to prove to Abel the love that flooded her heart once she gave herself permission to believe she could be loved?

She waited with Nugget for an hour or so, not wanting to draw attention to herself by entering the hotel too early in the morning.

The longer she waited, the more the questions peppered her brain. *Oh, God, please give me another chance with Abel and the children.*

His stomach growled, protesting Abel's decision to forgo a meal. But he had to hurry along and catch the show before the day ended. Food could wait, he insisted again. Finding Mercy could not. As he reined about to resume his journey a woman stepped in front of him.

He jerked back on the rein, bringing Sam to a sudden halt. "Sorry."

The woman looked like Mercy. The way she walked, the tumble of mahogany hair down her back, everything about her.

He rubbed his eyes. Was he dreaming? Seeing her in every adult female? This gal wore trousers and a fringed shirt. No doubt a part of the Wild West show. He wasn't dreaming. It was Mercy, but why was she here? Had she missed the show? She moved with a purposeful step. Was she trying to locate the show, catch up to it?

He sat back on his saddle. If this was what she wanted, could he take it from her? No. He'd learned that lesson well enough with Ruby. But he couldn't let her go without talking to her, telling her how he felt.

"Mercy." His call rang out.

She drew to a halt and slowly turned to face him. Surprise and shock wreathed her face and then she gasped and ran toward him. He dropped to the ground to meet her.

"The twins?" she gasped. "Are they sick? Is Allie...?"

"They're fine. I came for my own sake." He grasped her upper arms and held her close but not too close. He must not be distracted by hugging and kissing. "Mercy, I was hasty and wrong in accusing you of putting Ladd and Allie in danger. I know you wouldn't do that." He let the words sink in as he filled his lungs.

Her eyes widened as if she found it difficult to believe his words.

He rushed on, determined to make her understand. "I

feared everyone would be like Ruby, putting their own interests ahead of the children. But more than that, I feared trusting what my heart said."

She tipped her head slightly to the side and studied him with guarded eyes. "What does your heart say?"

A smile drew his mouth wide. He drank in her features—her dark eyes, beautiful skin, lovely lips, then realized she waited for his answer. "My heart says..." He tried to sort out the many things he felt. "It says you are the best thing that ever happened to me. I can trust you. And enjoy life with you." His voice deepened. "Mercy, I love you and I want to share my life with you."

She laughed softly. "Took you long enough to figure it out."

"I had a lot to sort out." He stroked her cheek. "I know you want to join a Wild West show and I would never ask you to give up your dreams. But I'll come, too. I'll bring the children. We'll help you."

There was a sheen of tears in her eyes. "Abel, you'd do that for me?"

"I'll do whatever you need."

She lifted a hand and cupped his face, warm and possessive, and he turned into her palm.

"Abel, I found the show. I was invited to join them. It was awful." A shudder ran up her arm and he pulled her closer.

"If someone hurt you..."

"No. Our friendly woodsman rescued me." She filled in the details.

"I'm so grateful you're safe, but there are other shows."

She shook her head. "You don't understand. I don't want to join a Wild West show. I don't want to perform.

I don't need the attention, because I found what I need with you and the twins."

"You did?" He ached for her to say she returned his feelings or at least welcomed them but he wasn't sure what she meant.

"Abel, I found acceptance with you. I found something worth being a part of."

He wanted more, but was he being greedy?

She chuckled. "Abel, just in case you aren't understanding what I'm saying, let me be clear. I love you. I want nothing else on earth but to share your life."

He stared. "You love me?"

She nodded, her eyes sparkling with joy. "You and the twins."

He leaned forward, but realized how very public the street was. "Let's find someplace private."

She led him to the back of the hotel where Nugget waited.

He pulled her into his arms, looked deep into her eyes. "Say it again."

Her soft laugh danced across his heart. "Abel Borgard, I love you and I want to share your life."

He caught the last word with his lips and claimed her mouth with a heart full of gratitude and anticipation of the future.

Cupping his cheeks with her hands, she offered him all her love in a kiss that threatened to explode his heart.

He eased back enough to smile into her welcoming gaze. "I love you, Mercy Newell. When can we change it to Mercy Borgard?"

She trailed her fingers along his jawline sending joy into every corner of his mind. "Do you suppose someone in this town could perform a ceremony?"

He roared with laughter. "You don't want to wait?"

"I have been waiting all my life." Her eyes filled with such need he hugged her tight to his chest and leaned his head against hers.

"You have my love now and always."

She clung to his shirtfront. "I don't want to ever leave you. Or have you leave me."

"I won't, except maybe to go hunting or get firewood."

She laughed.

His tension eased. "That's better." He wiped the tears from her eyes. "Wouldn't want the bride to appear teary." He tucked her in at his side. "Now let's go find a judge or preacher or someone to marry us."

She leaned her head on his shoulder. "I'm deliriously happy."

"Are you sure you aren't just overtired?" She'd told him how she'd sat awake all night waiting for a chance to escape.

"I'm wide-awake now. Thanks to your kiss."

They grinned at each other then restricted themselves to holding hands as they reached the street. They found the Mountie in his office and made their inquiry.

"You are indeed fortunate. The circuit judge is here today to hold court. He'll be glad to perform a marriage ceremony." He directed them to the hotel.

An hour later they stood hand in hand while the stern-looking judge married them. "I now pronounce you man and wife. You may kiss."

She turned and wrapped her arms around her husband. He claimed her mouth in a gentle promise of forever.

Epilogue

"Do I look like a fancy riding lady?" Allie asked.

"You certainly do." Even more important, she looked the picture of health. Miss Oake's doctor cousin had visited and examined Allie and given the word that her heart was as sound as Ladd's.

Marriage to Abel was beyond anything Mercy had dreamed possible. He was thoroughly attentive, affectionate and caring. Within a few weeks, Mercy discovered she could think of her parents without the sharp pain she'd grown so familiar with she barely noticed it.

They had moved into the new cabin before the first snowfall. Mercy had made it homey with framed pictures, a collection of books and the quilts she'd finished for the children in time for Christmas. And what a Christmas it had been. For the first time since she was very young, Mercy celebrated the season with a heart overflowing with joy and excitement. The twins were so eager for the day that many times they brought chuckles to the lips of Abel and Mercy. Sharing the anticipation with the twins and Abel was the best

Christmas gift she could ask for. With his ax, Abel had shaped a statue of a boy and girl sitting arm and arm on a bench. It was clearly the twins. She'd never seen anything more beautiful and told him so.

Every day she rose with a smile on her lips. Abel always traced the smile with his fingertip before kissing her.

She sighed.

Ladd tugged at her sleeve. "You gonna get ready?"

She brought her attention back to their task. "I'm about ready."

Abel worried so much about her not being able to join a Wild West show that she'd planned this surprise for him. "Let's go."

Allie rode Nugget while Ladd and Mercy walked on either side swinging lariats. They entered the area where Linette had staged her party after the roundup. They'd chosen a springlike day. It still amazed Mercy how the weather changed so quickly and unexpectedly.

The cowboys and residents of Eden Valley Ranch joined Abel for the show. Beside Abel sat Clay Morgan. They had located his crude camp after their return as a married couple. He had only a tent, which he had banked with earth to provide protection for the winter. Mercy and Abel had persuaded him to accept the use of the old cabin and, after a bit of demurring, he'd accepted.

They'd found him to be a good and trustworthy friend.

She and Allie and Ladd performed riding and roping tricks. Then as their finale, Allie stood on Nugget's back and rode around the enclosure. Mercy stayed at Allie's side, making sure she was safe.

When they were finished, they bowed to the sound of applause.

Mercy barely noticed. She sought Abel's gaze. They smiled at each other across the space.

She'd found what she wanted and needed in his love.

A little later, they walked with everyone to Linette and Eddie's house for dinner. Linette glowed with joy at the birth of their baby boy. Eddie was so proud he walked about with a swelled chest, Grady at his side imitating his every gesture.

As they reached the door, Abel pulled Mercy to one side. "Let the others go in first."

She gladly did so. Although she wasn't sure why he made the request, she trusted him so completely she didn't question it.

The door closed behind Roper.

Abel turned Mercy into his arms. "That was a wonderful performance. Are you sure you don't want to join a show?"

She shuddered. "Very sure. Besides," she said, and grinned up at him. "I don't think I'm going to have time. What with you and the twins and a baby to care for."

"A baby? Where—" He realized what she meant and touched her cheek gently. "Are you sure?"

"I'm sure. And it's about time. I want lots of little Borgards. I find my heart so full of love I fear I will smother you and the twins if I don't divide it up more."

He laughed. "My heart rests in your palm and it is safe. You have made my life everything I always wanted and dreamed of." He looked deep into her eyes. "I only hope I satisfy you as fully as you satisfy me."

She pulled his face close. "I don't mind letting you prove it."

He kissed her. "Does that prove it?"

She tucked her hand about his arm and reached for the door. "It's a very nice start, although I fear it will take a lot of kisses each and every day to make your point."

He pressed his chin to her head. "You are getting quite greedy."

"Hmm. Maybe not greedy. Just reveling in your love."

They entered the house amidst more applause. She wondered if they clapped for the show she and the children had put on or if they meant approval for the love that glistened from Abel's eyes and, she was quite certain, from hers, as well.

* * * * *

Dear Reader,

Mercy was a fun character to write. A young woman who thought adventure would give her what she wanted. I laugh when I think of her and murmur, "Have mercy on us," because she is the kind of person who keeps others on their toes. And maybe that's just what Abel needed. I like to think so. I also like to think that we all can add a little spice to our ordinary lives without hurting ourselves or others. I hope you enjoy following Mercy and Abel on their adventure.

I love to hear from my readers. You can contact me at www.lindaford.org, where you can also see what's coming next in my books.

Blessings to each of you.
Linda Ford

Questions for Discussion

1. Mercy wants to perform in a Wild West show. What is she hoping to find by doing so?

2. What do you understand about Mercy's family background? How has she reacted?

3. Do you think Ambrose, the preacher's son, treated her fairly? Does Mercy think so? Do you think she might have changed her mind about him by the end of the story?

4. Why does Abel see Mercy as a risk to himself and his family?

5. What do you think of Abel's concern for Allie? Is it founded? Understandable?

6. What is your favorite thing about the twins?

7. What did Mercy find in caring for the twins that she perhaps didn't expect?

8. Who did you think the man in the woods might be? Were you surprised at the role he played?

9. Mercy tried to change for Abel's sake. Do you think this was a wise move? Do you think she would have been happy if she'd continued? Why or why not?

10. What lessons did Mercy and Abel have to learn in order to be ready to love each other and become a family?

11. How did their faith change during the story, or did it?

12. Do you see them living happily together in the future? Will there be problems? If so what might they be and how do you think Abel and Mercy will handle them?

REQUEST YOUR FREE BOOKS!

2 FREE INSPIRATIONAL NOVELS
PLUS 2
FREE
MYSTERY GIFTS

Love Inspired
HISTORICAL
INSPIRATIONAL HISTORICAL ROMANCE

YES! Please send me 2 FREE Love Inspired® Historical novels and my 2 FREE mystery gifts (gifts are worth about $10). After receiving them, if I don't wish to receive any more books, I can return the shipping statement marked "cancel." If I don't cancel, I will receive 4 brand-new novels every month and be billed just $4.74 per book in the U.S. or $5.24 per book in Canada. That's a saving of at least 21% off the cover price. It's quite a bargain! Shipping and handling is just 50¢ per book in the U.S. and 75¢ per book in Canada.* I understand that accepting the 2 free books and gifts places me under no obligation to buy anything. I can always return a shipment and cancel at any time. Even if I never buy another book, the two free books and gifts are mine to keep forever.

102/302 IDN F5CN

Name _____ (PLEASE PRINT) _____

Address _____ Apt. # _____

City _____ State/Prov. _____ Zip/Postal Code _____

Signature (if under 18, a parent or guardian must sign)

Mail to the Harlequin® Reader Service:
IN U.S.A.: P.O. Box 1867, Buffalo, NY 14240-1867
IN CANADA: P.O. Box 609, Fort Erie, Ontario L2A 5X3

**Want to try two free books from another series?
Call 1-800-873-8635 or visit www.ReaderService.com.**

* Terms and prices subject to change without notice. Prices do not include applicable taxes. Sales tax applicable in N.Y. Canadian residents will be charged applicable taxes. Offer not valid in Quebec. This offer is limited to one order per household. Not valid for current subscribers to Love Inspired Historical books. All orders subject to credit approval. Credit or debit balances in a customer's account(s) may be offset by any other outstanding balance owed by or to the customer. Please allow 4 to 6 weeks for delivery. Offer available while quantities last.

Your Privacy—The Harlequin® Reader Service is committed to protecting your privacy. Our Privacy Policy is available online at www.ReaderService.com or upon request from the Harlequin Reader Service.

We make a portion of our mailing list available to reputable third parties that offer products we believe may interest you. If you prefer that we not exchange your name with third parties, or if you wish to clarify or modify your communication preferences, please visit us at www.ReaderService.com/consumerschoice or write to us at Harlequin Reader Service Preference Service, P.O. Box 9062, Buffalo, NY 14269. Include your complete name and address.

LIHI3R

SPECIAL EXCERPT FROM

Love Inspired.
SUSPENSE

*The marshals are closing in on the illegal adoption ring,
and Serena and her partner Josh must team up to bring it
down for good.*

Read on for a preview of the exciting conclusion to the
WITNESS PROTECTION *series,*
UNDERCOVER MARRIAGE by Terri Reed,
from Love Inspired Suspense.

U.S. marshal Serena Summers entered three-year-old
Brandon McIntyre's room with a packing box in hand. Her
heart ached for the turmoil the McIntyre family had recently
suffered. Danger had touched their lives in the most horrible
of ways. A child kidnapped.

But thankfully rescued by the joint efforts of loving parents and the marshal service.

The McIntyre family no longer lived in Houston. The
U.S. marshal service had moved them for a second time
when their location had been compromised.

Only a few people within the service knew where Dylan,
Grace and the kids had been relocated.

Serena and her partner, Josh, were among them. It was
their job to pack up the family's belongings and forward them
through a long and winding path to their final destination.

Serena's fingers curled with anger around a tiny tennis
shoe in her hand.

So many deaths, so many lives thrown into chaos.

The thought that someone she had worked with, trusted,
had stolen the evidence and had been leaking information
to the bad guys sent Serena's blood to boil.

If her brother were alive, he'd know how to compartmentalize the anger and pain gnawing at her day in and day out.

But Daniel was gone. Murdered.

A sharp stab of grief sliced through her heart. Followed closely by the anger that always chased her sorrow.

"Hey, you okay in here?"

Serena glanced up at her current partner, U.S. marshal Josh McCall. He'd taken off his navy suit jacket and rolled the sleeves of his once crisp white dress shirt up to the elbows. His brown hair looked like he'd been running his fingers through it again, the ends standing up. She'd always found him appealing. But that was before. Now she refused to allow her reaction to show. Not only did she not want to draw attention to the fact that she'd noticed anything about him, she didn't want him to think she cared.

She didn't. Josh was the reason her brother had been alone when he'd been murdered.

Turning away from Josh, she said briskly, "I'm good."

Taking the two ends of the sheet in each hand, she spread her arms wide and attempted to fold the sheet in half.

"Here," Josh said, stepping all the way into the room. "Let me help."

He reached for the sheet, his hands brushing hers.

An electric current shot through her. She jerked away, letting go of the ends like she'd been burned. "I don't need your help."

His hand dropped to his side. "Serena." Josh's tone held a note of hurt.

Glass shattered.

Someone else was in the house.

Pick up UNDERCOVER MARRIAGE by Terri Reed, available June 2014 from Love Inspired® Suspense.

Love Inspired
SUSPENSE
RIVETING INSPIRATIONAL ROMANCE

Hometown secrets

Was the explosion that took the lives of Sarah Russell's parents an act of murder? Her teenaged daughter thinks so and is determined to seek answers in their sleepy small town. Sarah fears her daughter will uncover a secret she's not ready to share: everyone—including Sarah's daughter—believes the girl is Sarah's kid *sister*. Even the child's father doesn't know the truth. But as Sarah reunites with Nick Tyler to look into the mysterious deaths, she knows she'll have to tell him—and her daughter—the truth. Yet someone wants to ensure that no one uncovers *any* long buried secrets.

COLLATERAL DAMAGE
by
HANNAH ALEXANDER

***Available June 2014 wherever
Love Inspired books and ebooks are sold.***

LIS44599